Diamonds And Pebbles

By

P. B. Slater

This novel is entirely a work of fiction. The names, characters and incidents portrayed are works of the author's imagination. Any resemblance to actual persons, living or dead, events or localities, is entirely coincidental

Published by P. B Slater 2010

P.B Slater asserts the moral right to be identified as the author of this work

Copyright © P.B Slater 2010

A catalogue record for this book is available from the British Library
ISBN Number: 978-184426-810-8

All rights reserved

Printed in the UK by Print On Demand Worldwide

This book is dedicated to Georgie, with love always

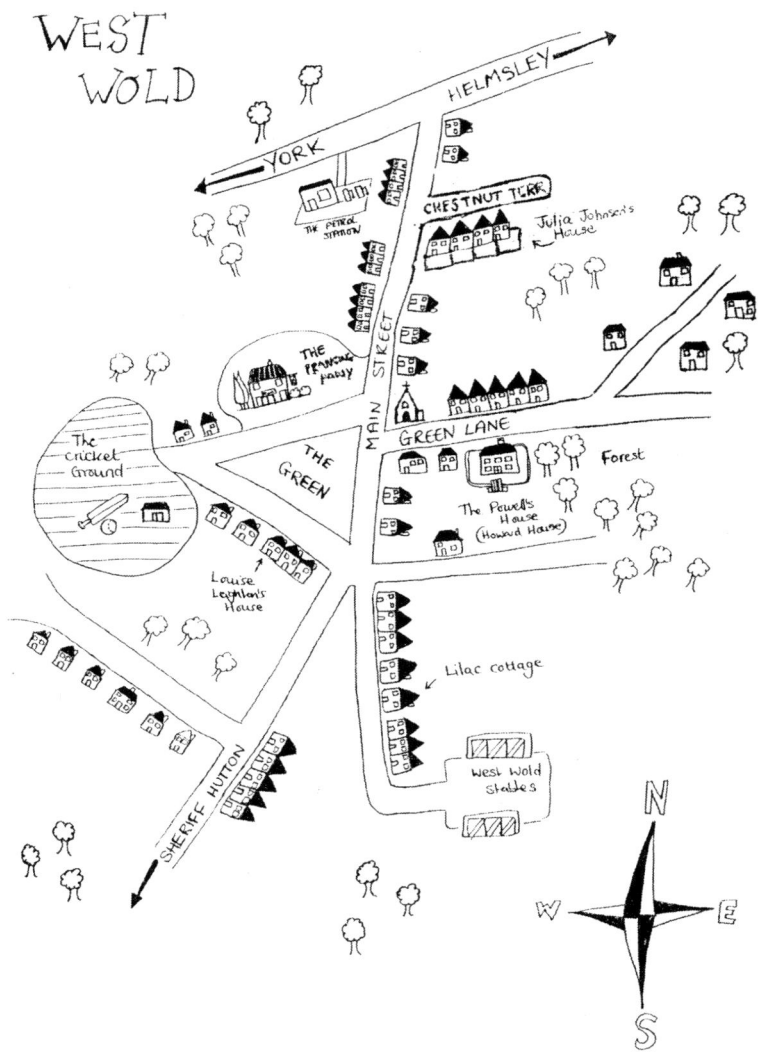

Prologue

A violent, August thunderstorm was turning day into night in North Yorkshire. The golden fields, recently (and providentially) harvested, lay flattened under charcoal skies. The hedgerows and the longer grass swayed constantly as though ruffled by a giant, unseen hand. The distant purple moors loomed closer. It was only four o'clock in the afternoon, but the street lights had come on in the small village of West Wold, nestling in the Howardian Hills. The wild power of the storm rolled down the valley, and battered the outside of a pretty stone cottage (called Lilac Cottage after two fine specimens which stood in its front garden), smashing at the small casement windows. A thin, but unceasing, cascade of water poured down noisily outside of a window, where a gutter was broken and had been uncharacteristically neglected for too long by the owners. Inside Lilac Cottage, the lightning flashed, illuminating the gloomy sitting room, like a set in a black-and white horror film, but there was also a preternatural stillness, apart from the ticking of the clock, marking, as all clocks do, the march of time and the brevity of each soul's sojourn on the Earth.

The sitting room was expensively, but quite sparsely, furnished. It was luxurious, with two large, brown-leather sofas set at right angles, a Victorian chair upholstered in amber velvet, an expensive glass coffee table, a large television, polished wooden floorboards and several Persian rugs. A few, well-chosen oil-paintings were displayed on the cream walls, and every small object gave the impression of taste and wealth. An old-fashioned chintz-patterned vase containing fresh chrysanthemums stood in the deep recess of the casement window. On the stone mantle-piece there stood a mahogany striking clock, two small photographs in silver frames (one of a bride and groom, and one of an elderly lady), and a single silver candlestick. In one of the recesses next to the chimney breast there was a large black-and-white photographic portrait of a woman. Her dress was low-cut, her beautiful hair had been carefully arranged, and her make-up had been expertly applied. Her gaze was frank and friendly, with a slight smile.

The ferocity of a human heart, and not just the forces of Nature, had been unleashed that afternoon. One area of the polished wooden floorboards was turning deep red as thick, sticky blood seeped into it from the body of the woman who lay there face down, with her arms sprawled in front of her, and her head turned to the side. The blood was dripping from several deep gashes in the back of her head and was matted into the long, red hair which had been her pride and joy. She was dressed in a long Mac, as though she had just come in from the rain. Beside her were her hat, which she had been dropped as she fell to the floor, and a second silver candlestick, its square base streaked with coagulating blood. The woman looked a little younger than her forty years. She had an expression of surprise on her face and her skin was still faintly pink. Her remarkable, turquoise-blue eyes, staring forlornly at the floor, would soon slowly fade to opaque.

The rain battered at the window, and the clock ticked loudly on the mantle-piece as her heart faltered, and her life ebbed away. Inside her womb, a tiny flickering heartbeat also stopped. The storm still raged outside, but inside Lilac Cottage it was as though nothing would ever stir again.

Diamonds And Pebbles

Friday

Diamonds And Pebbles

Chapter 1

There is a saying that it is better to have a flawed diamond than a perfect pebble; this is especially true of people, and discerning the former from the latter can be the occupation of a lifetime. These were the thoughts of Detective Chief Inspector Frank MacDonald, sitting with his feet on his desk, leaning back with eyes closed. It was his mother's saying, and one which had lodged in his consciousness through many years of repetition. On the other side of the clear glass wall of the small room which served as his office there was a large, open-plan office with a dozen desks, each one cluttered with a computer, telephone, files and paperwork. It was after seven o'clock on the Friday evening of the storm, and the telephones were still ringing constantly in York police station, keeping Frank's colleagues at work when their shifts were long over. The weather that afternoon had caused chaos in York and the surrounding villages, with flooding, accidents, traffic jams and the petty, opportunistic crimes which ensue when people are distracted and distressed. After eight weeks of unprecedented heat, with the frail and the weak expiring daily, Nature had finally boiled over in spectacular fashion.

Frank should have gone home several hours ago, but he had decided to stay and tackle some of the untidy piles of paperwork which were stacked around the edges of his office floor. Having spent two hours at the task, he was preparing to leave. He was tired, hungry and hot.

"Something here for us, sir," said Detective Sergeant Steven Brown, walking into Frank's office, holding a piece of paper in his hand, "A body's been found in West Wold. A forty year old woman in the living room of her own home. It looks like it was definitely murder; she was hit on the back of the head. The husband found her about an hour ago when he got in from work. The Scene-Of-Crime Officers are there now. The Super said he wanted the best brains on this one!"

Frank put his feet on the floor and rubbed his eyes with his hands to rouse himself, then ran them through his short, thick brown hair which was just beginning to go grey at the temples. It was warm and humid again despite the storm, and he would have liked to have a shower and change his shirt.

"But he chose us instead, don't tell me. There goes my weekend," he said, with a sigh, "I was supposed to be seeing Nate." Nate, short for Nathan, was his sixteen year-old son.

Steven Brown nodded, and said, "I'm not going to be popular, either."

Having voiced his disappointment, Frank then began to feel the familiar flutter of excitement in his stomach which always accompanied the start of a new case. He knew that a murder enquiry would test his intellect and intuition to their limits. It was a challenge which he relished.

"Okay - let's go. You can give me the details in the car," Frank said. Rising out of his chair and picking up his jacket, mobile phone and keys, he followed the younger man out of the office. "Your turn to drive?" he said, throwing the car-keys towards his long-suffering colleague. He always avoided driving whenever he could. He preferred to gaze out of the window at the passing streets or countryside, and think about whatever came to mind.

Detective Chief Inspector Francis Albert MacDonald, known as Frank, was forty-one years old, of average height and build, with soft brown eyes and a good-natured smile. He was named after Francis Albert Sinatra by his father, who regarded Sinatra as the greatest singer who had ever lived. Frank wore expensive striped shirts, coloured silk ties and dark Italian suits and shoes to work, which made him look smart and clean-cut. However the tie, which started off each day so neatly fashioned, was always eventually pulled away from the collar, and the loop loosened to a less restricting length. He pulled at it now, in a vain attempt to feel cooler. He had taken off his suit jacket much earlier in the day.

The Detective Sergeant, Steven Brown, was twenty-eight years old. Bright and personable, he was tall and thin with legs and arms which looked too long for his body. He also usually wore a dark suit to work but, in contrast to the elegance of his boss, it had the effect of making him look like an overgrown schoolboy. He had short, fair hair and a boyish, freckled face with pleasant blue eyes. This mild exterior disguised an impressive brain, and he had an assertive enough manner when circumstances demanded it. He was not a native of York, having been born in Devon, but he loved the northern city, and the county of North Yorkshire, and had married a local girl, with whom he had a four year old daughter and a three-month old baby girl. He and Frank MacDonald had been partners for some three years and had forged a good working relationship, both being decent, honest men. They shared a sense of honour, a sense of humour, and a determination to get the better of whichever criminals strayed into their path. They both preferred to use 'Wits, Not Fists', as one of Frank's old Superintendents had put it, and between them they had a considerable combined intelligence to put to good use. If Frank occasionally pulled rank in order to avoid some of the more wearisome aspects of police work, then Steven accepted this as Frank's privilege. Frank was a good policeman; better than good because he had hung onto his conscience and his instincts, and Steven was happy to learn. Frank had sacrificed a lot to his career; a marriage had ended, and other relationships, particularly that with his son, had been tested to the limit. Steven respected Frank for his devotion to duty, if not for the way he conducted his life.

Steven drove the unmarked police car the short distance out of York, and they were soon travelling along the country roads north of the city. The earlier traffic jams had dispersed. Harvested wheat fields basked in the late evening sunshine. Beyond the fields broad tracts of grass, nibbled short by sheep, reached up into the dense woodland on top of rolling hills. The coolness brought about temporarily by the storm had gone. They wound down the car windows and enjoyed the pleasant rush of air. The narrow lanes, which rose and dipped as they threaded through the gentle hills, were lined with hawthorn bushes and dry-stone walls. Pheasants wandered in a desultory fashion on the grass verges, whilst occasionally a small, brown rabbit sat and sniffed the air before scurrying away. Frank had often seen deer, stoats, foxes, hares and badgers along these lanes, as well as owls, kestrels, pied-wagtails and a host of other feathered varieties. He admired the scenery as they went along and tried to ignore his hunger. The two policemen duly arrived in the village of West Wold some thirty minutes drive to the north of York on the way to the lovely market town of Helmsley. Like many others in North Yorkshire, it was a small, pretty village with houses built mainly from the local pale stone, and decorated with window boxes and hanging baskets overflowing with orange pelargoniums, pink fuschias and blue lobetia. After turning right off the main road, the village high street ran north to south and about half way down, to the west, there was a triangular green, one side of which was divided from the road by a ditch, usually dry in summer, but recently replenished by the storm. On the right-hand side of The Green there was a public house - *The Prancing Pony* - and on the left-hand side a row of small cottages. Opposite The Green, on the east side of the main street, there was a small row of shops, including a tea-room, village stores and post office, and a fine, old church set back in a small churchyard with a couple of stately old Yew trees. The entrance to the churchyard had an elaborate, oak lych-gate topped by a low-pitched slated roof. The church was on the corner of Green Lane, a road which branched off the main street and ran east towards Slingsby. Frank knew the village well; he had family and friends who lived there. West Wold was growing fast, putting out shoots into the surrounding countryside with new roads and houses to satisfy the demands of a prosperous York. At the southern end of the high street, going towards Sheriff Hutton, the two policemen found the address which they had been given; Lilac Cottage. The cottage was on a narrow road, more of a cinder track, which forked off to the left and ran parallel to the main road separated by a bank covered in grass and

Diamonds And Pebbles

shrubs, and ended at a gate which led to the local stables. Some dozen cottages ran along the side of the road facing the bank and the main road. Lilac Cottage was about half way down. The small front garden contained two superb lilac trees, standing on either side of a central path. However, the storm had stripped the last of the wilting blossoms, and the grass which grew beneath the trees was strewn with lilac petals, faded and brown at the edges. The cottage had a central, black-painted door with casement windows either side on both ground and upper floors, and a low, rosemary-tiled roof. The short, gravelled path ran from the front gate to the front door, then turned to the right, and lead round to the back of the house. The cottage and its garden were cordoned off with red-and-white SOC tape which flapped in the gentle evening breeze. The two men lifted the tape and, with a nod at the uniformed constable standing guard at the front door, took the disposable overalls and accessories which he handed to them. Having donned the garments, they went into the front doorway of the cottage. They entered a small hall with a stone-flagged floor, with a wooden staircase running straight up in front of them, and heavy wooden doors to left and right. The right-hand door was open and led into a sitting room. They turned right into the room, where two officers in white overalls were taking photographs and collecting samples of fibres and tissue.

Frank stopped just inside the room and looked inside. It was a pleasant sitting room, typical of a cottage, with a single oak beam running across the ceiling, a stone fireplace with a clock, two photographs and a silver candlestick on the mantle-piece, and a small casement window with a deep sill. A large vase of appropriately funereal chrysanthemums, in shades of red and bronze, stood on the window sill. A small Victorian chair stood beneath the window. The walls were plain with one or two oil paintings of country scenes, and a striking black-and-white photographic portrait of a woman in the recess between the chimney breast and the window. Two large leather sofas formed an L-shape; one facing the window, one facing the fireplace. There was a woman's body lying on the floor between the sofa which faced the fireplace and a glass coffee table. Her long red hair was matted with blood which had also soaked into the polished wooden floorboards around her head. Her eyes, with their colourless irises, stared unseeing. The sight of her made a shocking contrast to the serenity of the room. She was sprawled on her front as though she had been attacked from behind. Frank saw that she was dressed in a green waxed coat; not far from her body there was a green waxed hat with a large brim, and a silver candlestick lay on a red Persian rug. One of the SOCOs turned around and stepped forward. He was an officer that Frank had worked with before.

"Good to see you again," he said.

Frank nodded. "Right, what have we got?"

"The deceased is Jane Sinclair. She's forty years old. Her husband Roger found her about two hours ago, just after six o'clock. He had been at work, and that's his normal time for getting home. She looks like she's been dead about three or four hours - the pathologist is on his way, he'll obviously be able to tell you more. Killed by one or two blows to the back of the head by the looks of it; I should think with that silver candlestick."

"Any prints on the candlestick?"

"Hopefully. We'll let you know. Just waiting for the pathologist before we move anything. You've just missed her husband. He's gone to stay at his mother's house in the village. I said I'd send you along there."

"Okay. There doesn't seem to have been a struggle. Any signs of forced entry? Burglary?"

"No. Everything's neat and tidy."

"The killer's somebody she knew then, probably."

"Looks that way."

"Or at least trusted enough to let in," said Steven.

Frank agreed. He asked the SOCO, "How did the husband react?"

"Upset and baffled. Genuinely upset, I'd say."

"Did any of the neighbours see anything?" asked Steven.

"Mrs Mountjoy next door saw Mrs Sinclair taking the dog for a walk just before the storm. Uniformed are seeing the other neighbours along the row now."

"Just before the storm. That would be about half past three? About an hour before she died then?"

"The Met Office says the storm hit at three forty-seven and lasted until thirteen minutes past four. It looks as though she had just come in from the rain when the killer struck from behind."

"Did she come in the front door or the back do you think?"

"Well, there's no mud or stains near the front door. Roger Sinclair said that they usually used the back door with the dog; it has a porch with Wellies, boots, towels for the dog and so on, so it looks as though she probably came in that way."

"And the killer came in and went that way too, presumably," said Frank.

"Yes. The family dog is currently missing, by the way, we're not sure whether it arrived back at the house with her after the walk, or went missing during the walk," said the SOCO.

"If it was here at the time the killer must have taken it. Why would a killer take a dog?" said Frank.

"Unless he or she let the dog out because it was getting in the way," said Steven.

"Hmm," said Frank, "right, let's have a closer look at her."

He carefully stepped forward towards the body. He knelt on one knee and peered closely at the woman's face, then slowly inspected her and the surrounding floor, the hat and the candlestick without touching anything. She looked younger than forty years old with good, clear skin. She was of average height and slim build. He was used to looking at bodies, and had seen them in far worse states than this one, but he still found it disquieting. He reminded himself, as he always did, that here was a woman with hopes and dreams, family and friends; all snatched away from her by the will of another person. As always, it hardened his resolve to find the perpetrator. He looked up at the photograph of Jane Sinclair (it was clearly her) on the wall next to the chimney breast. She was bursting with life and confidence; a sorry contrast to the pathetic body on the floor.

Frank got up and nodded to his sergeant, "Right, Steven. Let's have a quick look round the rest of the house, and then go and see Roger Sinclair. In the morning we'll have a chat with the neighbour, Mrs Mountjoy."

They went through a door at the back of the sitting room into a large kitchen, which was housed in a later extension to the original cottage. The kitchen was expensively modern with oak units, and a round, wooden table and chairs on a slate floor. Through the window, they could see a long, narrow garden which was mainly lawn with a few shrubs in the borders. The garden was neat and functional; not the province of a gardening enthusiast. From the kitchen, there was a door leading out into the garden, via a porch. The kitchen was extremely tidy and betrayed nothing about the life which went on there, other than the comparative wealth of its owners. The only decorative touches were a cream vase with pink roses in it placed on the window ledge, and a calendar showing a photograph of Whitby harbour hung on the wall next to the garden door. There was no evidence of the paraphernalia of cooking. Everything was neatly stored away in the numerous cupboards. Frank and Steven turned to their left and entered another doorway next to the sitting room door, which lead back into the original part of the building, and into a formal dining room. There was a large rectangular dining table and eight chairs made of yew. More pictures of country scenes were on the plain cream walls. A yew sideboard held more framed photographs, many featuring the murder victim. They passed through the room, back into the hall at the front of the cottage and turned left up the stairs. At the top of the stairs, to the left and right of the small landing, there were two mirror-image rooms. They each had a low casement window to the front, a large dormer-window to the back and an en-suite bathroom. These rooms occupied both the original part of the cottage and the same modern extension which housed the kitchen, and were decorated with the same cream walls and polished wooden floorboards as the downstairs rooms. Soft, luxurious, pale rugs softened the effect of the wooden floors. The two bathrooms were expensively fitted out with white and chrome fixtures and neat stacks of fluffy white towels. Both rooms were furnished with cream French beds, wardrobes and dressing tables with ornate mirrors. The room to the right of the landing showed signs of occupation, with a woman's towelling dressing gown on the bed, cosmetics, jewellery and trinkets on the dressing table, and other ephemera on the deep front window sill. Another black-and-white portrait of Jane Sinclair adorned the room, smaller this time, and less formal. Frank was not surprised to see a print of Dante Gabriel Rossetti's portrait of Alexa Wilding as *La Ghirlandata*, radiant with a halo of red hair. She and Elizabeth Siddall and Jane Morris were the archetypal flame-haired Pre-Raphaelite beauties, much admired, and much copied. Elizabeth Siddall had almost died for her art, catching cold when John Everett Millais had her immersed for too long in cold water as she posed for his portrait of Ophelia drowning. She had later died young of a broken heart after losing a baby. Jane Morris also died young. Obviously Jane Sinclair had identified with their looks. Frank doubted that she had foreseen a similarly tragic fate for herself. The two men walked into the other bedroom, which was devoid of personal items, and was presumably used as a guest room. Frank and Steven had a quick look without touching anything, and then made their way downstairs back into the sitting room to talk again with the SOCOs.

"Right, let's go and talk to Roger Sinclair. We'll come back tomorrow with him and have a proper look around. He can look through her papers and things with us," said Frank presently, reluctant to start looking through the Sinclairs' personal belongings without the owner being present. Having obtained the address of Roger Sinclair's mother, they walked out of the cottage, ducked under the fluttering red-and-white tape and walked back to the car. It had been a long day, and they were still not finished. Frank tried not think about how hungry he was.

Diamonds And Pebbles

Chapter 2

It was after nine o'clock when DCI Frank MacDonald and DS Steven Brown drove back up the main street heading north, and continued past The Green to the address which the SOCO had given them for Roger Sinclair's mother before they left Lilac Cottage. It was almost dark and the shimmering, pale blue sky of the early evening had faded to indigo. Frank could see Venus shining close to the Moon. They found the house; a detached building a few doors up from the row of shops on the right-hand side of the road. They rang the bell, and were shown into a spacious hall by Roger Sinclair. They introduced themselves, and he directed them towards the door to the sitting room. As they walked across the hall Frank could hear voices in the kitchen at the rear of the house .

"My sister and her husband have come to see us," said Roger, explaining the voices, "and a couple of neighbours have popped in to make sure I'm okay."

He led them into the room, invited them to sit down on the sofa, and offered them a drink. They both accepted a cup of coffee - they needed stimulants at this time of night after a tiring day - and he went off to the kitchen. The room in which they were seated was well-appointed if rather cluttered and old-fashioned, with chintz sofa and armchairs, patterned curtains and a patterned carpet; all in soft shades of pink and green. Frank and Steven made themselves comfortable. As they waited Frank wondered what sort of man Roger would turn out to be; spouses were always prime suspects in a murder enquiry. He took his tie off altogether, folded it up and put it in his jacket pocket, and undid another button on his shirt. He was looking forward to the next day so that he could really get started on the investigation. There was a strong chance that he would meet the killer in the next few days; he felt again the familiar sense of excitement and apprehension. Steven Brown took out his notebook and pen in preparation for taking notes.

Roger returned with three mugs which he placed on a coffee table in the centre of the room. He sat down wearily in an armchair.

"My mother has gone to bed I'm afraid. She's rather frail, and this has been a terrible shock. Did you want to speak with her?" he said.

"In due course, Mr Sinclair. We'll probably see her tomorrow. We are both very sorry for your loss," said Frank.

"Thank-you. I'm so shocked. I just don't know what to think. To come home and find her like that. It's unbelievable. Why would anyone want to kill Jane?" he said, and rubbed his eyes with his fists, looking suddenly very tired and bewildered. Steven Brown started to write quickly and neatly into his notebook.

"You found her at about six-thirty, is that right?"

"Yes - I'd just got home from work. I knew there was something wrong as soon as I opened the door. It was too quiet. Our dog, Charlie, has gone missing too, by the way; that's very odd. I walked into the sitting room and there Jane was. She was just lying on the floor, in her Mac. She must have just come in to the house when she was killed. I rang the police straight away."

"Did you notice anything unusual? Anything out of place? Anything missing?"

"No, nothing at all, just Jane lying there with blood oozing into the floor," Roger said forlornly, his eyes suddenly misting over.

Frank sympathised with Roger Sinclair's grief. Even so, he sensed that it was the exhaustion and resignation of a man presented with a huge set of problems, rather than real desolation. Roger was a tall, imposing man of about forty-five years with neat, dark hair with an old-fashioned side parting. He was immaculately dressed, even at this late hour and in such extraordinary circumstances, in shirt and tie and expensive trousers and shoes. He had the air of someone who would have been at home in a company board room.

"I'm sorry it's late, sir, and you've had a shock, but the sooner we start this investigation the sooner we'll catch Mrs Sinclair's killer. Could you tell us about Jane, about your marriage, about her family and friends and neighbours, or anyone else who might be able to help us? Do you have children?" said Frank. He had assumed from the unoccupied second bedroom and lack of memorabilia in Lilac Cottage that the couple were childless.

"No, we don't, regrettably. My fault according to the doctors. It will become obvious to you both that Jane and I had a less than perfect marriage, and I often wonder if that was the major cause; the fact that we couldn't have children," he admitted.

Frank nodded and said, "Tell us about the people Jane knew well."

Roger gazed at the patterned carpet for a few seconds, pausing to gather his thoughts, "Well, Jane knew just about everyone in West Wold. I've lived in West Wold most of my life - in this house, when I was a boy - and I moved back to the village, with Jane, from York not long after we married, and bought Lilac Cottage. She really threw herself into village life. She was always organising something; she was very actively involved in everything. She runs - I mean, ran - a small dress shop in the village, in the row of shops opposite The Green, and she helped organise the village fête and other fundraising activities. She didn't need to work - I own a software company in Wetherby, and my business is very successful - but she wanted an occupation, and she enjoyed it. She was well-liked I think, although she could be a bit bossy, I suppose," he said with a small smile. "She could also be very good company. We are on nodding terms with everyone and know all of the immediate neighbours. We entertain a lot, and I play golf with a couple of them. In terms of family, she has a sister, Julia Johnson, who lives at the top end of the village - Number 4, Chestnut Terrace. Julia was often at our place. Their mother lives in a nursing home in York, their father died years ago. They manage their mother's affairs jointly, but other than that they weren't particularly close really, as sisters go. We have friends in the village - there are the Powells; Stella and James. We often meet them on Sunday nights in the pub, with another couple called Phil and Samantha Watson, and a few others. Stella Powell and I have known each other since we were children, both born and bred here. Jane's known Stella since she moved here, and - " he paused and examined his well-manicured hands,

" - I may as well tell you that Jane had an affair with James Powell about a year ago. It's just that I'd rather you didn't mention it to my mother unless it is absolutely necessary. She's rather old-fashioned about that sort of thing, and she and Jane were a little cool with each other at the best of times. I don't want Mother to think even more badly of her."

"We'll bear that in mind, sir," said Frank. "They didn't get on?"

"Well, Jane wasn't exactly the type to mince her words, and neither is my mother, so perhaps they were too similar to ever get on really well," Roger rubbed his eyes again. "Strong women you know, Mr MacDonald, never easy…"

"Indeed. You were saying about James Powell? Were you aware of the affair at the time?"

"No, but Jane told me all about it afterwards. She didn't want people talking behind my back; for me not to know what other people knew. She was always very discreet. The affair was no longer an issue. I didn't kill her in a fit of jealousy if that's what you are thinking. James is a photographer - celebrity portraits, fashion shoots, that sort of thing. Quite well-known. He took the portraits of Jane in Lilac Cottage which you may have noticed? The Powells live in a house down Green Lane - Howard House - the turning's just opposite The Green."

"What was the relationship like between you and James Powell?"

"We've all known each other for a long time, and we both play for the village cricket team, that sort of thing. By the time Jane told me about the affair it was all over, so it didn't seem worth making a huge fuss about. I went to *The Prancing Pony* less often, and he and I were cooler with each other when we did meet, I suppose."

"Okay. Anyone else we should talk to?"

"Jane had another friend called Louise Leighton. She's a teacher in York. She lives on The Green; the row of houses across from the pub. Number six, I think. She's been friends with Jane for a couple of years since she moved to the village. She was often round at Lilac Cottage. Jane started inviting her to our dinner parties. She felt a bit sorry for her I think, not really knowing anyone. Not my cup of tea, but Jane liked her well enough. A bit pushy for my liking. She was determined to get into village life, and latched onto Jane straight away. She worked in *The Prancing Pony* for a while when she first moved here. Louise even wanted to become Jane's business partner in the shop at one stage, but I advised Jane against it, and she took my advice. James Powell has moved onto *her* now, I hear."

Frank reflected that James Powell certainly had a tangled love life. Was that why Jane was dead?

"Had Jane's behaviour changed in any way recently?"

Roger considered for a moment and said, "Yes, strangely enough, I think it had. She was rather quiet actually, these last couple of months."

"Can you think of anyone who would wish her harm?"

"I've been thinking about that and I really can't. It's been puzzling me all evening. Who on earth would want to kill Jane? Could it have been just some random psychopath who didn't even know her?"

"It is possible, and it's something we'll bear in mind. There was no evidence of forced entry or a struggle in the cottage, so it was probably someone she knew. If it is a psychopath, they will probably have killed before or will do so again. We'll check against other murder cases for similarities with this case. Is there anyone else we need to speak to?"

Roger thought for a moment and shook his head, "She has other friends in York and elsewhere, but she doesn't see them often. Her life was very much here in West Wold."

"That's fine," said Frank, "please let us know if you think of anything else that might be relevant," he paused, knowing that the next question was going to be difficult for Roger to hear, "I'm sorry to have to ask you this , Mr Sinclair, but where were you between four and six thirty this evening?"

The other man took the question in his stride, however, "Well, I was at work all afternoon until I left just before six to come home - my company is in Wetherby as I said. I discovered Jane when I got home at about six-thirty. My secretary will be able to confirm everything."

Frank decided to change tack and said, "Tell us about your marriage, Mr Sinclair. How did you meet?"

"We've been married for twenty years. I met Jane through Julia, her sister, as it happens. I went out with Julia for a while, nothing serious. Later, I asked Jane out, and it went from there. She was very attractive, and very good company. I wanted a home of my own by that time, and I asked her to marry me. We lived in a flat in York for a while, and then bought Lilac Cottage. I had lived here in West Wold from childhood, of course, but it was all new to Jane. She and Julia had been brought up on a council estate in York. She took to West Wold straight away, though. She had some doubts about living so close to my mother, but it worked out alright."

"Jane had a normal childhood?"

"Yes, pretty much. As I said, her father died long ago and her mother struggled to bring them up, financially and in other ways. Julia was always jealous of Jane, I think. Jane seemed to have been blessed from birth with good looks and personality. She did reasonably well at school, but she wasn't academically minded. When I met her she was still living at home, and working in an office in York. She came up with the idea for the dress shop shortly after we moved here, and I encouraged her. I lent her the start-up money which she insisted on paying back once the business was up-and-running. Julia and her husband followed us out to live in West Wold. They've been divorced for a long time. We've had a happy life on the whole, except that I think Jane would have liked children, and so would I. But we've enjoyed lots of holidays - places like Australia, China, Bali - and done things we wouldn't have done with children, perhaps."

"When did Jane start to have affairs?"

Roger Sinclair looked a little embarrassed and hesitated, "We hadn't been married long, actually. Just a couple of years. I didn't know until later. When we had been married for about ten years I confronted her about her latest lover, and she told me everything. I had stopped being jealous by then. She just wanted a bit of romance and excitement in her life, and clearly I wasn't providing it. She attracted men wherever she went as well, which didn't make it easy for her to be faithful. I'm not condoning her behaviour. I suppose I felt partly to blame..."

"Did you never think of adopting a baby?"

"Jane was reluctant to give up hope of us having our own child one day."

"Thank-you, Mr Sinclair. We'll stop there for tonight. A constable will come to take a formal statement tomorrow, and we will come to see your mother at some point. We'd also like you to go back to the cottage with us first thing tomorrow to help us find Jane's bank statements and so on. Did Jane keep a diary?"

"She wrote appointments and other things on the wall calendar in the kitchen - she had one at the shop as well for business appointments. But if you mean a private journal - no, not that I'm aware of."

"Okay - we'll bid you goodnight."

Steven Brown closed his notebook and put it away in his pocket. They all rose, and Roger saw them to the front door, and quickly closed it after them.

As the two policemen walked back to the car, Frank asked, "What did you make of him?"

Steven Brown replied, "He seems pretty genuine. He has a motive though - the affair with James Powell."

"Yes - our Mr Powell is beginning to sound like the key to Jane's death. Tangled relationships can lead to strong emotions, and strong emotions can lead to violent acts. We'll see Roger Sinclair again and talk to Mrs Mountjoy first thing in the morning - find out exactly what she saw. Then James and Stella Powell, Jane's sister Julia, Roger's mother and Louise Leighton. Now - please - take me home, I need a shower and my bed, and I could eat a horse!"

Diamonds And Pebbles

Chapter 3

They drove in relative silence back to York, and Steven Brown dropped Frank MacDonald at his flat on the west bank of the River Ouse. They arranged that Steven would pick him up at seven o'clock the next morning to go back to West Wold, to start questioning the people that Roger Sinclair had mentioned. Frank wearily climbed up to the second floor flat. He let himself into a spacious hall with doors to right and left. The first door on the left opened into a large sitting room with double French doors which led out onto a balcony overlooking the river, and a view which made the climb up the stairs worthwhile. His flat was part of a prestigious Nineteen-Eighties development in the heart of the city, with views across the river and over the rooftops towards the beautiful York Minster, some half a mile away. The Minster dwarfed everything around it. The price of the flat was out of even Frank's salary bracket, but he had purchased it thanks to an inheritance from his maternal grandmother. The sitting room, like all the rooms in the flat, was simply furnished with wooden floors. He had bought the Nineteen-Eighties, black-ash furniture from the previous owner with the intention of replacing it, but had never had the time. Wooden Venetian blinds at the windows were functional but not cosy. The only purchases of his own were two red-leather reclining chairs, a large television, some prints, and an expensive stereo system which sat on two long, black-ash shelves along with his collection of CDs and vinyl albums. On the walls were a large print of Rousseau's *Surprise!*, Hockney's *A Bigger Splash*, a water-colour painting of a bleak moor depicted in greys, blacks and purples painted by his sister Sophie, and a black-and-white photograph of Steven McQueen on his motorcycle in the film *The Great Escape*. He loved the Rousseau for its richness of colour and its depiction of the rawness and vibrancy of Nature, the Hockney for its luminous colours, striking simplicity and air of mystery, and the McQueen portrait for his effortless 'cool'. On one of the shelves was a framed photograph of Frank's son, Nathan, who was the donor of the McQueen print. The flat contained a modern, functional kitchen, two bedrooms, one large with the same view of the Ouse as the sitting room, one small, and a small bathroom. The larger bedroom was pleasant and comfortable, the starkness of the cream walls relieved by richly coloured curtains in bronzes and oranges, warm wooden floorboards, and a print given to him by his father, after Frank had seen the original in Edinburgh and enthused about it. It was *Lady Agnew of Lochnaw* by Sargent. She was a dark-haired beauty. The portrait had a rare intensity and its subject, sitting in a cream armchair, and dressed in a lilac gown, her arm draped nonchalantly on the arm of the chair, had a tantalising, enigmatic gaze which was both reticent and challenging, provocative and innocent, all at the same time. The picture never failed to impress and intrigue him whenever he looked at it.

At home on that Friday night, Frank MacDonald had a shower, put on jeans and a sweater, and sat for awhile in his favourite, reclining chair with a tumbler of single malt whisky. He thought about Nathan, his son. Frank had got married to Nathan's mother, Nichola, some eighteen years before. She was a solicitor and they met on a case. He was not long out of his police training after University. He had studied the History of art at University, a fact which had caused much mirth at the police college, so much that Frank occasionally changed it to 'Physics' when asked. He had announced to his parents that he wanted to be a policeman when he was four years old, and had not changed his mind since. It seemed to him, even as a child, that there could be no nobler calling than protecting good people from bad people, as he saw it. However, his father had encouraged his interest in Art, and persuaded him that it would do no harm to indulge his interests for a while before embarking on his life's work. During the police training, and afterwards, he had carefully constructed the necessary mental insensitivity that enabled him to do his job, but in hindsight it had distanced him from his wife. Nichola was slightly older than him, dark-haired, slim, and vivacious. She was ambitious, and Frank was attracted by her drive and sense of purpose. They met, married and set up home within a year. Not long after, Nathan came along and Frank adored his little boy. Cracks began to appear in the marriage, however. It became apparent that he and Nichola actually had very little in common. Frank liked art, music and reading; she rarely picked up a book, saying that she spent the whole time reading at work. She had returned to work when Nathan was three years old. She preferred to meet with her friends for a bottle of wine as her way of unwinding. They both worked long hours and juggled

Nathan's care between themselves and two sets of willing grandparents. They saw less and less of each other. Frank's long and unsociable hours, necessary if he was going to gain promotion, caused friction between them. Frank missed Nathan, and tried to spend time with him, but he was torn in too many directions.

Frank did not entirely understand how and why Nichola and he had drifted apart - it happened gradually, like the contents of a bowl of water leaking away one drop at a time, through a tiny hole which no-one notices is there. The first glow of romance lasted until well after an unexpected and joyous pregnancy and then the birth of Nathan, their wonder-boy. After that, they had each taken a different turn and lost each other. Nichola's moods had intrigued him as a young man, and he was happy to wheedle and tease her out of her occasional fit of the blues, but later he was bored by them, and left her to them whilst he busied himself with something more interesting. Day-to-day life was similar on the surface, but the undertow had changed from a warm familiarity to a puzzled apathy. It was so long since she had hugged him or held his hand that he had forgotten how it felt - and because he had forgotten he no longer needed it. At first his long absences from home were grievous for Frank, then masochistically enjoyable because of the rapturous re-unions, then bearable except for missing Nathan, then, finally, welcome, because whilst he was away he could forget that he was in trouble. There were times when he and Nichola talked in the old way, but mostly they avoided being alone together. Nathan was a buffer between them - a source of conversation and joint action. It was as though neither of them could make the first move towards or away from each other, or could even be bothered to try. They circled around each other like cats

- wary and blasé in equal measure. They finally parted and divorced when Nathan was nine years old, and the intervening years had been tough. Frank looked after Nathan whenever he could, often taking him to stay with his own parents in Sheriff Hutton, where Nathan was also able to spend time with his aunts, uncle and cousins, but Frank struggled to maintain his relationship with his son for the same reasons for which his marriage had foundered; too many hours dedicated to a job which he loved, and a determination to make it as near to the top of his profession as he was able. When he looked back on that time, Frank had deep regrets; in hindsight he felt that his priorities had been wrong. It was a source of sadness to him now. After the divorce, Nichola got married to a decent man whom Frank liked, and chatted to about common interests, on the rare occasions when they met. Frank was happy that Nathan was well taken care. Frank had had relationships with other women since the marriage had ended, but no-one that he cared to introduce to Nathan.

Frank had two sisters, one of whom, Alison, known as Ali, was a year older than him and married with two adult sons, the other, younger, and still living at home with their indulgent parents; he was never short of invitations or opportunities for socialising. Whereas Sophie, his younger sister, stomped her way sure-footedly through life, Ali was as thin and skittish as a fawn. Ali was attractive in a wasted kind of way; she chain-smoked and drank more than was good for her. Both of Frank's sisters had large brown eyes and lots of brown, curly hair, but Sophie was altogether more solidly built than Ali. Sophie, now aged thirty, had been a late baby for their parents. With middle-age, Frank had grown even closer to his parents. He was aware of time spent with them being sweetly precious, and enjoyed relaxing with them in his childhood home in Sheriff Hutton.

Thinking about his marriage, Frank remembered one catastrophic day with absolute clarity. He and Nichola and Nathan were on holiday for two weeks on a Greek island. They had been married for ten years. Ali and her husband David were with them. Ali sunbathed whilst David played with their boys, then fourteen and fifteen years old. David was an indifferent husband, in both senses of the word, but an enthusiastic father now that the boys were growing up. He was keen to join them in whatever pursuit they chose; to swim, snorkel, dive, and wind-surf. Sometimes David forgot where fun ended and dictatorialness began, and occasionally one of the boys slunk off to sit with Ali to be soothed and mothered. The first few days of the holiday had calmed them all, and, to Frank, he and Nichola seemed especially close that day. Nichola seemed more relaxed than she had been for months. They sunbathed and swam, with Nathan, always near each other, always touching. They smiled at each other a lot and remembered private jokes. In the evening, after a few glasses of retsina, she became more affectionate than of late and they were engrossed in each other. Frank hoped that, after all, they could rekindle what they had lost; that he could be a good husband, and not just a good policeman. That evening, at the end of a wonderful day, Nichola confessed that she had met someone else and that she wanted them to part. Frank cried; a physical pain crushed his chest, and he felt sick at her betrayal, but he knew that she was right.

After this, he lost confidence in his ability to have a close relationship with a woman, and instead ploughed relentlessly on with his career, hardening and adding layers to the protective shell of toughness; growing slightly more cynical, and slightly less idealistic, with every year that passed. He was a red-blooded man, but for the present, he had buried and sealed up his sexuality in the foundations of an edifice constructed of work and family. His ardour was a stream damned up with the boulders of constraint, morality and honour. This did wonders for his self-respect, but nothing at all for his sense of humour. He felt a sense of marking time, of waiting for something; something spied, fleetingly and wistfully, something waiting to be brought properly into focus.

Frank turned on the CD player and sat in his favourite chair. He listened to Bruce Springsteen, patron saint of strangled passion. It was his habit to listen to music late at night. He had a visceral reaction to music; he felt it course through his veins. He mulled over the Sinclair case for a while, then went to bed.

Diamonds And Pebbles

Saturday

Diamonds And Pebbles

Chapter 4

The storm of the previous afternoon was forgotten, and it was a beautiful Saturday morning, with a clear blue sky and a playful breeze. Frank MacDonald leant back in his seat in Steven Brown's car and looked at the countryside, as Steven drove efficiently and smoothly. North Yorkshire is a beautiful county; from the thrusting cliffs of the coastline and the pretty resorts of Scarborough and Whitby, to the brooding, mystical moors of Rosedale, from the patchwork gold and green of the view from Staxton Hill to the craggy hills and waterfalls of the Dales, there is so much to please the eye. The working people who live there are rough-and-ready perhaps, but they have an ancient nobility, and are no fools, neither do they suffer fools. North Yorkshire also has its share of wealthy people who enjoy the good life in a beautiful place which provides them with every opportunity for pleasure and leisure. August is a glorious month in the county, the fields are shorn and bask in golden sunlight. Much as he enjoyed the sights and sounds of the world's cities, the culture, the shops, the theatres, the edginess, the café society, the sheer vibrancy of life lived at breakneck speed, Frank could never imagine living his remaining years far from these hills.

The two policemen arrived presently at West Wold, and drove straight to Lilac Cottage to meet Roger Sinclair at eight o'clock. They all ducked under the red-and-white-tape and walked past a uniformed officer and into the house. Turning right into the sitting room they could see that Jane's body had been removed, but the blood stain was still undisturbed. She was now in the police mortuary, entombed in stainless steel. Unlike Snow White in her glass coffin, in merely a dream of death, Jane could not be woken by a gallant prince's kiss.

Roger went over and leant against the mantle-piece, and hid his face with his hand for a moment.

"I'm sorry," he whispered, turning to face them, "it's just that it's all so shocking. I can't believe this is happening to me."

Frank was moved by the sheer force of the other man's emotions, and said kindly, "We understand, sir, just take a moment."

Roger soon recovered his composure, and offered to show them around. Over the next hour or two they all sifted through Jane's belongings and papers together to find anything that might be important, and one of Frank's team arrived to take the items back to York to be looked at in detail. After Roger had completed a tour of all of the rooms with them, and again confirmed that nothing was missing or untoward, he went back to his mother's house, having packed a suitcase of his belongings to take with him. Then the two policemen called in to see Mrs Mountjoy, the Sinclair's next door neighbour. Her cottage stood next to Lilac Cottage, in the direction of the stables.

Sitting in the kitchen, and squashed in at a very small,

round dining table with stiff wooden chairs, Frank said, "Mrs. Mountjoy, we need to ask you a few questions about yesterday." Their *modus operandi* in preliminary interviews was for Frank to ask most of the questions, and for Steven to write down the salient points, and ask additional questions if necessary. Members of the investigation team would then call to take written statements. Any person of particular relevance to the investigation might be asked to cooperate voluntarily with fingerprints and DNA samples. Those who refused could be made the subject of a warrant applied for to the courts.

"Oh, call me Sadie," said Mrs Mountjoy, wiping a tear away, "that poor girl - I can't get over it."

"Tell us exactly what you saw, Sadie."

Sadie Mountjoy carefully placed a bone china cup and saucer in front of each of the two officers, and filled them with tea from a china teapot, then added milk. She was a small, slight lady with curly white hair, wearing a floral-patterned overall over her dress, with thick tights and slippers, despite the clement weather.

"Well, like I told the other policeman last night, I saw Jane going along the lane towards The Green about a quarter to four."

"Can you be precise about the time?"

"Yes, I can. The thunderstorm struck at a quarter to, and this was about five minutes before."

"So you think about twenty to four?"

"Yes, that's right."

"What was she wearing?"

"That long, green Mac that she always wears to walk the dog when the weather's bad, and a green hat with a brim that matches. You know, like a waxed material."

"And you are sure it was her that you saw?"

"Of course - there's no mistaking that red hair of hers - hangs all the way down her back, at least it did, poor soul. She was good to me, you know. She was always giving me things - little things - biscuits, magazines, chocolates. She often popped in to say hello. In fact, this time yesterday she was sitting where you are now, drinking a cup of tea," she said to Frank, pointing to his chair. He felt momentarily overwhelmed by this; the randomness of fate was shocking. Life and death, separated by a heartbeat.

"Do you know where she went when she left here?"

"Yes, she was on her way to open up the shop. Lovely things she had in there, you know, too expensive for me of course, but lovely. She had good taste, she did. Well, you've only got to look at that house of hers to see that," Sadie dabbed at her eyes with a handkerchief which she fished out of one of the many pockets in her overall, "very upsetting, you know, very upsetting."

"It is, Sadie, but anything you can tell us will help us catch the person who did it."

"You don't think it could have been a burglar, do you? He could still be hanging around for all we know."

"It is possible," said Steven Brown, "but there were no signs of it. Did you notice anything at all unusual? We think Jane may have been killed very shortly after you saw her yesterday afternoon."

"Well, yes actually, there was something - a few things really. First of all, I couldn't understand why she was going out in the first place. It was obvious it was going to thunder, and pour down with rain any minute. It had gone really yellow and quiet, like it does before a storm. Then a wind blew up suddenly. That's how I came to see her. I went out to shut the front gate properly 'cause it was rattling. As I stood at the gate, I saw her walking up the lane towards The

Green, and the first few spots of rain started."

"She had her back towards you?" asked Frank.

"Yes."

"And what else was there that was odd?"

"Odd? Oh, yes - it was the dog - he loves his walks normally - any weather - doesn't bother him - but she was having to drag him along - he didn't want to go. Just sat down and wouldn't budge. She had to really keep pulling. And also it was her shoes. Usually, she wears Wellies or boots to walk the dog in bad weather, but she had high heels on. It didn't look right."

"What sort of shoes?"

"Them fancy shoes - what do they call them? - court shoes, that's it, black court shoes with high heels."

"Did you see her come back?"

"No. Once I'd shut the gate I went inside, and stayed away from the windows during the thunder and lightning. What a storm that was! I've seen some bobby-dazzlers in my time, but that took the biscuit I can tell you!"

"And did you see anyone hanging around during the afternoon, before or after the storm? Especially at the back of the cottage?"

She looked doubtful, and shook her head, "No, dearie, I didn't. I can't see much at the back anyway because my trees have grown so tall. My son used to keep them cut back low for me, but he died. My grandchildren are good to me, but they don't have time. Nobody has any time these days, do they? Everyone is so busy."

"You didn't see anyone you didn't recognise, any strangers?"

"No, I'm sorry."

"Thank-you, Sadie. You've been very helpful."

"Well, I'm just glad I can help. I'm so glad that you're

here to sort it all out," she said, patting Frank's hand, "You both seem like very clever young men. You just go and catch whoever killed that lovely girl. They should bring back hanging, they really should."

The 'clever young men' exchanged a look with deadpan faces.

"Anything I can do, dearie, just ask," continued Sadie Mountjoy, lifting up the teapot, "now then, would you like another cup of tea?"

As Frank and Steven stepped out of Mrs Mountjoy's cottage, Frank was disappointed to see a group of reporters and photographers waiting across the road, along with several large television news vans equipped for live transmissions to their various organisations. A uniformed officer had prevented them from actually venturing down the un-adopted road that the cottages were built along, but the reporters and photographers were as close as they could be without incurring his wrath. Normally, crimes in the North of England were not of sufficient interest to tempt London journalists away from the comforts of home, but a recent event had made that part of North Yorkshire of rather more interest than usual. A local Member of Parliament (who was also temporarily a member of the Cabinet), a local rock guitarist, and a female 'model' had been discovered, and photographed, *in flagrante* at the rock guitarist's country pile, and the outraged public reaction to the politician's behaviour had pushed an already beleaguered Government to the brink of a forced, and unwanted, General Election. As a result, anything which happened in the said politician's back yard was of immense interest to the national newspapers and television companies, being anticipated as the final straw which was going to send the Government down. This was also the reason that Frank, one of the best and most experienced officers in the North Yorkshire force, had been assigned to what could become a very high-profile case. Frank sighed at the sight of the huddle of reporters. Intrusive reporting always made his job harder, and increased the pressure to get fast results. As the two policemen made their way back towards The Green, Frank recognised a particularly critical and outspoken reporter walking towards him. The man's name was Roy Parsons. He was a large, blonde haired man in his mid-thirties. He and Frank had crossed paths before, and he was relentless when he thought he smelt indecision, confusion or incompetence. The man, dressed in a Hawaiian styled shirt, baggy shorts, flip-flops and sunglasses, strode casually towards Frank.

"Morning, Mr MacDonald. Got a statement, sir?"

"Chief Inspector MacDonald, Mr Parsons. A statement was made at York Police Station this morning, as you know."

"We understand the victim was an attractive red-head, is that true? Are you close to making an arrest?"

Frank chose to ignore the man as he and Steven got into the car, and Steven quickly drove off. A tall man called Don Green, a photographer who often worked with Roy Parsons, took several photographs.

"That's all we need," groaned Frank, as they drove along the main street of West Wold, "they'll be dogging our footsteps all the way from now on, especially when they find out that a celebrity photographer like James Powell is involved."

Diamonds And Pebbles

Chapter 5

Frank MacDonald and Steven Brown left the car at The Green, and walked down Green Lane looking for the Powell's house. The sun was fully out now, with no clouds to break up the heat, and the temperature was rising steadily after the temporary respite which the storm had brought. Frank sighed and, loosening his tie, he undid the top button of his shirt. He knew it was going to be another long day. Although he did not mind hard work, and enjoyed the intellectual challenges of his job, he felt a real sadness at not being able to see his son as planned. It was mid-morning as their feet crunched on the gravel of the semi-circular drive in front of Howard House, the home of Stella and James Powell. It was a pleasing and beautifully-proportioned Georgian house; modestly-sized, square and symmetrical, built of local stone with a stone portico in the centre, and with tall windows either side on both ground and upper storeys. The enclosed portico had low shelves on either side which were full of Wellingtons, tennis racquets, riding hats and other paraphernalia. The wide front door was already ajar, and just as Frank was about to knock politely on the door-frame, a female figure came rushing out, accompanied by two dogs, and almost collided with him. For a moment they stood nearly chest-to-chest.

"Gosh, sorry!" the woman said, "I wasn't expecting you to be there."

Frank smiled inwardly. He could not remember the last time he had heard anyone say 'gosh' in real life. He maintained his professionally blank expression, however.

"I'm Chief Inspector Frank MacDonald, and this is Detective Sergeant Steven Brown. Your husband is expecting us I think. We're investigating Jane Sinclair's murder."

Her face fell immediately. "Of course - terrible business," she said, offering a hand, "I'm Stella Powell. James is my husband. He's waiting in the house for you."

He shook her hand and noted a nice, firm grip. He was always amazed at how many robust-looking people had weak, effeminate handshakes. He studied her for a moment. She was carrying a riding hat and crop, and dressed in beige jodhpurs and a masculine, short-sleeved checked shirt which contrasted strongly with the curves of her figure. Her thick, dark hair was scraped back untidily and tied with what looked suspiciously like a shoe-lace. She was in her late thirties with an open face, large green eyes, a slightly aquiline nose, and a generous mouth.

"Were you wanting to speak to me? I was just going riding, but I can stay if you like," Stella said, with a smile.

"Later will be fine." It was the opposite of what Frank had wanted to say, but his mind had gone blank, and he felt suddenly powerless to form the sentence which he had intended to deliver. He felt very hot, and slowly ran a finger between his neck and his shirt collar.

"Okay. Goodbye, then. Go straight in. The door's open. Come on, boys," she signalled to the two dogs, a grey lurcher and a brown-and-white Jack Russell terrier, and strode off across the gravel.

Both men stood and watched her retreating derrière until she went through the open gate, and onto the street. Next to him Steven Brown emitted a low whistle, raised his eyebrows and grinned at Frank. Frank shook his head, and rewarded him with a wide smile.

As Stella disappeared from view, Frank and Steven entered the stone portico of the Powell's house, and Steven knocked on the already open door. The two men stepped inside.

"Hello? Anyone there?" Frank shouted.

They stood in an impressive hallway with doors to left and right and a wide wooden staircase running up on the right-hand side. A door at the far end of the hall opened, and a man emerged, waving them forward.

"Yeah, come in, come in. They said you were on your way. I'm James Powell." He offered his hand to them both, and Frank made a mental note of the flimsy handshake.

James Powell led them into the back of the house into a large room which was a kitchen on the left hand-side and an informal sitting room on the right. In the space between the two halves of the room was a large farmhouse table surrounded by mismatched chairs. In the centre of the back wall there were French windows looking out onto a sprawling garden. They were open, and the sun shone very pleasantly into the room. Motes of dust floated in the shafts of sunlight. The kitchen units were modern and expensive, but the rest of the room was rather cluttered and battered-looking.

"We've come to ask you some questions about Jane Sinclair," said Frank, after introducing himself and Steven Brown.

James Powell nodded. His handsome face looked red and puffy, like a man who had been crying or had very little sleep, or both. He was of average height and wiry build. In his mid-forties, his blonde hair was turning white, and he wore it in a style which he had probably had since his teens; short around the face and sides and much longer at the back. He wore a gold earring in one ear, a heavy gold necklace and bracelet, and several gold sovereign rings on his fingers. When he smiled he showed one gold-capped tooth at the right upper side of his mouth.

Ageing rock star, thought Frank.

"Yes, of course," said James Powell, "fire away. Please - sit down, can I get you a drink?"

They declined, still being awash with Sadie Mountjoy's tea, and sat down at the kitchen table. James Powell sat down opposite them and began to fidget. He seemed ill at ease, as well as upset.

"I understand that you and Mrs Sinclair had a relationship sometime last year?" Frank decided to get straight to the point.

"Yes, we did. For about six months. Then we broke up."

"Whose decision was it?"

"Mutual really. It all got a bit difficult. Too many other people involved. You know - family - I have two teenage daughters. They are at University now, but I was worried about what it would do to them if me and Stella split up; they feel it when these things get gossiped about, you know?"

"When was the last time that you saw Jane?"

"I see her all the time around the village. A crowd of us meet in the pub regularly. I haven't seen her alone recently." He shifted uncomfortably in his seat.

Frank doubted that James Powell was telling him the

truth.

"Did you see her alone yesterday?"

"No, I didn't. Like I said, it's been a while."

"Where were you yesterday between four and six o'clock?"

James Powell looked as though he was about to protest, but thought better of it, "I was on my way back from Manchester, I had to pull over for a while during the storm, then arrived here about five o'clock. Stella had gone to the stables."

"So no-one can corroborate your whereabouts?"

"No, but if you're thinking that I murdered Jane you couldn't be more wrong. I loved Jane. In fact," he hung his head in his hands for a moment, and then lifted his head, "look, you may as well know, Jane and I had been seeing each other again for about the last four months. We were trying to keep it quiet. Only Stella knows."

Frank looked at him seriously. "It really would be better if you tell us the whole truth, sir. I understand you are also now having a relationship with Louise Leighton," he said coldly, "You have a busy life. What does your wife think of your affairs?"

"Stella and I have an open marriage, we are not really man and wife any more - we're more like close friends. It's hard for other people to understand."

"Perhaps, sir. You're a photographer, I believe?"

"Yes - portraits and fashion shoots mainly. I go abroad a lot, you know? I've got a studio over in Manchester that I stay at sometimes."

"Can you think of anyone who might want to harm Jane?"

"No, I really can't. Why would they? She was a lovely girl."

"What about Louise Leighton? Is she the jealous type? Was she aware that you and Jane had started seeing each other again?"

"She and I weren't that seriously involved, so she had no reason to be jealous. She didn't know about me and Jane getting together again. Anyway, she's a teacher, for God's sake. This is a small Yorkshire village. People don't go around killing each other."

"But somebody did exactly that, Mr Powell. I ask you again, can you think of anyone who might have hurt Jane?"

"No, no," James said, wiping his eyes with his hand, "I'm sorry, I'm just not handling all of this very well."

Frank suppressed a sigh. James Powell was either genuinely grief-stricken or a plausible performer. It was too early to tell which.

James Powell got up and walked over to the open French windows and nervously lit a cigarette, inhaling deeply, and blowing the smoke out into the garden.

Poor Jane, thought Frank, it seems that when she chose to follow her heart's desire she was as cursed as the Lady Of Shallot, daring to leave her enchanted mirror. James Powell returned to the table and Steven Brown asked more questions about his affair with Jane Sinclair, and about his work, and his life in the village.

"Right, Mr Powell," said Frank, finally rising from his chair. "Please keep us informed of any trips other than to Manchester, and also if you have any plans to go abroad."

As the two policemen walked away from the house, Frank puzzled about the Powell's marriage.

"Bit of a weird relationship, sir?" said Steven Brown, echoing his own thoughts. "Him," pointing towards the house, "and her," pointing up the road in the direction which Stella had taken.

"Succinctly put, Sergeant," said Frank with a wry grin.

Diamonds And Pebbles

Chapter 6

Having walked in the oppressive heat towards the north end of the village, DCI Frank MacDonald and his Detective Sergeant turned down an unpromising path which led off the main street. The path was initially flanked on both sides by overgrown leylandii, and then opened out to reveal a row of four terraced houses which ran along the right-hand side. Number 4, Chestnut Terrace, was at the end of the row. The first three houses were neat, tidy, and well-maintained with manicured lawns and shrubs in their tiny front gardens, and a plethora of window boxes and hanging baskets, all over-flowing in their late summer profusion. Each plot was sharply defined by a white picket fence and gate. The last house in the row had an air of neglect, in stark contrast to the others. The front garden and a large area to the side were covered in long grass and edged with brambles. The garden, if such it could be called, was strewn with rubbish, and a half-dismantled motor-bike stood forlornly in one corner. A makeshift washing line was strung across from the house to a falling down shed, and assorted grey underwear hung there disconsolately. The front door, its paintwork peeling and cracked, did not look as though it had been opened for a very long time, so they walked round to the side of the house to the kitchen door which was open, and looked directly into a small kitchen. Frank knocked on the open door (leaving the door open was a habit in West Wold it seemed) and was answered by a 'Come in' from a female voice. The two men passed through the very dirty and untidy kitchen into a rather bare living room with windows to front and back. To the left there was a cheap dining table and four chairs, to the right a three-piece suite, television and coffee table - all of which had seen better days - arranged around a mantle-piece with an ancient gas fire. The white walls had faded to a nicotine yellow. Every available surface was littered with mugs, used plates and dirty ash-trays. A greater contrast to Jane Sinclair's immaculate home was hard to imagine.

On the sofa sat a woman, the owner of the voice, and a boy of about eighteen. The boy was dressed in funereal black, with black hair and metal studs in his eyebrows, lips and ears, and was playing desultorily on a hand-held games consul. The woman was watching the television, which was on very loudly. She looked up at the men, but did not bother to get out of her seat.

"Mrs Johnson?" asked Frank, "we'd like to speak to you about your sister Jane." He briefly introduced himself and Steven.

"I'm Julia Johnson," she replied unenthusiastically, with an unlit cigarette dangling from her mouth. Since she did not invite them to sit they did anyway. Frank regarded her. Like her son, she was dressed in black, in a baggy T-shirt, jogging pants, and black clogs. Her hair was short and spiky, and dyed an unlikely and unfortunate shade of plum. She was very overweight, and the ash-tray beside her was overflowing with cigarette ends. Frank struggled to reconcile the difference between this woman and her sister. In the many photographs which he had seen in Lilac Cottage, Jane Sinclair appeared to be a vivacious and attractive woman; he preferred to think of her that way, as opposed to the saddening memory of her lifeless corpse. He could, however, see a similarity in the facial features which spoke of a family resemblance. Julia, sitting placidly on her sofa, did not have the air of someone who had just had a sister murdered.

"In private if you don't mind," said Frank, indicating the boy.

"Oh, there's nothing I can't say in front of Jason."

"Nevertheless," said Frank in his steeliest voice.

She sighed, "Go on then, Jason. Go upstairs." The boy sloped off reluctantly and clomped upstairs into the bedroom above, and Frank got the distinct impression of an ear pressed to the ceiling above him. The noise from the television was annoying him intensely.

"If you could turn the television off please, Mrs Johnson?"

She sighed again, and reluctantly aimed the remote control at the set. A blessed silence descended.

"Go on then," she said ungraciously, finally lighting the cigarette, and inhaling with an air of grim satisfaction.

"You are aware that your sister was murdered last night?" The woman was so unconcerned that Frank wondered if there had been some terrible mistake, and she did not know.

"Yes. Roger rang me last night."

But you couldn't be bothered to go and offer your condolences, thought Frank.

"We are trying to build up a picture of Jane to enable us to find out who killed her. What would you say she was like?"

"What was she like? Now there's a question. Look, you may as well know that there was no love lost between me and Janey. We're sisters yes, and we live in the same village, but that's about as far as it goes."

Poor Jane, thought Frank, no family to grieve for her.

"But her husband said that you were a frequent visitor to Lilac Cottage."

"Oh, Lilac Cottage! More like Buckingham-bloody-Palace. Janey really thought she was something special. Like the Lady-of-the-Manor, when after all it was only a two bed-roomed cottage. At the posh end of the village, of course."

"Why *did* you visit her then?"

"We had to sort out our mother - she's in a nursing home - crippled with arthritis and senile, poor thing - sad, really. Anyway, there's always something needing doing or sorting out - money, all her belongings, insurances, solicitors and that - what's it called - Power of Eternity - so we had plenty to talk about. Mind you, it was me that got lumbered with most of the visiting - and I'll have to do it all now - "

"So you weren't close? She wouldn't have confided in you if she was in trouble of any sort?"

"Trouble? What sort of trouble?" She wriggled in her seat expectantly, hungry for a piece of gossip.

It gave Frank great pleasure to disappoint her, as he said, "Nothing specific. We just need to know what was going on in her life - why someone would want to kill her."

Julia pulled a face, and dotted the ash from her cigarette into the already-full ash-tray. "There'd be quite a few I should think. She was good at putting people's backs up was our Janey. She thought she was a cut above, even though she was born in a council house same as me. It was all champagne-this and Chanel-that. I wasn't impressed, and neither was anyone else. That clothes shop of hers was a joke. Nothing in there under two-hundred pounds, and she only managed to open it about three hours a day. Too busy doing other things if you get my meaning. She was no saint my sister. That James Powell was the latest in a long line, another rich one of course; she wasn't interested in paupers. (That bloody Stella Powell's another one; thinks the sun shines out of her own arse.) Roger spoilt Janey rotten and she didn't appreciate it a bit."

"You were aware of her relationship with James Powell, then?"

"Yes, not that she told me anything, but I saw them a couple of times in the pub, sitting together thick as thieves and trying to pretend that nothing was going on. That all started last summer but soon petered out. Janey was enough to get on anybody's nerves after a while. Why Roger put up with her all those years I don't know. Bossy isn't the word! I don't know what she thought was going to happen in her little romance. There's no way that James Powell was ever going to settle down with Janey. He's been giving Stella the run-around for years, he has, with all those models and celebrities that he photographs. He moved on to Louise Leighton this year, anyway."

"What do you make of Louise?"

Julia considered, "Don't know her that well, but she seems a bit of a cold fish if you ask me. Like she's not really with you half the time. Always got something else on her mind."

"Did Jane talk to you about James? Or the fact that he had got together with Louise?"

"Nah, we didn't talk about private things really, we

weren't really sisterly like that."

"You were her elder sister; is that correct? What was she like as a child?"

"Yes, I was six years old when Janey came along and spoilt everything. She was always the favourite, with that red hair down to her waist in no time. She had everything, and I got nothing after that. Not only did she get the looks and the love, but then she stole Roger from me. I met him first - I introduced them, more fool me. She dropped her knickers for him alright, not till after the wedding of course, wanted to make sure he'd marry her. She wasn't stupid, Janey, I'll give her that. Got all his money as well. She was tight with it, never offered me a penny when my husband left me with three bloody kids to feed," she pointed towards the ceiling. "Thank God he's the last, and he'll be gone soon."

"She was quite active in village life, I believe, your sister? Fundraising and so on?"

"Oh, yes, a cross between Rapunzel and bloody Mother Theresa, our Janey!"

Frank decided to bring this rant to a close, "Mrs Johnson, can you think of anyone who might have wanted to harm Jane?"

She thought for a moment, "Nah, not really. She was a pain sometimes, but murder - that's not right, is it?"

"If you had to choose someone from her family or friends, who would you say? Someone from here in the village."

She thought for a moment, before saying, "Well, if I had to pick it would be Stella. Stands to reason really; Janey had been screwing Stella's husband, probably still was for all I know, so Stella put a stop to it. Yeah, she comes over as all Miss Prissy Pants, but she's a dark horse really - oh, horse!

that's good! - yeah, I reckon she could whack somebody over the head if the mood took her. (Roger told me it was probably a candlestick that killed Janey!) Louise Leighton had better watch out in that case - she could be next!" Julia seemed quite animated by this prospect.

Frank left a silence, and watched Steven Brown writing in his notebook for a few moments before saying, "And where were you between the hours of four and six yesterday afternoon, Mrs Johnson?"

She looked dumbfounded, "I was sitting here minding my own business, if it's got anything to do with you."

"It has, Mrs Johnson. This is a murder investigation. We'll need you to make a written statement."

"As you like," she shrugged her shoulders, and took another deep drag on her cigarette before stubbing it out into the ashtray beside her.

The two men stood up and left shortly afterwards, saying goodbye. Julia Johnson immediately switched the television back on, and lit another cigarette. She still had not moved off the sofa.

Diamonds And Pebbles

Chapter 7

Shortly afterwards, they stood outside Louise Leighton's tiny terraced cottage, one of a row of six overlooking the triangular village green and across from the public house, *The Prancing Pony*. The sun was fully overhead in a cloudless blue sky, and the heat was creating a haze which floated a foot above the melting tarmac of the road. Frank had taken off his jacket with relief and tossed it onto the back seat of the car as they walked past it. He pushed the doorbell and they heard it ring inside. A figure appeared through the opaque glass of the door, and it swung open. A young woman in her early-thirties beckoned them in, and held out her hand to Frank.

"I'm Louise Leighton, Jane's friend. Pleased to meet you. You must be Frank MacDonald." Her handshake was very firm.

Frank nodded, "We've come to ask you about Jane Sinclair."

They stepped inside, straight into a small, but immaculately clean and tidy sitting room decorated with stripped wood, white walls, and black-and-chrome furniture. The chimney breast had a rectangular recess cut into it, and instead of a fire there was a pile of carefully arranged stones. The ground floor of the house was entirely open-plan with a steel, open-tread staircase running sideways across the middle of the space, dividing the front from the back. The walls had examples of what Frank thought of as 'supermarket art', picked up on the same trip as the groceries; large box canvases featuring magnified leaves in improbable colours.

Seated on one of two black leather sofas was a woman of about fifty, smoking a cigarette. Louise pointedly handed the woman an ash-tray, and introduced the two policemen to her as being her mother. The woman stood and nodded at them. She did not smile or hold out a hand.

"I'm Karen Leighton." She was small and extremely thin, to the point of scrawniness, dressed in leopard-skin leggings, a thin pink top and rather precariously high gold sandals which still did not make her tall. She had wrinkled, orange skin. Her short hair was bleached to a brassy yellow with dark roots, and she wore a pale pink lipstick which did not suit her. She was heavily decorated in gold with large hooped earrings, necklace, bangles and many rings.

"Mum's come to stay with me for a few days," said Louise Leighton. Her expression did not betray whether this arrangement was to her liking or not.

"I'd like to speak to your daughter alone, if you don't mind," said Frank to the older woman.

"Suit yourself, I'm sure," sniffed Karen Leighton, "I doubt if it'll make any difference. The police never catch any real criminals these days, do they? Too busy arresting motorists for speeding, in my opinion. Fancy a murder happening in our Louise's village! It's so nice here as well. You're not safe anywhere these days, are you? You could be murdered in your own bed, easy as breathing. That Jane was a lovely girl as well. Very fond of my Louise, she was. Always doing something, organising this and that, for the village. Well, I'll leave you in peace. I'll just nip over the road, Louise, and have a drink with Brian." She picked up her packet of cigarettes, a gold lighter, and a rather gaudy, gold handbag, and tottered out of the front door.

"She's going to the pub," explained Louise, "She rather likes Brian Sykes, the landlord. Come through."

She led them to the back of the house, which had the same décor as the front, and contained a modern pale wood and steel kitchen. She offered them a cold drink, and indicated the peninsular breakfast bar which jutted out into the room and was flanked by chrome bar stools. Perching somewhat precariously (and ridiculously as far as he was concerned) on a stool, Frank watched her as she took a plastic container out of the freezer, filled three glasses with ice and poured orange juice over.

Louise Leighton was a mousey blonde with immaculately cut and highlighted shoulder-length hair. She was of medium height and slim. She was wearing a blue vest-top, white jeans and no shoes and her skin was a perfect, golden brown. She had pale blue eyes and a blandly pretty face. She wore a little make-up, expertly applied, and her finger and toe-nails were painted a delicate shade of pink. She soon joined them with the drinks, and sat on one of the stools opposite them. Steven got out his notebook and rested it on the breakfast bar, ready to take notes.

"I'm so upset about Jane," she said, "I just don't know what this is going to mean for me, really. It's terrible news." The sensibilities expressed in her words did not quite reach the expression on her face.

"Yes, it is. We're trying to form a picture of Jane so that we can gain some insight into her life, and hopefully find out who killed her. I understand that you are a teacher?" said Frank as he sipped the cold drink, grateful for something to parch his thirst.

"I'm a Geography teacher in York. I've lived in West Wold for about two years."

"How did you and Jane meet?"

"I worked in *The Prancing Pony* for a while when I first moved here. The Sinclairs were part of the crowd. We got chatting, and it went from there."

"And would you say you were close?"

Louise hesitated, and then said, "Yes, I would. Jane organised a lot of activities in the village and she roped me in - I was very happy to help." She spoke in a polite, measured voice. Every now and then there was a catch in her throat, as though she was trying to control her emotions. (No real tears though, thought Frank.) She had an immobile face which did not change expression when she spoke.

"I understand that you were quite keen to go into partnership with her at one stage - in the dress shop?"

Her hands fluttered a little in surprise, "Oh, that. Well, I thought the fashion business might be fun, and she seemed to need help. Roger put her off the idea though, I don't know why. It's a shame, it would have been 'wicked', as my pupils would say."

He changed tack, "Was she in trouble of any kind? Was there a change in her behaviour?"

"I don't think so. There might be one thing though; it may not be significant. It's just that I've seen her a few times lately getting in or out of a silver BMW. There was a man driving, I didn't see him clearly, and I didn't recognise him."

"Thank-you for that. Did you happen to notice the

registration number?"

"No, I'm sorry, I didn't think it might be important."

"Miss Leighton, can you think of anyone who might want to kill Jane?"

She hesitated, and said, "Look, I may be out of line here, but I think Stella Powell had as good a motive as any. Jane had an affair with James not that long ago and Stella was very jealous - I've seen her looking daggers at Jane in the pub."

Frank judged it to be the right time to turn up the heat a little, "I believe you yourself are now having a relationship with him?"

Again, she seemed surprised that Frank had been appraised of the gossip quite so quickly, and shifted uncomfortably on her stool. "Well - yes, I have. It's obviously no secret."

"You said that Stella was jealous of Jane, and therefore presumably of yourself, but the Powells claim to have an open marriage?"

"That's just Stella's way of covering up her mortification at the way James behaves."

"With women like you," said Frank quietly, looking her straight in the eye.

Her expression did not change, and she said, "If you like." She hesitated and then made up her mind, "Look, there's something else. I hate to do this to James, but I have to tell the truth. I think Jane's been pestering him lately - wanting them to get back together, wanting them to live together. I've seen her trying to corner him in the pub. James couldn't stand it, he just wanted to concentrate on me," she said, batting her eyelashes and trying to look bashful, "I hate to think he got so stressed out by her, and Stella, and everything, that he did something terrible."

"So you think both of the Powells had a motive for murdering Jane?"

"In different ways, yes," she said.

"Interesting - thank-you for being so frank with us, Miss Leighton," Frank said. A thought occurred to him, and he continued, "Jane must have known about you and James Powell?"

"I don't know - we didn't discuss it. It was a subject that was hard for us to broach, I suppose."

Not that close a friendship, thought Frank.

"You were rivals for the affection of the same man. That must have affected your friendship, surely?"

"I didn't see it that way, Mr MacDonald. Jane was part of his past as far as I was concerned. Jane and I chose not to discuss it, as I've said."

"Where were you yesterday tea-time, Miss Leighton?" he asked.

She took the sudden change of direction in her stride, "Well, I had a hair appointment in York at four fifteen. I left here, and went to the petrol station on the main road at about half-past three. I can probably find the receipt if you like. I was late for the hairdressers because the storm caused problems on the roads."

"Thank-you. Yes, the receipt would be useful if you still have it. Can you tell us a little about your own background?" said Frank, changing the subject again.

"Yes, - I've been teaching for about six years. I left school at sixteen without many qualifications. I left home pretty soon afterwards and worked at different jobs for a while - waitressing and bar-work. I was married briefly but it didn't last. I went travelling abroad and drifted round for a while, then came back and decided to work with children, so I trained to be a nursery nurse. I was a nanny for a few years - with two or three families - and then I decided to train to be a teacher, got my qualifications at night-class and applied to University."

"What made you move out here to West Wold?"

"I felt like a change from the city, I suppose. I've lived in and around York for most of my life. I thought it would be an opportunity to meet some new friends."

Louise Leighton struck Frank as a rather lonely person. He said, "And did you? Make friends?"

"Yes," she smiled, or assumed the expression which approximated to a smile in her curiously emotionless face, "everyone's been very nice. Especially Jane." She reached over and got a tissue from a box which stood on the kitchen counter, and wiped an imaginary tear away.

Frank decided to change tack, and said, "When did your mother arrive? Was she here yesterday?"

"No. She drove here this morning. She lives in York with her latest boyfriend. They argue a lot, and she comes here whenever things get too difficult. I think she'd like to live here permanently, but I couldn't cope with that, I'm afraid." Frank looked at her for an ironic smile to soften this statement, but one did not appear.

She saw the look, and said, "There's no love lost between my mother and me, Mr MacDonald. She's behaved badly to me in the past. She used to try to steal my boyfriends off me when I lived at home. She used to go to the pub and leave me on my own in the house when I was a child, from as young as I can remember. She left me on my own for two weeks to go on holiday every year, from when I was twelve years old. We were always moving around as well when I was small, gathering our things together in the middle of the night, moving in with whoever was her latest man, or someone would move in with us. I was always having to change schools, start again, try to make new friends. It wasn't easy. I only put up with her now because - well - she's family. I have no brothers or sisters, and I never knew my father. She might have been rubbish as a mother, but she's all I've got, I'm afraid. She's a liar, too. Don't believe a word she says to you. I left home at seventeen, and married very young to get away from her. It didn't last, of course. But I managed to straighten my life out eventually, and now I've got a nice home and a good job, and James."

"And do you think you and James Powell will stay together? Perhaps move in together?"

She shrugged her shoulders in a rather churlish way, and said, "I don't know. Stella's not going to let go without a fight, we'll have to see."

Frank thought it best to finish for now, and looked at Steven for his agreement. "Thank-you, Miss Leighton. You've been most helpful."

They said their goodbyes, and the two policemen stepped out of the little house into the bright sunshine.

Someone else who is not telling us the whole truth? thought Frank, as they walked across The Green to Roger's mother's house. He just did not know.

Chapter 8

Roger Sinclair's mother, Daphne, sat facing the door in an easy chair by the fireplace, as the two policemen entered her comfortable sitting room once more. Roger had shown them in, introduced them, and then discreetly withdrawn. It was now about two o'clock on Saturday afternoon. The sunlight crept nervously in through the heavily-draped windows. It was hot and airless in the room.

Daphne Sinclair appeared moderately composed despite her daughter-in-law's untimely and violent death the previous day. She did not offer them a drink.

Frank was surprised that James Powell seemed to be the only person genuinely grieving over Jane. Even that could be a sham considering that he was on the list of suspects.

Frank and Steven sat down opposite Daphne Sinclair on the sofa. Steven took out his note book and pen. Frank was feeling decidedly jaded, and sighed inwardly. He felt hot and grumpy. He had rolled up his shirt sleeves on the walk across The Green in an effort to cool down, and now, faced by Daphne's imperious stare, he wished he had kept his tie and suit jacket on. He cleared his throat and began, "Tell us about Jane. Did you and she get on?"

"She was Roger's choice and I warned him at the time, but he would have her. He could have had the pick of the crop, with our good name in this area, but no, he had to go off to York and find somebody who had been dragged up goodness-knows-where," she said, her voice loud and strident. She was a plump woman in her mid-seventies with tightly-curled, grey hair and a plain face that was used to getting its own way. A wooden walking stick leant against her right leg. She wore a pink cardigan, pink blouse, thick brown skirt, tights and brown leather shoes. She had led a largely useless life, being both vain and selfish. Born at the beginning of the Second World War, she had been lucky not to have suffered its deprivations or those that followed in the post-war world of the Nineteen-Fifties, coming as she did from a relatively wealthy family. The flamboyance and permissiveness of the Nineteen-Sixties had passed her by, and she had made a dutiful and successful marriage to someone suitable, as her family had expected. Her most significant achievement had been to bear two children, but raising them had afforded her little pleasure. She had attended church, and joined in its associated activities such as the Mother's Union, in a grudging way all of her life, but the joy of religion, the joy of *anything,* had never entered her soul.

"She defied me from the start. She liked her own way, did Jane," Daphne Sinclair continued petulantly (I think that makes two of you, thought Frank). "She had Roger wrapped around her little finger. She wasn't even faithful to him. Oh, he thinks I don't know but I do, I know everything that has gone on over the years. He would have been better off with Julia as it turned out, he brought her out here to meet me first. Don't look so surprised. She is a lot more down to earth than Jane, and she was alright before she got so fat and dyed her hair that dreadful colour. Flighty, Jane was. Flighty, self-opinionated, and never lifted a finger for me. I'm very bad on my legs these days, but never got any offers of help from that quarter."

"But did she have any enemies?"

She thought for a moment, "No, not that I know of. She had disagreements with a few people over the years, but nothing that serious. With all her faults, she didn't deserve to be killed like that. I don't know what the village is coming to. A defenceless woman killed in her own home by goodness-knows-who."

"If you had to choose someone here in the village, who would you say? Just between us, of course," Frank asked.

"Well," Daphne considered, "Logically, it would have to be Stella Powell. Jane was having an affair with her husband, after all. By the way, when can we have the funeral? The arrangements must be made. Roger said it could be weeks before her body is released for burial. That's not right. We simply must have a proper funeral soon. I really must insist. The Chief Constable is an acquaintance of mine and I could get the matter taken up - ", her voice grew louder and more strident.

"I'm afraid it won't be possible just yet," said Frank patiently, "We must be completely sure that we have all the forensic evidence, or actually catch her killer, first." He decided to change the topic, "How often did you see Jane? Had you noticed any change in her recently?"

"Well, she was here most Sundays, I suppose. She and Roger took me out for lunch quite often. Roger comes to church with me most Sundays. Not Jane, though, quite the heathen she was. I saw her last Sunday and she seemed - well, now you mention it - she did seem rather subdued. I even asked her if she felt unwell, she was so dull. Normally, she was very chatty."

"And what did she say?"

"'Just a headache' she said."

"Do you think your son was happy with her, Mrs Sinclair? Were there problems in the marriage?"

"Apart from her constant infidelity, you mean?" she barked, giving him a withering look. "I hope you are not suggesting that he killed her. Absurd! He was a good, caring husband and better than she deserved, I can tell you. She wanted for nothing."

"They had no children though?"

"No, it is a shame, I would have liked grandchildren. My own daughter would not oblige me, either. Jane didn't seem to mind though. She kept herself busy with that shop of hers. She was always cheerful, I'll say that for her. But selfish too, she never looked after Roger properly. Not to my mind."

"But he was content with his life, you think?"

"Yes, at first. He was besotted, like the cat that got the cream. She was an attractive girl - very vain though - all that hair! They settled down alright together I suppose, and he seemed happy enough. She made a fool of him a few times though, that I know of – "

Frank sensed that he would get nothing more from her that was of any relevance, and swiftly brought the interview to a close. The two policemen said a brief farewell to Roger Sinclair and left the house, stepping out into the fresher air with relief.

Chapter 9

James Powell showed them into the large kitchen at Howard House again later on that Saturday afternoon. It was their last interview of the day, and Frank was already feeling exhausted, but he found himself looking forward to seeing Stella Powell with a sense of anticipation, which, if he had examined his feelings closely, he would have realised he had not felt for a long time. Mixed up in this was the growing comprehension that, if Louise Leighton and the others were right, then Stella had to be considered as one of his main suspects. Now dressed in T-shirt and shorts, she was standing at the sink, and invited them to sit at the dining table whilst she made them a cup of tea. Frank and Steven were sated with beverages by this time, but politely accepted nevertheless. James Powell, his handsome face still reddened with grief, quickly left the room.

Stella joined them at the dining table, sitting opposite Frank.

"Mrs Powell – " Frank began.

"Call me Stella, please."

"Stella, we're just trying to form a picture of Jane, and talking to the people closest to her, to see if we can start to understand who might have wanted to kill her. When was the last time you saw her?"

"Yesterday lunchtime. It must have been not long before she was killed, I suppose," Stella said and looked upset, suddenly, "I bumped into her as she was closing the shop, and she invited me back for a coffee."

"How did she seem?"

"Perfectly normal. We had a drink and a chat, and I left after about three quarters of an hour."

"And you noticed nothing unusual? Anyone hanging around who shouldn't have been there?"

"No, I'm sorry. I really wish I could help."

"You and she were friends?"

"Yes, sort of. Not close friends, though. It's complicated. The thing is, we have both known each other most of our adult lives, but we were not really close. I've known Roger since we were young children, although he's a bit older than me. When Roger came to live back in West Wold with Jane we all got friendly. She could be good fun, when she chose. You need to understand, Jane didn't have female friends really. She was far more interested in men. A room full of women was an empty room as far as she was concerned."

"But you did spend time together?"

"Yes, we both sat on the village fête committee, did the cricket teas, that sort of thing, and I used to see her and Roger regularly on Sunday nights in *The Prancing Pony*."

"What was your opinion of their marriage?"

"Like any other twenty-year old marriage I should think," she replied levelly.

"Do you think she had any enemies?"

"No! I'm sorry, I really don't. Jane was a bit loud sometimes; a bit arrogant and self-opinionated maybe, but I don't know why anyone would want to kill her."

Frank MacDonald paused, the next question was going to be tricky, "Mrs Powell, Stella - we have been told that Jane had an affair with your husband last year. I have to mention it in case it is relevant to the case."

"It's alright, I know. I knew at the time."

"Were you jealous?"

Her eyes flew to his in surprise, "You think *I* killed her out of jealousy?" The green eyes narrowed, and the slight, rosy flush of anger which bloomed on her cheeks enhanced her striking looks. "What you have to understand is that James and I don't have a conventional marriage," she said, slowly and carefully, "we are just really good friends. I realised when the girls were small - we have two girls - that he was never going to be faithful to me. He's a photographer; he meets beautiful women all over the world. We haven't - that is - we've had separate rooms for years. This house is mine; it belonged to my parents. James earns a lot of money. I earn a little."

"What do you do?"

"I give riding lessons at the stables, and I write articles for magazines like *Yorkshire Life* and *Horses*, and occasionally a feature for a newspaper." She relaxed and became more animated, "I started writing pieces about horses when I was about eleven years old for the Pony Club, and it went from there. Then someone asked me to write something about my garden. It was my mother's garden; her pride and joy, and I took it over when she died. The editor likes me to 'Yorkshire' it up a bit for the gardening articles. I'm meant to be a younger version of Hannah Hauxwell, I think! I'm lucky enough to be able to write about two things that I really love - gardening and horses - but what I earn wouldn't keep the family, especially with my daughters at

University. So, in financial terms, I have the house, James has the money - enough of it that I don't have to go out and seriously earn a living. I'm really grateful for that. I get to enjoy my children, my animals, my garden and my writing - James gets to come home to a loving family life whenever he chooses to. That's the bargain. It wouldn't suit everyone but it suits us. So, yes I knew about Jane, and no, I wasn't jealous."

"Jane sounds a bit more formidable than your average model," observed Frank.

The intelligent eyes met his, "James likes beautiful women and Jane was stunning - even if she did tend to push the Titian beauty thing at you a bit - she did like to flick her hair around a lot," Stella smiled, she had recovered her composure by now, and Frank could not stop himself from smiling back, "besides, she had balls, and he likes that."

Frank suppressed another smile. The part of him that was not a policeman, the small part that was able to relax and consider his surroundings, was enjoying sitting at the table in Stella's kitchen. It felt cool compared to the blistering heat outside. The large French windows lead outside onto a stone patio and gave views out over the garden and beyond, and there were more windows above the sink, which made the room bright and airy. The half of the room that did not contain the kitchen units and appliances had the appearance of a den with sofas, television, CD-player, and ceiling-to-floor shelves filled haphazardly with reference books, school books and novels, as well as a chaotic display of memorabilia. Frank could see the spines of the Tolkien trilogy, several Austens, Brontes, and some Dickens, a handful of John Grishams, and a neat row of fat Jilly Coopers. The walls had a selection of James

Powell's photographic portraits of well-known celebrities, minor royals, and musicians, as well as other artwork. He recognised a large print of the splendid bay horse *Whistlejacket* by Stubbs, and another of *St George and the Dragon* by Moreau with its dashing hero riding a charmingly fey white stallion, both of which paintings Frank had seen in the National Gallery. In the background of the Moreau there is a princess praying earnestly for salvation, wearing a stupendously large crown, and with long, long hair that even Jane Sinclair might have envied. A rather effeminate and beautiful St George is killing the dragon, which cringes in terror. At the centre of the picture, however, is the horse. He is not interested in the princess, St George, or even the dragon reeling in submission at his feet. He is looking straight at the viewer with a knowing eye and he wants you to see how handsome he is. He is a dandy. He wants you to admire his flowing mane, his flying tail, his bejewelled harness. If truth be told he would not look amiss on a fairground carousel, but he does not know that. He just wants you to admire him. He just wants you to think what a fine boy he is. The horse in the other painting, *Whistlejacket,* is an altogether more serious beast. He famously won a race at York in 1759. He rears against a putty-coloured background, showing off every sinew and muscle. For once he is free, and unfettered by saddle, jockey and whip. If you moved towards him he would bolt. He is magnificent, but he does not know it.

Frank inclined his head towards the pictures, "I like your prints. Have you seen the originals?"

"Oh, yes, many times. I adore the horses! I like other paintings as well of course. I wouldn't want you to think I was a straw-chewing philistine!"

Frank chuckled good-naturedly, but then reminded

himself that Stella could be a killer. He decided to change the subject.

"Where were you yesterday afternoon around four o'clock?"

"I was here alone - James had gone to Manchester. I was writing at the kitchen table, and I suddenly lifted my head up and realised how dark it had become outside. I thought about going down to help at the stables - I knew they would be trying to get the horses sheltered - but then the rain and the thunder started. I just stood at the windows and watched the storm - it was awe-inspiring. I walked down to the stables when the rain stopped about quarter past four."

"So you walked past Lilac Cottage? Did you notice anything unusual?"

"Yes, I did walk past, but it seemed fine."

Frank said. "Tell us some more about Jane and your husband."

"Well, it all started about a year ago. They were seeing each other secretly for a while, and then James told me about it. He asked me to keep it quiet because Roger didn't know. They were very discreet. They did spend a couple of week-ends away in the Lakes. James seemed very happy for a while. Then all of a sudden it was finished - just before last Christmas. James told me that he liked her very much. I don't really know what the problem was, but I think it was mutual. Then earlier this year, I realised that things had started up again between them. Louise Leighton was also here by then. I didn't think James really knew what he wanted. One day he sat me down and told me that he loved Jane, and was seriously considering some sort of future with her. He wanted to give me a chance to get used to the idea. Nothing was going to be decided immediately. We had to consider Ellen and Grace - our daughters - and how they would react. Again, he asked me to keep it to myself for the time being. It was awkward for me and Jane for a while. Then I told her that I knew. It made things slightly easier. She wanted me to be okay with it, but it wouldn't have made any difference if I wasn't. Jane wasn't one to let anything get in her way. My disapproval or hurt wouldn't have stopped her for a moment."

Frank nodded. Through the open French windows he could see a large, well-stocked garden, divided into haphazard sections, each with lawns and borders filled with shrubs and trees. At the back of the main lawn the land seemed to fall away downhill and he assumed there were more divisions and terraces. At the back of the main lawn there was a magnificent horse-chestnut tree; despite the storm it was still covered in the green fruits that would shortly become the treasure-filled conker-cases of the autumn. The only shrubs that Frank could identify were the roses that bloomed in profusion throughout the garden, of every size and colour. He knew from having spent time with his mother in her garden that the beauty and seeming naturalness of the display was the result of a lot of hard work. Stella's house and garden were so much a reflection of their owner; warm and generous.

Reluctantly, Frank acknowledged that it was time to go and nodded to Steven to wrap things up. They left Howard House and walked back towards The Green. Frank decided, at the end of that long, hot Saturday afternoon, that a cool pint of best bitter might be just the thing that he needed. It never did any harm to get acquainted with the local landlord. They were normally good sources of village gossip and unlikely bits of information. Also, it seemed as though Jane Sinclair had been a regular visitor to the public house, so it was worth having a look.

The Prancing Pony was on one side of the triangular village green; an old stone construction with a large stone porch on the front. They ducked under the low lintel of the door into the cool shade of an old-fashioned interior. Black beams, horse brasses, antique plates and humorous notices gave a welcoming, cosy feel to the place. The bar was furnished with round, copper-topped tables, small stools and plush banquettes around the walls. Beyond the bar was a large room which housed a busy restaurant.

"Afternoon, gents," said a burly, balding man behind the bar, "What can I get you?"

"Two pints of your best bitter, please," said Frank. He got out his warrant badge, as did Steven Brown. "I'm DCI Frank MacDonald, and this is DS Steven Brown. We're investigating the death of Jane Sinclair."

"Oh, aye?"

"And you are?"

"Brian Sykes, landlord."

"You knew Jane Sinclair, I believe?"

"Aye. A real looker, she was. Organised just about everything that happened in the village. Had us all in our place, good and proper. When she said 'jump' you jumped, if you know what I mean. Nice enough girl, I suppose," he said noncommittally, "her and Roger often dropped in here. Bit of a tease, if you know what I mean."

Frank nodded curtly, and he and Steven moved away from the bar and over to the far end of the room to sit at one of the small tables.

"Shades of a spurned lover, sir?" asked Steven Brown.

Frank sipped his pint and nodded, "Yes, he can go straight on the suspect list."

They chatted and relaxed for a while. Frank took advantage of this rare opportunity to speak to Steven at length about his young family. As they talked Frank cast an eye around the bar. A couple of regulars, sitting on the high stools at the bar, dressed in T-shirts and jeans, looked like the type of customer who may as well pay their ill-gotten gains straight into Brian Sykes' bank account. Round the other side of the bar, some golfers stood chatting and an older man, dressed smartly in shirt and cravat, and slacks, was reading a paperback book as he drank. Otherwise the bar was empty. Frank and Steven sat companionably and finished their drinks.

As they drove back to York at the end of a long day, Frank mentally reviewed the people he had met and the stories which they had told him. He felt covered in a fine film of opinion and deceit, like a cobweb on his face; he could not wait to have a shower and wash it all away. He felt the familiar sense of trepidation which was usual at this stage of an investigation, and also overwhelmed by personalities, facts and conjecture. However, he had faith in his own ability to unravel the mystery. Someone he had spoken to today had been the killer, he felt sure. Someone, or possibly everyone, had lied, but who? And how the hell was he going to find out?

Diamonds And Pebbles

Chapter 10

Later, relaxing in one of his reclining chairs, Frank thought about his son Nathan. When Nathan had reached the difficult age of thirteen, and hit puberty like a wall, he turned from a sweet, chatty boy into a silent hermit almost overnight. He no longer wanted to spend extended periods with Frank, especially at his grandparents' house, but admitted that Frank's flat was 'cool'. Frank almost gave up hope of ever having a proper conversation with his son again. After a series of monosyllabic outings and cancelled trips (cancelled by Nathan), Frank despaired of having any kind of relationship with his son and, to his regret, had virtually stopped contact for a long time; almost two years.

During this estrangement, Frank had fallen in with the crowd at the police station who were always willing to go for a drink after work, either in the local public house or in the city centre, and for months he only used his flat to sleep, shower, and lie low during hangovers. He did not listen to music or read a book. The morning that he woke up with his fourth hangover in a row, in some ungodly suburb of York, with a woman whose name he could not remember, he told himself that it was time to stop. He was deeply ashamed of himself, his work was suffering - his brain barely functioned some days - and he missed Nathan.

Walking through the middle of York one day shortly afterwards, Frank was drawn into a camping exhibition, and, looking around at all the latest tents, rucksacks, camping stoves and other paraphernalia, he wondered whether this might be a way to re-establish contact with his son. On an impulse, he bought a tent and two sleeping bags. Later he rang Nathan with much trepidation and proposed a one-night stay in the Yorkshire Dales. He expected teenage scorn, but Nathan, a little older and wiser, had agreed. They later spent an enjoyable afternoon in a camping shop buying anoraks, and rucksacks, and waterproof trousers, and woolly hats and all manner of expensive gear. Frank had done a bit of fishing as a boy, and decided that this might be a suitable diversion, so they set about buying rods and reels and baskets with relish, too. The first trip had been a little tentative, but had gone quite well. Frank was worried that Nathan would find the fishing boring, but he appeared content, spending much of the time with the speakers of his personal stereo pressed firmly into his ears, whilst they sat on a riverbank waiting for the fish to bite. The trips became a regular occurrence, at weekends and during school holidays, and Frank looked forward to them, arranging them as often as his caseload would allow. Frank had started off with the romantic idea of surviving in the wild, and that they would live off what they could catch or find. This notion had quickly disappeared in the face of reality, and they were just as likely to ditch the tent and stay in a country inn at the first drop of rain as brave the prevailing conditions. Equally, their survival often entailed tucking into steak and chips at a restaurant, when the local wildlife had failed to co-operate.

Frank wisely did not try to force conversation or false intimacy during the first few trips, but allowed a not-so-comfortable silence to evolve into a comfortable one. Then, slowly, Nathan began to talk - about school, friends, television, films he had seen, the books he was reading - nothing much, but Frank felt a huge relief. After several trips they were at ease. Nathan was emerging from his hermit years, and did not seem to bear a grudge that Frank had neglected him so badly for so long. Gradually they found a shared sense of humour - putting up the tent always caused fits of giggles - and a real pleasure in each other's company. Nathan turned out to be ten times more practical than Frank, and if anyone had survival skills it was he. Frank imparted the little knowledge he had about the native habitat, learned from his father in his own childhood. He even managed to drag some of the Latin names from his memory. This seemed to light a spark in Nathan, and he started to learn about the natural world for himself. Before long his knowledge outstripped Frank's and it was Nathan who taught Frank about Botany, Biology, and Ecology. Nathan's interest had become so strong that he was intending to study Botany at University if he succeeded in his exams. Frank was delighted that his son seemed to have found a vocation. In the evenings after they had eaten and the campfire was glowing, they sat and talked. Nathan was interested in Frank's work and Frank had lots of stories to tell. Slowly, they began to talk about real issues; about Nathan's mother and step-father, the divorce, and Frank's life. The best day for Frank was when Nathan started asking for his advice about school, girls, and intimate matters, and he finally felt like a father again.

Frank was much happier of late; he felt that his life was back under control. He enjoyed his work, he enjoyed being with Nathan and his family, and he enjoyed spending time alone in his flat. He rarely socialised with colleagues, and kept away from alcohol for the most part, only allowing himself a glass of his favourite single malt whisky at night, reclining in his chair, listening to music, musing about his current case, or thinking about his family.

Chapter 11

Extract from a diary;

I DID IT. I KILLED HER. I PLANNED IT ALL. SHE'S DEAD. SHE DESERVED IT, THE BITCH. SHE WON'T KEEP HIM NOW. HE'S MINE NOW. OR THE OTHER THING. SHE CAN'T HAVE THAT NOW. THAT WASN'T FAIR. NO, NOT FAIR. SHE NEVER EVEN KNEW WHAT HAD HAPPENED. SHE LOOKED SO SURPRISED. I NEARLY LAUGHED. I HIT HER. REALLY HARD. I HIT HER TWICE TO MAKE SURE. PLENTY OF BLOOD. NONE ON ME THOUGH. I WAS REALLY CAREFUL. BLOOD ALL OVER HER LOVELY HAIR. SHAME. THE CANDLESTICK WAS HEAVY. THAT BLOODY STORM! IT ALMOST RUINED EVERYTHING. AND THE WELLIES! TRUST HER TO HAVE SUCH SMALL FEET. THEY WON'T GUESS IT WAS ME. THEY'RE TOO STUPID. THAT STUPID POLICEMAN. I'M TOO CLEVER FOR HIM. HE'S ANOTHER ONE WHO THINKS HE'S SO CLEVER. NOW I'LL SHOW HIM. THE OTHER ONE'S NEXT. I'LL GET HER

TOO. SHE THINKS SHE'S SO LOVELY. I'LL HIT HER TOO. REALLY HARD.

Sunday

Diamonds And Pebbles

Chapter 12

"Right everyone, listen up, let's go through what we've got so far. I assume you've all read and inwardly digested yesterday's interview notes." Frank MacDonald was addressing the members of his investigation team. It was eight o'clock on the Sunday morning after Jane Sinclair's death. The team consisted of some four or five Detectives Constables and a liaison officer from the uniformed branch, and was meeting in the designated investigation room for the case at York Police Station. The team were grouped informally on chairs around a table in front of three whiteboards. Coffee mugs and plates, with the remains of breakfasts, were on the table. One or two younger members of the team looked distinctly hung over, as though they had gone straight to work from whichever club they had found themselves in, as the dawn broke over York. Frank and Steven Brown sat in front of them, facing the group. After a good night's sleep, Frank was feeling exhilarated at having a new case to work on, to crack, and to end by bringing a killer to justice. Murder was far from common in North Yorkshire, and he had had his share of the more pedestrian Serious Crimes recently. He was reasonably happy with what they had achieved the previous day, and had an instinctive feeling that the murderer was one of the people that they had already spoken to in West Wold.

The buzz of conversation in the room stopped as everyone settled down to listen. "I'd like to spend this morning going through in fine detail what we know so far; the interviews, house-to-house enquiries, etc. Steven," said Frank, "Would you do the honours?"

Steven Brown stood up, tall and ungainly, unravelling his long limbs as he rose from the chair. He picked up some marker pens, and began to speak and write on the central whiteboard. "We have the victim - Jane Sinclair - aged forty, medium height, slim, distinguishing feature; long, red hair. Apparently killed in the living room of Lilac Cottage, West Wold, by two blows to the head with a blunt object, most likely a silver candlestick found next to the body," ("Mrs Peacock in the library" quipped some wag at the back), "as per the photos – " Steven quickly spread a dozen or more large photographs of the crime scene on the table " - approximate time of death is thought to be between four and six on Friday evening, which coincides with just after the time of the thunderstorm, by the way. No reason to believe that she was killed elsewhere and taken there afterwards, at the moment."

"Any news on the fingerprints?" asked Frank.

"No forensics back yet, sir. They're stretched with so many people being off on annual holidays. They're trying their best for tomorrow. All the main players and suspects will be fingerprinted and DNA-ed, but the SOCOs thought that the site of the murder was pretty 'clean' in DNA terms. In any case, most of our current suspects were regular visitors to the cottage, so DNA will not necessarily be helpful. Jane was married to Roger Sinclair, and having an affair with James Powell, a well-known photographer who lives in West Wold. They had started an affair last year but parted; things started up again recently. She seems to have had quite a strong personality, rather out-spoken, and well-known in the village. Roger Sinclair discovered the body, and claims to have been at work all day until he got home. This was later corroborated by his secretary." He nodded at DC Emma Smith, a bright twenty-five year-old, whose job it was to co-ordinate all the tasks identified during the investigation and report back to Steven. "James Powell has no alibi, he says he was in Manchester alone, and then driving back to West Wold," he continued, "We'll come to suspects and motives later. James' wife, Stella Powell was a friend of the victim, and says she was at home at the time in question, but later passed Lilac Cottage on her way to the stables. She was probably the last person to see Jane alive; she was at the cottage with Jane earlier and left around one o'clock. Louise Leighton, also a friend, also having an affair with James Powell (busy boy!), reported seeing Jane Sinclair in a silver BMW several times during the last few weeks, so we need names and addresses for all owners in a twenty mile radius to start with. Also, there is a petrol station just north of the village, see if they've got the CCTV footage for Friday, and work backwards from there. Louise Leighton had a hairdresser's appointment in York at quarter-past four, and has a petrol receipt for the petrol station at three twenty-nine. Jane Sinclair has a sister, Julia Johnson, who also lives in West Wold. They don't appear to have been particularly close, although Roger Sinclair said she was often at the cottage. In terms of suspects; Roger Sinclair must be top of the list as things stand, because he was her husband and he found the body, although motive is uncertain at this stage, unless it has to do with Jane's affairs (of which there were many, according to his mother). James Powell appears to be very upset, but Louise Leighton reckoned that Jane may have been pressing him for a reconciliation that he did not want; not a particularly strong motive but there may be more to it. Stella Powell's motive would have been jealousy, although the Powells claim to have an open marriage. They've been married for twenty years but James seems to have always been a pretty 'free' spirit, shall we say. Louise Leighton's motive would also have been jealousy, although the affair between her and James seems to have been short-lived and lukewarm at best, but she told us herself that Jane Sinclair and James Powell seemed to have unfinished business. Julia Johnson was extremely envious of her sister's looks and money, and her favoured role within their family; as the elder sister Julia felt usurped when Jane was born, so sibling rivalry could be a factor, but the question would be, why now? The Sinclairs were friends with another couple, the Watsons, but they have been in Cyprus for a fortnight, and arrived back yesterday, so that rules them out. That just leaves our friend in the BMW."

Frank added, "My feeling is that the little triumvirate around James Powell is key to this; Jane, Stella and Louise, but we can't rule out any of the others at this stage, and of course we may not even have spoken to the killer yet. I'd like a detailed history taken from all of the main suspects - everywhere they've lived and worked, employers names and telephone numbers etc. There may be a previous connection between them which could provide a motive. Run us through what the neighbour said she saw, Steven."

"Mrs Mountjoy lives next door to Lilac Cottage, and saw Jane at about three forty taking her dog for a walk. The

Met Office timed the storm at three forty-seven. She was surprised to see Jane going out when it was obvious that the storm was imminent."

"So, Jane could either have gone straight home during the storm, or taken shelter and gone back later, which would put the murder much later," said Frank.

"The storm lasted until four thirteen, sir, and she was seen from a distance by several other witnesses up towards The Green, so presumably she did not get back to the cottage until after that."

"Whereupon her killer was either waiting in the house for her, or followed her in," said Frank. "That pretty much rules out Louise Leighton, then. Let's double check what time she arrived at the hairdressers. Anything else, Steven?"

"The neighbour also noticed that Jane was wearing dressy, black shoes rather than her normal boots to walk the dog, which she thought was strange."

"Perhaps she was all ready to go out, and decided to take the dog for a last minute walk?" suggested Emma Smith.

"Perhaps," said Frank, "in which case we need to find out where to, and who with. Which reminds me, Roger Sinclair does not think that Jane kept a private diary, and was able to explain all of the appointments marked on their calendar (there were none for Friday incidentally). Jane ran a dress shop in the village. Steven and I will go there and have a look round after this, to see if she kept any private papers there. Roger Sinclair has also given us Jane's bank statements to have a look at, and reckons the business papers will be at the shop. We need to see whether she had any financial problems, whether she was being blackmailed, or anything that could indicate a motive for murder. We also have her mobile phone if someone can check that out, and all calls made on the Sinclairs' landline over the last couple of months, please. Apparently there is a village cricket match on this afternoon, where most of our current suspects should be, so we'll call in on that too."

"What type of person do you think we're looking for, sir?" asked Emma Smith. She was blonde with the piercing blue eyes and chiselled face of a Viking princess. She was referred to as 'The Terrifying Emma Smith' by lesser mortals such as the uniformed branch of York's constabulary.

"In terms of psychological profiling?"

"Yes."

"It's early days, yet. This is a complex one; some of the main suspects seem to have jealousy or other emotional reason as a motive, which would suggest a crime of passion; perhaps someone who was temporarily out of control and acted on the spur of the moment. Yet at the same time there is something very controlled about the whole thing – there seemed to be very little forensic evidence at the cottage; there was no real mess, there didn't appear to have been a struggle. The murder was carried out quite carefully, maybe even completely planned and pre-meditated. The killer has him-or-herself completely under control, and will probably appear to be very normal and calm on the surface."

The team sat around the table for several hours, and went painstakingly through the evidence, putting forward theories, and planning the way the investigation should go forward.

At length, Frank said, "So, that's it for now, folks, no clear leads at the moment. Hopefully, the forensic results will push us forward when they come. Keep pressing on with what we've discussed, and also processing what we've had from the house-to-house enquiries as well. Steven, you and I need to have another look at Lilac Cottage, and go to a cricket match!"

As they were about to leave, DC Emma Smith called them back, "Sir, the Super wants to see you urgently before you go. He's come in specially."

Frank left Steven, and went and knocked on the Superintendent's door, and then entered his superior's office. The man, short and stocky, stood behind his desk in casual clothes. It did not look as though he intended to stay long. He and Frank rubbed along together, but did not share a natural affinity, nor a common view on how the job of a policeman should be done. Superintendent Drake admired Frank MacDonald's intelligence, diligence, and his ability to get results, but that was as far as it went. Frank did not admire anything at all about Superintendent Drake.

Drake looked at Frank from beneath knitted brows, and threw a copy of *The Observer* across the desk, saying furiously, "What the hell is this?"

Frank picked up the paper, expecting to find a critical report on the West Wold investigation, its lack of progress and possibly a ridicule-inducing photograph of himself. He was puzzled to find that it was a copy of the paper from the previous Sunday, almost a week before the murder. He inspected the page and was surprised to find an article by Stella Powell.

Is Feminism Dead?

Someone had drawn around the second part of the article with a pink fluorescent pen, and he quickly read through that part first;

Diamonds And Pebbles

...*because the underlying aim behind all of this is surely male oppression; this obsession with perfect looks infantilises women and keeps them in their place; the sub-culture of constant shopping is an adjunct of this. You can't be plotting revolution whilst you are busy in Top Shop can you? You can't be practising with your Kalashnikov when you've just painted your nails, can you? Modern women's weekly magazines are a disgrace. There is something sinister in the new obsession with the mainstreaming of topics such as domestic violence, female violence, dysfunctional family relationships, kinky sex, bizarre events etc. One can only assume that the male ownership of the publishers are using them as a means of undermining and oppressing women and pulling them back into line. What most of these magazines are saying is - look, you are not even safe at home! Perpetual female anxiety is the aim. Similarly, we live in a Western society where a man can keep his own daughter in a cell for twenty five years, rape her 3,000 times, father seven children with her, and nobody noticed? Then we have two examples of men in South London, raping and sexually assaulting literally hundreds of women, and the police fail to carry out simple DNA matching, and 'lose' data which would have caught them so much sooner. It seems to me there is a conspiracy here; a decision to let these people carry on frightening women. Frightened women don't cause trouble. At some indefinable point in time the role of the police subtly changed from protecting us to oppressing us, and protecting their political masters.*

There must be a male agenda behind all of this; some sinister sub-committee in the heart of Government is surely peddling this creed of terrifying women with a vengeance. Or is there simply a universal testosterone-fuelled telepathic brotherhood, which enables men to strategise individually in a way which is for the universal good of the dominant male? Even if all of this is just the result of the natural male impetus to protect women, and is essentially benign, unfortunately the end result of being over-protected is infantilisation. Or is the truth much simpler? - that the conspiracy is a female one, that women are hormonally programmed to be subservient, and fundamentally don't want their freedom? I hope not. Paranoid conspiracy theory versus hormonal fog - not much of a choice is it?

In terms of politics, yes we have more female MPs than ever before - but what an anonymous bunch they are! When they do make it to the front bench they seem little more than men-in-skirts. What we really need is more women involved in grass-roots politics. There is an enormous vacuum to be filled there as it seems as though no-one is really interested anymore. Membership of political parties is falling and the number of people voting is at an all time low. Now would seem to be an excellent time for ordinary, decent women to grasp the power that nobody else seems to want; men only seem to be interested in the trappings and perquisites of power, not the exercising of it for the common good. It must now be a case of 'cometh the hour, cometh the women'.

No, feminism is not dead; punch drunk and reeling, certainly; quietly regrouping, definitely; waiting in the wings - oh, yes. Whether the call to arms is precipitated by a religious war, or an apocalyptic event, or just a universal cry of 'enough-is-enough' - next time there may be blood. Do the ordinary, decent men of the world want women fighting beside them to vanquish common foes, or against them because they have become the enemy?

Frank quickly scanned the article whilst Drake glared at him. When he had read enough to get the gist, Frank whistled under his breath. Stella Powell - an unlikely freedom fighter, he thought.

"Who the hell is this woman?" Drake exploded, "Have you interviewed her? Arrested her? Have you established that she did the murder? It has to be her, doesn't it?"

"Her political views don't make her a murderer, sir. Yes,

I have interviewed her, and she is certainly a suspect by virtue of being James Powell's wife. You know that he was having an affair with the victim?"

"Yes, yes, I've read your reports. This has caused quite a stir I can tell you. Our little corner of the world is already causing enough concern in high places with that idiotic Cabinet Minister, without this kind of thing going on. I'll be watching you very closely. We all will. I want results and I want them fast. Keep her under close watch. And don't waste too much time looking further a-field if you get my drift. The sooner we get people like this locked up the better," he grumbled.

"Will that be all, sir? May I?" Frank said, indicating the newspaper.

"Yes, yes, away with you," said Drake, waving his arm to dismiss Frank, "I've wasted enough valuable golfing time as it is."

Frank folded the newspaper and tucked it under his arm so that he could read the article properly when he got back to his office, and then show it to Steven and the team. He settled in his chair and put his feet on the desk. From the beginning of the article it read;

Is feminism dead? Feminism definitely had to happen. Women are intelligent, capable, practical beings. The wonder is not that they demanded emancipation in the 20th century, but that they had not done it long before. Of course there are those who argue that women have always managed to get what they want by stealth. This may have been true of the middle classes, because money makes everyone's life easier. But for the vast majority of ordinary working class women, life has always been a constant round of drudgery and hard work, whose burdens were eased or worsened by the personality of the man they happened to be dependent on; be it father or husband. Your life was circumscribed by the mere fact of whether you were married to a bully, an oaf, a miser or a sloth. Of course women can be these things too. Of course there were ordinary, loving husbands as well, but this was dependent on good fortune, and the affection was conditional in many cases. Many women have spent their married lives walking that delicate tightrope where the level of comfort in their lives could be given or withdrawn depending on their biddableness. How many a young wife has gradually had her hopes dashed, as the true personality of her seemingly benign husband begins to emerge after the honeymoon period. The simple, and sad, fact is that what it all boils down to in the end is that men are bigger and stronger than women. Men have subjugated women from the dawn of civilisation by dint of being bigger than them; 'do as I say or I'll hit you'. This does not need to mean 'hit' in its most literal sense either; control comes in many guises. This is the most basic and primeval exchange between a man and a woman, and it still underlies many conversations.

As for getting what you want by stealth – why should we? Why can't we claim as a right the ability to live in freedom and safety, to fulfil our talents and interests, and to be financially independent, if that is what we choose? Of course with rights come responsibilities. Women, like men, must work to put a roof over their heads, to put food on their tables, and clothes on their backs. We are all hunter-gatherers now. Women must support their own children, if they choose to have children alone. Relying on the State is simply not good enough. It makes women weak and subjugated – merely substituting the State, for a husband. Working class women must disassociate themselves from the culture of sponging.

For money is the root of everything – good and evil. If you have money you have power, even the power to overcome the male's physical dominance. You simply pay another male to protect you. You have power to choose how you live your life ; who with, where, how, everything. This is not about a woman becoming Chairman of *the Board or an entrepreneur. This is about working class women getting onto the next few rungs of the ladder as teachers, nurses, solicitors, accountants and administrators. This will be done through education, hard work and support. Support from families, peers and Government. Of course this always brings up the subject of childcare, and this is where the Government must step in to provide access to good, affordable childcare.*

The family unit is key to this, too. If working class men can reconstruct themselves, so that women can trust them, and feel safe enough to give up their financial independence to stay at home to raise children, then the future of the nuclear family will be safe. If not, working women will have to organise themselves into economic units, or communes, to provide safe, nurturing homes for bringing up children, where those who want to work support those who are looking after children, (and incidentally elderly women could be provided for in this set up as well). I do not personally advocate separatism (as Germaine Greer did in her book The Whole Woman*), but the behaviour of some men makes it seem an attractive option at times.*

I stress 'working-class' because in general I think that the middle-class nuclear family is in better shape. A little money goes a long way towards easing the tensions and friction that a close relationship can generate. Middle class couples can afford to get away from each other periodically. The term 'golf widow' suggests that the woman is unhappy with her day alone, but I think the golfer might be surprised at how merry his temporary widow is. A middle-class woman may have access to her own funds, whether inherited or earned, and is not so financially dependent on her husband; money also gives her some status. This is the crux; with no money behind her the woman has no status whatsoever in her husband's eyes. A woman with her own money must at least give him pause before he raises his fist. I am not saying that middle class men are not violent (or lazy, or miserly or oafish) - they can be. But a woman with money has so many more choices - she can walk out of the door. This is a choice denied to a woman with children and no money in her purse, let alone a bank account.

Feminism rarely gets a mention these days. The assumption seems to be that equality has already been achieved, so why bother talking about it? - or it can never be achieved, so why bother talking about it? Either way, and as usual, men just want women to shut up about it. The result is that working-class women are just as downtrodden as they ever were but, due to the subtlety of their oppressors, mistakenly believe that the outspokenness and licentiousness in which they can now indulge is indicative of freedom. Thus these women can go out and behave as outrageously as they dare, but their husbands still want their tea on the table when they get home. I think each woman has to decide for herself what equality means to her and what she want to do with her life. Perhaps, in that sense, we have achieved equality, since never before in history have women had that basic economic choice, or the mindset to exercise that choice. Unfortunately, the ability, or even the desire, to make that informed choice is still largely limited to middle-class or better-educated girls.

The rise of the 'ladette' has Middle England in apoplexy, but I say, where is it written that girls have to behave better than boys? The female lager lout is undoubtedly a reflection of a swing of the pendulum too far, but it should correct itself over time. I abhor their behaviour in so far as it impacts on anyone else, but I still defend their right to act that way if that is their choice and they harm or disrespect no-one but themselves. Oh, but they are harming themselves. How it saddens me to see them; poor, lost, bewildered girls, not a shred of self-esteem, or an inking of what is in their own best interest. Unloving, unloved and unlovable.

The 'ladette' phenomenon seems to go hand-in-hand with the so-called 'celebrity culture' and the endless obsession with looks. How we came to this after forty years of feminism is a mystery worth investigating. The feminists of the Nineteen-Seventies hoped that, through liberation, women could abandon artifice and be appreciated for what they were, for the beauty within, not what they looked like. We seemed to have moved a million miles in the opposite direction. Our teenagers and young women have to be perfectly coiffed, perfectly made-up, perfectly dressed, perfectly thin, and almost totally depilated, at all times. Magazines reflect this in their ruthless dissection of celebrities; perfectly normal phenomena like weight gain, cellulite, and bad dress sense are held up to derision. The underlying message to the women they so hypocritically pretend to support is; let yourself go (ie. step out of line) and you too will be ridiculed, or found wanting. Interestingly, the 'ladette' behaviour is subtly condoned; you don't need to be oppressed by someone else when you are your own worst enemy, do you?

So where does this leave feminism? We are still physically the weaker sex. The more that economic wealth is spread more evenly between the sexes, the more power women will wield over their own lives. Money equals power, it is as simple as that. How far have we come? In some ways, not far; 'do as I say or I'll hit you'. Globally many women are as oppressed as they ever were; female circumcision remains a dreadful and hidden scandal that nobody wants to tackle. And the little way we have come is so tenuous; sitting in Britain today there are groups of men determined to put us all into burkhas, if and when they get the chance. There has been a little progress; women can be bus drivers or surgeons if they want to, and many men are deriving real pleasure from greater involvement with their young children. Whilst there are certainly still some old dinosaurs not revealing the contents of their wage packets to their wives and refusing to change the nappies, many modern marriages are based on an equal partnership. It may be that, if we come to a civil war over religious tolerance, women will be the ones who take up arms to fight for their independence; after all, a gun negates mere muscle power completely; 'don't touch me or I'll shoot you' would turn that primeval exchange on its head. The issue with the burkha is that of freedom; not just freedom in the political and ideological sense, but literally the freedom to walk and run and move untrammelled; to perform the basic human act of lifting one's face up to enjoy the sun. Interestingly, some supporters of the veil cite one of its benefits as that of being a leveller; that women are not judged on their femininity, their beauty, their desirability and will therefore be taken more seriously. Ironically, this directly echoes those feminist ideals of the Nineteen-Seventies. But the point here is that the personality, 'the beauty within' if you like, which the feminists wanted to shine through the outward appearance and make it irrelevant, cannot be displayed either. Let us be clear; the veil turns a woman into an object, a non-communicator, a non-human, literally into a 'non-entity'; and as such the woman can be ignored, dismissed, used and abused. In an ironic and sinister twist on this, the current interest in plastic surgery is attempting exactly the same thing from the other end of the scale; the face is exposed but is so immobile, so deadened, so fixed, that the personality has no chance at all of being seen. Plastic surgery is yet another self-negating strategy which women are adopting, encouraged of course by greedy male surgeons and controlling husbands, in a desperate quest to stay youthful. Again, the beauty that comes from a life, well-lived and etched onto a happy face, is no longer valued. Why are women doing this to themselves? Are we crazy? There is little wonder that men dismiss women as brainless. A little make-up and lipstick to boost the confidence is one thing, the rest is just madness...

Frank was startled by this unforeseen side of Stella Powell. Clearly, she was much more than just a mother and a home-maker. But how much more? Was she also capable of murder?

Later, Frank and Steven made their way to West Wold. The two policemen stood in the back garden of Lilac Cottage looking at the building. A kitchen door and a window overlooked the garden, as did two dormer windows above.

Frank turned to look back towards the end of the garden. "Do you think the killer got in and out this way? No-one seems to have noticed anything."

"Most probably, sir. Let's see where the path leads."

They turned and walked down the long, narrow garden until it met a scrubby field with only some long grass and a well-worn path to mark the boundary. All of the back gardens of the houses along the lane ran parallel to each other and stopped in a line along the edge of the field, some with fences or hedges, some not. Many feet had worn the path that ran along the bottom of the gardens. Red-and-white SOC tape staked out an area enclosing the end of the Sinclair's garden and the path. As the two men stood with their backs to the houses, the path to the right led down to the stables, and to their left to a short side-street, which had no houses and petered out completely after fifty yards into a mere footpath leading into trees.

"Easy access in and out here, sir," said Steven, "The gardens are long and screened by trees and hedges, which means someone could park in that little side street, walk down the path and into the Sinclair's garden without being seen."

"Yes, particularly during a wet, dark thunderstorm. Better make sure the SOCOs had a look around here."

They lifted the tape and walked the full length of the path both ways but found nothing of interest. They agreed that Steven would walk back along the path and have a look around the stables, whilst Frank went to look around Jane's shop. As he left the path and walked up the short side street towards the main street, Frank rounded the corner and saw Roy Parsons hovering there. The blonde haired man, still dressed in a Hawaiian styled shirt, shorts and flip-flops, ambled towards Frank.

"Morning, Mr MacDonald. Got a statement, sir?"

"It's still Chief Inspector MacDonald, Mr Parsons. Another statement will be made at York Police Station in due course."

"We understand the victim was having an affair with James Powell, the celebrity photographer, is that true? Are you any closer to making an arrest?"

Frank did not reply, as he walked quickly off in the direction of the village green. Don Green took more photographs .

"Not him again," muttered Frank to himself, as he hurried away, "Doesn't he have Sundays off?"

Diamonds And Pebbles

Chapter 13

At noon on Sunday Frank MacDonald let himself into Jane's shop with a key which Roger Sinclair had lent to him. It was another hot August day, and the little shop was stiflingly warm when he stepped into it. He propped the door half open to let in what little breeze there was, but left the white blinds closed. It was a small shop with its stock - dresses, suits, tops, trousers, and accessories - tastefully displayed. This season's colours seemed to be lemon and taupe. There was a black floor and black shelving and a black counter with an electronic till. Jane had provided two bentwood chairs and a coffee table with fashion magazines for her customers. He made his way to the back of the main shop where there was a storeroom, a toilet, a small office, and a kitchen area where Jane obviously made tea and coffee.

Frank wanted to see whether Jane kept personal documents or other papers at the shop which she did not want to be seen at home. There was also the possibility that the killer had been a business acquaintance. It was important to know who her business contacts were. He started to open drawers in the office desk. He had barely begun when he heard the shop bell ring as someone pushed the door further open. He stepped back into the shop to find Louise Leighton standing there. He was surprised to see that she had a small dog with her. He looked expectantly behind her, but there was no Karen Leighton bring up the rear.

"Hello, I hope you don't mind," Louise said, "I saw that the door was open. I offered to take Charlie here for a walk - it's Jane's dog. The shop is nice, isn't it? I've asked Roger if I can take it over. I'll put someone in to run it. He said he would think about it." (Jane's dog, Jane's shop, Jane's man, thought Frank.) Louise pulled herself up to sit on the counter and crossed her legs. She was wearing a dark blue top, blue shorts and sparkly blue flip-flops which showed off her perfect tan. She smiled, or at least turned up the corners of her mouth, and said, "Are you looking for anything in particular? Perhaps I can help." She twirled a piece of blonde hair between two fingers and stared at him.

Frank wondered if she was trying to be seductive. It was not working. He had decided he did not like Louise Leighton much. When she was not talking, she was as still and watchful as a cat stalking a mouse.

"That won't be necessary, thank-you. If you'll excuse me, I need to press on. After a few further attempts to engage him in conversation, which he did not respond to, she took the hint and left.

Frank went back to the office desk, sat in the chair and looked around at the walls. There were two shelves holding large lever-arch files and coloured plastic wallets. He worked his way quickly through the files, selecting a few that might be worth a more thorough look. There were various printed lists, notes, postcards and adverts on the walls, and an appointment calendar with one month to a page, currently showing a view of Castle Howard. He took the calendar off the wall, and looked at the entries for August. Nothing much there. He flicked back through July and then June. Some dates were marked with the names of cities like Manchester or London for trade fairs or fashion shows. Some with names and times. (Deliveries or sales reps, maybe? I wonder if our friend in the BMW could be a rep? Worth a look, Frank thought). He looked as far back as the month of May. The second Friday was marked with a circle and the number '1' inside. Each subsequent Friday was circled and numbered sequentially all the way through June, July and August. The last Friday that she had worked, the Friday that she died, she had written the number '14' in the circle. (What was she counting and why start in May?) He continued looking through the files and drawers but could find nothing of any immediate significance. The shop did not appear to have a personal computer, and they had already found Jane's laptop computer at Lilac Cottage. Taking the calendar and some of the shop's business files and wallets with him, he locked the door and went to meet Steven Brown.

It was two o'clock on Sunday afternoon by the time Frank and Steven arrived at the cricket ground, which was situated just off The Green. The entrance to the field sat between Louise Leighton's row of cottages and *The Prancing Pony* public house.

Wispy clouds, blown by a warm breeze, shaded the intense heat from time to time. As a concession to the weather and to the occasion, Frank had forsaken his charcoal grey work suit for beige chinos and an open-necked blue shirt that morning. Steven wore black denims and a grey T-shirt. The game of cricket between West Wold and a neighbouring village was, literally, in full swing and the scoreboard showed that the 'Away' team had their first and second men in. The cricket boundary was marked out in a large field of grass, with ample room to spare. The field was encircled by horse chestnut trees blowing gently in the breeze. A small community hall, which also served as a pavilion, stood to the left of the entrance to the cricket ground. A number of green deckchairs, some occupied some not, were scattered under the shade of three oak trees which grew near the pavilion, and also along the nearest part of the boundary.

Frank had no firm idea of what he wanted to achieve, but he thought it would be useful to watch the main suspects for the murder, or at least the main people in Jane's life, at play. As he looked around he confirmed that most of the people he wanted to see were there. James Powell, who was not in cricket whites, and had presumably declined to play, stood talking to a couple whom Frank did not recognise, perhaps the Watsons. Louise Leighton sat nearby, dressed in the same T-shirt and shorts showing off her tanned legs, seemingly not interested in the cricket, with her eyes closed, enjoying the sun. Karen Leighton sat next to her, squinting in the strong sunlight, smoking a cigarette, and looking around at the crowd. Julia Johnson, all in black, was talking animatedly to two or three women on a cluster of deckchairs near the pavilion. (Drawn by the promise of free food, no doubt, thought Frank). He could see her son, Jason, across the field with some youths with their bikes. Stella Powell was nowhere to be seen. As the two policemen stood watching the match, Frank was surprised to see Roger Sinclair coming towards them. He had not expected Roger to be socialising whilst Jane was still lying in the police mortuary.

"Hello Mr MacDonald, I just came along to see if you were here. I wonder if I could have a word?"

"Of course - why don't we walk?" said Frank, indicating the open spaces beyond the field of play.

The three men set off slowly round the cricket boundary, and as soon as they were out of earshot of anyone in the crowd, Frank said, "What did you want to tell us, Mr Sinclair?"

Roger looked down hesitantly, and made a steeple out of his hands, "I - er - I'm afraid I wasn't completely truthful on Friday night when I told you I was at work on Friday afternoon."

"In what way?"

"I was actually at my secretary's house. We go there most Friday afternoons. We are - that is - well, Sarah and I have been lovers for a while, actually. I lied to you because I don't want my mother to find out if I can possibly avoid it. She is so fussy about that kind of thing. I am so very sorry, Mr MacDonald, I'm afraid that Sarah and I both lied when we gave our statements to your constable. Sarah only did it for my sake, of course. You mustn't blame her."

Frank decided not to let him off the hook too easily; Roger Sinclair was, after all, one of his main suspects. Spouses were always under suspicion in such a case, and having a mistress gave Roger Sinclair a strong motive for killing Jane.

"This is a very serious matter," Frank said, deliberately hardening his features, "You will both have to amend your statements, and it may have to be mentioned in court, if it becomes relevant to the case."

"Yes of course. Again, I really am sorry."

"Is there anything else you have misled us about?"

With a difficult confession over, Roger Sinclair relaxed a

Diamonds And Pebbles

little, "No. Believe me, there isn't. Thank-you for being so understanding."

"Very well, sir."

"Actually, I did come to say as well that I have a video of Jane taken earlier in the year at the village fête. I wondered if it might be useful for you to have a look at? I thought you might feel you knew her a little bit better."

Frank agreed that it could be very useful, and they agreed to meet at Roger's mother's house at five o'clock to view the video. They all walked back towards the pavilion together, and Frank and Steven sat down on a couple of deckchairs to watch the game, as Roger Sinclair walked away. The away team was fairing badly and had lost their fifth man for a current innings of forty-eight.

"What are you looking for in particular, sir?" asked Steven Brown, sitting back in his deckchair and putting his sunglasses on.

"Not sure, but I'd like to bet that our killer is here. What do you make of him? Think he did it?" Frank asked, indicating the retreating figure of Roger Sinclair.

"Him and the secretary getting rid of the wife, you mean?"

"Exactly."

"Don't know. Divorce is easier and less dangerous, surely?"

"Yes, and if he was a killer, I think his mother would be under the patio by now."

Steven grinned, "He certainly seems keen to keep her happy. Maybe there's a lot of money coming his way. Perhaps he didn't want to give Jane half of his money in a divorce settlement so got rid of her instead?"

"Losing half of his money would be better than going to prison, surely? Does he seem the type to kill, do you think?"

"Not really, but does anyone here?" Steven replied, looking around, "It's quintessential England, isn't it?"

"The way England used to be, perhaps. Roger belongs here, certainly. If we're talking about someone who doesn't belong, that would be Julia Johnson or Louise Leighton. Louise is essentially still an outsider. She could have jealousy as a motive, but she doesn't even seem sure that Jane was seeing James again, only suspicious. It was odd that she claimed that she and Jane were such good friends, when Stella Powell said that Jane didn't have female friends."

"Probably just wishful thinking," said Steven. "Louise wanted to be associated with Jane in the eyes of the village." He scanned the spectators and his eye fell on James Powell, "What would Mr Powell's motive be?"

"Well, if the re-union wasn't as happy as he'd have us believe, then maybe Jane was asking him for more than he wanted to give."

"Why not just end the relationship? Unless Jane had some other claim on him? Blackmail, maybe?"

"Yes, or - " Frank suddenly thought about the calendar from Jane's shop with its numbered weeks, " - maybe she was pregnant. Roger said that he was the one to blame for their not having any children, not her, so it's possible. Perhaps James Powell wasn't happy at the prospect of being tied down with a young child. It would have cramped his style a bit. Right, who else?"

"What about Julia Johnson? In her own eyes, she had every reason to hate Jane."

"As we said before, though, why now? What did Jane do that pushed Julia into murder?"

"Must have been something to do with money; it seems

to be Julia's favourite topic of conversation. Which leaves us with Stella Powell," said Steven. "She's got the motive - Jane was a rival, and threatening to disrupt Stella's whole life, even more so if Jane was pregnant. It depends whether or not you believe that she doesn't mind about James' infidelities."

"Affairs are one thing, but James Powell and Jane seem to have been on the brink of something much more serious. Perhaps, when it came to the test, Stella was unable to give James up, after all," said Frank, dubiously.

The two men subsided into silence. They both leant back in their deckchairs and soaked up the sunshine, watching the cricket, and the crowd.

Frank had not been sitting there for long before he saw Stella Powell entering the cricket ground. She was dressed in a white shirt and jodhpurs and had her hair untidily pulled back off her face into a pony-tail. She looked relaxed and self-possessed. *Still waters run deep*, he thought. He reminded himself of Superintendent Drake's instructions to keep a close watch on her, and politely beckoned her over, rising to meet her.

"Hello, Mr MacDonald, Mr Brown."

Steven Brown said hello.

"Mrs Powell," said Frank, indicating a deckchair next to his own, "Won't you sit down?"

She acquiesced, and sat down gracefully next to him.

"I've just had the pleasure of reading your article in last Sunday's Observer," he said noncommittally.

She raised her eyebrows and laughed, "Really? I bet that's gone down well back at the police station."

He smiled, despite himself, "Yes, it certainly made for interesting reading."

"I was really fired up the day I wrote that," she said,

"The editor asked me to write something punchy."

Frank paused, and said more seriously, "You don't seem to rate the police much."

"I take people as I find them, Mr MacDonald. As so often these days, I believe most individuals within organisations are perfectly good people, but there seems to be a 'wrongness' at the top which pervades downwards."

Frank could not disagree. For some time he had been dismayed at the way his job was increasingly manipulated by politicians and civil servants. It was not simply about good people catching bad people anymore; there were shadows, and nuances, and relativism, and agendas, and manipulation. When he thought about the personal sacrifices which he had made for the sake of his profession, he questioned whether it had been worth it. He wondered whether he was now more inclined to be Robin Hood than the Sheriff of Nottingham. He said, "You may be right. Do you really think there may be a civil war over religion, one day?"

They both surveyed the scene in front of them - the cricketers in their whites, the green hills surrounding the village, the spectators basking in sunshine.

"Probably not," she said equally seriously, "the current threat will probably all fade away given time; you know - thirty years ago it was the IRA, now it is Al Qaeda, in ten year's time it will be something else. But if it came to it, then you have to remember that the British fought bitterly - fought each other in fact - for religious tolerance hundreds of years ago. They're presumably not going to give it up without a fight. The trouble is that it would be a very complex situation; the yobs would be fighting the religious extremists, and I would be fighting them both."

"You're not ready for your burkha just yet, then?"

"No, thank-you."

"I think my mother would have something to say about it, as well."

"I'd like to meet her," said Stella sincerely, and added, "We need to get back to a firm concept of right and wrong. If I want to decide whether something is right or wrong I apply my 'cave' theory; that is - would a cave dweller have done that? For example, do we need a Royal Family which costs thousands of pounds of taxpayer's money? Did the cave dwellers have a Royal Family? No! Did the cave dwellers have a political system where some had more food and animal skins than others? No! Did cave women wear burkhas? No! Should I have a facelift? No! Do I need a £300 pair of shoes? No! Did the cave dwellers pool their resources for joint mutual benefit? Yes! Did they care for and nurture their children? Yes. Did they achieve results through hard work? Yes. You see; everything becomes clear. Really though, I believe that change should be brought about through the ballot-box, not through violence. Given that women form more than half the electorate, I doubt that extremists of any persuasion will ever form an elected government in this country. Besides, I think that the Middle East will implode before long, and the Arab world will turn inwards and have their own problems to cope with, which will take decades to sort out."

"Perhaps you should get into politics yourself?"

"Yes, perhaps, now that I'm not a full-time mother anymore. There is something about motherhood which makes you so - so dreamy, somehow - so distracted. Perhaps that is another reason why women are so easy to control. Do you understand?"

He nodded.

"Do you like cricket, Mr MacDonald?"

"Yes," he smiled, "my son plays for the schools' County team.

"You should get him to come and play for us. I'm sure our captain would like some new blood," she smiled and then paused, and looked more serious, "I hope you don't think we are being disrespectful by playing cricket today. The village does care about Jane. Everyone feels a bit helpless, I think, to know what to do, or what not to do. We are all in unknown territory. Sorry, excuse me, I must go."

She left them, and went into the small community hall.

"She certainly feels things deeply, sir," said Steven, "do you think she could have channelled that same anger into killing off a rival?"

"It's definitely possible," admitted Frank, deciding he must try to be totally detached and professional in his dealings with Stella from then on.

When the first innings finished the two teams and the spectators started making their way to the pavilion. Frank and Steven followed. Inside the small hall, people were waiting in a queue to help themselves to the buffet spread out on trestle tables, and then go to get a cup of tea or coffee or a cold drink. Frank saw that Stella Powell was manning the drinks table, chatting amiably with whoever she was serving. They walked over and, joining the end of the queue, waited their turn. They both asked for tea, and, as she served them, Frank took the opportunity to put his resolution into practice.

"By the way, any further thoughts about Jane? On who might have killed her, I mean?" he asked flatly, reminding himself that she was a suspect, perhaps the main suspect. Not waiting for an answer, he made his face more serious, and his voice sharper, "A constable will be coming to see

Diamonds And Pebbles

you to take a full history, fingerprints, and DNA from you and Mr Powell. It is voluntary of course at this stage, but we would be grateful for your full co-operation."

The usual ready smile died in her eyes, and she said coolly, "Yes, of course."

He was surprised how much it pained him to have killed her smile.

The two men took their drinks, and stood to one side of the room. It was a typical community hall with windows down the two longest sides, green-painted walls, and a wooden parquet floor. Frank scanned the room, and his eyes fell on Louise Leighton standing with James Powell. They both seemed tense and Frank wondered whether the village grapevine (aka Brian Sykes) had provided her with the news about James and Jane's recently renewed relationship. James was scratching his head in perplexity, and Louise soon moved away and stood on her own by the wall. She caught Frank's eye, nodded briefly and turned away.

All is not well in paradise, he thought.

Elsewhere in the room, Julia Johnson and her son Jason were standing together eating enthusiastically from plates piled high with food. Roger Sinclair was deep in conversation with a man wearing a clerical dog collar whom Frank recognised as the local vicar.

Karen Leighton went and stood close to Louise. She reminded Frank of a vulture waiting for carrion. She spotted Frank and made her way towards him, hobbling on her gold high heels, and holding a cup and saucer and an unlit cigarette in one hand.

"Caught Jane's killer yet, Mr MacDonald?" she said, "I'm surprised you've got time to watch cricket in the middle of a murder investigation. Thought you'd enjoy an afternoon off, did you? It's lovely here isn't it? I could really enjoy living in West Wold. Such nice people, specially that Roger Sinclair. What a fool Jane was messing about with James Powell when she was married to Roger. Yes, I like it here. I couldn't live with Louise though. Always been a trial to me that girl. Too fussy in her ways, in my opinion - she hates me smoking indoors - tries to make me go in the garden. She should have been married to a nice man and giving me some grandchildren by now. Course, that will never happen. It's just as well she can't have any because I can't imagine Louise with children anyway; much too selfish, and much too fussy, always cleaning and tidying up. It's time she started acting her age. James Powell would be a good catch, all that money and jetting off to tropical islands! Louise shouldn't wear that shade of blue, it really doesn't suit her. Do you have any suspects, yet? I'd look no further than that Stella Powell, if I were you. She's fiery, and as jealous as hell. If James and Jane were carrying on she would have put a stop to it, I reckon. Louise will have to watch her back, she might be next! Then I'll get her house, and live here with all these nice people!" Seemingly cheered up by this thought, she laughed and shuffled away again, appearing not to require an answer to her monologue.

Frank resumed his surveillance of the room. Which one of you is it? Or are we on the wrong track? Is it our man in the BMW, or really just a random killer?

"Time to go?" asked Steven, putting his cup and saucer down on a nearby trestle table.

"Yep," said Frank. He gloomily reflected that they had wasted their time.

As they left, the killer watched them with cold, cold eyes.

Diamonds And Pebbles

Chapter 14

Frank McDonald and Steven Brown met Roger Sinclair at his mother's house that evening at about five o'clock, and he switched on the television in the sitting room so that they could watch the videotape of Jane. The two policemen sat on the sofa, and Roger sat on one of the armchairs close to the television.

"This was filmed this summer in July. Jane was on the organising committee, of course" said Roger, ruefully, "I thought it might be useful for you to see Jane as she really was, in life."

"Thank-you. Yes, it will help us," said Frank. He had found in the past that it was so easy to forget that the deceased, whom one did not know when they were alive, was a real person with a separate role and a history, and not just a murder victim.

The video had obviously been taken by Roger Sinclair at a village fête on the cricket ground. Stalls, cheerfully festooned with multi-coloured bunting and selling a variety of produce, were grouped around the field. There was also a beer tent, a bouncy castle and petting zoo for the children, and a mobile café with tables and chairs arranged on the grass nearby. The video-camera's microphone picked up the sounds of music, children laughing and shouting, and people talking. Jane Sinclair walked in front of the camera and pointed things out to the viewer. She was lithe and slim, and the famous hair, a glorious combination of autumnal reds, hung in thick swathes down her back to the waist. She looked back rather provocatively at the camera from time to time, and flicked her hair. She was lively and attractive. As they watched the film, Frank looked across at Roger for his reaction. He looked pensive and upset. On the video Jane walked past a stall selling cakes and Frank recognised Louise Leighton and her mother, Karen, standing behind it. Louise looked rather bored, but her mother waved enthusiastically at the camera, always anxious to befriend Roger. Jane exchanged a few words with Louise and then moved on. In the background, Frank could see Stella, and two teenaged girls who looked like they must be her daughters, giving pony rides to the local children.

Jane pointed people out as she walked along, and chatted enthusiastically to those behind each stall. She seemed well-liked, and Frank puzzled as to which one of these people could have hated Jane enough to kill her. If indeed hate was the motive. He knew that people killed in cold blood as well as hot. There were many reasons for wanting someone out of the way, but in his experience it usually boiled down to either love or money; or pure insanity. On the video, Jane approached a stout old lady standing with difficulty with the aid of a stick, and Frank recognised Daphne Sinclair, Roger's mother. She ignored Jane, and started reprimanding Roger for messing about with 'that video contraption'. She shook her stick at the camera as though it was an animal she was defending herself against. Jane laughed and carried on walking. Frank heard Roger promising to come back to his mother later. Julia Johnson, dressed as always in black, came into view. She scowled at Jane and the camera, "Trust you to be cavorting around in front of a video! Fancy yourself as a film star?" she laughed sarcastically.

Jane laughed back at her sister, and carried on walking, with Roger dutifully walking behind, filming. Jane continued to point out people, stalls and attractions as though it was her personal project, and she was responsible for organising the whole event single-handed. The next person they encountered was James Powell, and, although they tried to hide it, there was an embarrassing unnaturalness to their greetings, with Jane's cheeks turning pink and James looking shifty. Frank again glanced across at Roger, sitting in the armchair, to see what his reaction was, but he seemed oblivious. On the video, James Powell moved off in another direction, and Jane carried on walking. The camera panned round to show the beer tent, manned by Brian Sykes, with a queue of people waiting to be served. Julia Johnson was standing there by now, engaged in conversation with the same group of women as Frank had seen her with at the cricket match. The camera panned again and showed Phil and Samantha Watson manning a tombola stall. Jane stood and chatted to them for a few moments, with promises to catch up soon, and some ribaldry at Roger's prowess as a cameraman. A group of older ladies waved and smiled, and Frank recognised Sadie Mountjoy, the Sinclairs' neighbour.

The scene shifted suddenly and it was obvious that Jane had gone off on her own, and Roger was filming alone. The camera panned around very slowly. In the foreground, Sadie Mountjoy was talking to the camera, ie. Roger, but in the background Frank noticed that Jane and James Powell were now standing together side by side and talking to each other in a seemingly nonchalant fashion which concealed something more serious. Jane seemed happy, and looked briefly into James' eyes from time to time. As the camera moved away it caught Louise Leighton in the foreground, standing by her stall, with her usual blank expression.

The images faded and re-appeared. Julia Johnson had joined Roger by this time and was walking alongside as he filmed. Frank could hear her chatting. Karen Leighton hobbled into view and took a place on Roger's other side, and began to accompany him also. Frank suppressed a chuckle at the picture they would have made parading around the field; Roger, the cameraman, flanked on either side by an admiring lady.

The camera panned around once again to show Stella and her daughters, in the foreground this time, and Stella laughed and waved to the camera, whilst stroking the mane of a small pony whose bridle she was holding. Dressed in a checked shirt and jodhpurs, she glowed with good health. Her eyes sparkled, and she grinned and called Roger 'Franco Fellini'. Jane then approached, alone now, and as Stella noticed her she stopped smiling, and she pointedly turned away. The video continued with some random shots of various activities, and Jane did not appear again. The picture faded for the last time, and Roger got up and switched off the television.

"You can see what a live-wire Jane was, Mr MacDonald," Roger said sadly.

"Yes, you are going to miss her very much, sir," said Frank.

"Yes, I will. I'm not being hypocritical. I know that you must think that because I was having an affair with Sarah that I no longer loved Jane, but that isn't true. It's just that the original feelings had gone out of our marriage. We were honest with each other. There was no anger involved. We were both reasonably happy, I think. There was a *status quo*."

"Was Jane asking you for a divorce?"

"No, it was something we had never discussed."

"Did you think that the affair with James Powell was serious?"

"No more so than any of the others. There have been three or four over the years."

"Perhaps we should consider whether one of the former lovers had resurfaced?" said Frank, thinking of the man in the silver BMW, "Could you give us their names and addresses?"

Roger sighed and rubbed his eyes before agreeing, "I'll let you have them tomorrow morning."

"That's fine. Well, thank-you for showing us the tape. It has been useful. Would you mind if we kept it for a while?"

"By all means, do."

Frank and Steven left Roger's mother's house and set off back towards York in the evening sunshine. Frank yawned and stretched as Steven drove the car smoothly and efficiently.

"What did you make of the video, Steven?" asked Frank.

"It was obvious that there was something going on between Jane and James. Stella didn't seem too pleased about it either, despite the open marriage, so-called."

"Yes, and Roger was turning a blind eye, it seems. Quite a steamy little place, West Wold, full of intrigue and shady goings-on, especially with our friend the Cabinet Minister!"

Steven dropped Frank off at his elder sister's house in Sheriff Hutton. Ali was giving a 'going away' party for her eldest son, Ben, who was going to Australia for a year.

Frank had promised, 'on pain of death', to put in an appearance, if only for an hour. It was seven o'clock and still warm. He walked around to the back of the modern, red-brick house into the neat garden, which was busy with groups of people dressed in shorts and T-shirts, eating buffet food and drinking from paper cups. He could see Ali's husband, David, manning a barbeque. He waved hello to his two nephews, Ben and Daniel, and their friends and was pleased to see that Nathan had arrived. He briefly said hello to Nathan, agreeing to talk later on, and then made his way over to his father sitting on the wooden-decked patio in a garden chair with a rug wrapped around his legs. Jack MacDonald was almost eighty years old, and had been in failing health for some time. He had been a handsome man, and still had the twinkling, brown eyes of his youth, albeit in a wrinkled, tired face. His once-thick hair was grey and thinning.

"Hi, Pops, how's things?" Frank bent down and took his father's hand.

Jack MacDonald's eyes lit up, and he shook Frank's hand enthusiastically and hung on to it, "Hello, Frank. Good to see you, son."

At that moment Ali and Joyce, Frank's mother, stepped out of the kitchen door into the garden, and greeted him enthusiastically, "Oh, well done, I know you are busy," Ali beamed, kissing Frank, and indicated with her thumb, "Help yourself to food at the barbeque, and to drinks in the kitchen. Sophie's in there, somewhere."

"See you in a minute, Pops," Frank squeezed his father's hand, greeted and kissed his mother, and walked into the house.

Frank's younger sister, Sophie was in the kitchen helping herself to gin and tonic, and squealed in delight at seeing Frank, and handed him a can of beer, at his request. By mutual agreement they moved back into the garden together. Sophie was as sweet as a Scarborough candy-floss. She ran a trendy café in York called Smiths. She was in love with Harry, a young friend of the MacDonalds', but she seemed incapable of acknowledging this fact to herself, much less of informing the object of her desire. Harry was in love with Sophie. They both belonged to that group of unfortunate people who are rendered speechless when the object of their passion hoves into view, and act as though this is the very last person on earth they would like to speak to. Ali tried to make sure that Harry was invited to every social occasion in order to get the unwilling lovers into the same room together. Unfortunately, all they ever did, when finally forced into shy proximity, was make small talk with great embarrassment, whilst Sophie stared at the ceiling and Harry stared at the floor, and then mutter incoherently as they went off in relief in opposite directions. Harry was tall, snake-hipped and gentle. Sophie thought she was not good enough for Harry, and Harry thought he was too poor for Sophie. A gifted carpenter and furniture-designer, but also a late developer, he was still striving to establish himself and build up his business. Commissions were hard to come by. Until he was successful, he would not allow himself to woo Sophie because he could not yet provide for her and the many fat, rosy babies that he wanted to give her. He was also somewhat put off by the fact that she seemed not to notice his existence. This was all the subject of quiet amusement for the whole family. Everyone waited impatiently for a breakthrough to this impasse, but could not foresee how it was to be brought about.

Ali, had been married to her husband David for over twenty years. Their marriage was like an egg which has had its contents sucked out through a tiny pin-prick in the shell; it still gives every appearance of being an egg, but inside there is nothing. It was no longer a marriage based on love, nor did it have the dignity of being based on mutual respect. They lived parallel lives, and had not had a meaningful conversation in years. The relationship had begun initially because of mutual need (his to have a family life and hers to be provided for) and lust, and as such it worked for a while. But they had both outgrown it long ago, and now they merely lived parallel lives in the same household and gave every outward appearance of being a couple, if not happy then at least contented, and united parents to their two boys. Ali's sons were very tall and slim and towered over her, one fair, one dark. Whenever Frank saw her with them she always seemed slightly bewildered, like a dog-owner who thought she had bought Yorkshire terrier puppies and ended up with fully-grown Great Danes. David was not a bad husband. He had even loved Ali a little at the beginning of the marriage. He was quite a good father. All he wanted was to lead a normal life, as he defined it. But he was a man obsessed with maintaining his standing in the world. He would not countenance any behaviour that might jeopardise a large inheritance that he thought so close to his grasp. His parents were elderly, old-fashioned and strict church-goers; stalwarts of the congregation in the Home Counties village in which they lived. Ali and Sophie maliciously believed that they had already cut their only son out of their Will in order to leave their considerable wealth to the local church, which so badly needed a new roof. By this they thought that they had guaranteed their place in the Kingdom of Heaven. David was a successful architect, and spent most of the working week in London. Whatever else was lacking in Ali's life, there was plenty of money, and she took pleasure in spending it. Ali had one major character flaw; she was lazy. Whilst she was being nurtured in a happy and loving home, this fault lay dormant and relatively concealed, but as she became a young woman it came to the forefront of her personality, to the detriment of her other, more endearing character traits. Out of this laziness came an absolute determination to find a rich husband and lead an easy life. Thus she had clung onto David like a drowning woman to a life-raft, and at first she deemed herself content. Over the long years of the marriage, however, she had paid a heavy price in terms of independence, self-worth and joy, serving needlessly under the heavy yoke of David's fastidiousness, when she could merely have refused to go along with it. His was not actually a strong personality; if she had been more resolute he would have backed down. He would have been glad to pass over the mantle of responsibility sometimes if she had been willing to accept it. But part of her could only be passive; she wanted him to make the rules. It was easier, it was safer. Since she was too blinkered to blame herself for her endless predicament, she blamed the rest of the world, and called her relentless unhappiness 'depression', and insisted that her doctor make her better with pills, which, needless to say, he could not do. Ali had reacted to the freedom that her sons' leaving home had brought, not by immersing herself in good works like her mother, but by developing sudden and crippling crushes on the men in her circle of acquaintance. These fantasies never developed into physical relationships, being mostly acted out in her head, but David had leapt the hurdle of infidelity long ago, Frank suspected. David did not interfere in Ali's life unless her behaviour threatened to betray the sham of their marriage. Then, he was hasty in pulling her back in line in order to preserve the appearance of their perfect marriage to his circle of friends, colleagues and neighbours and, particularly, his parents. From the safety of her marriage, Ali indulged in serial dalliances with the most unsuitable men she could find. Frank was concerned about her; he sensed a change recently, a growing lack of caution. Ali was becoming as reckless as Red Riding Hood on her way through the wood.

As Frank and Sophie returned to the garden, Harry was talking to Joyce, and he began immediately to ignore Sophie as though his life depended on it. Sophie, meanwhile, went over to the far end of the garden to talk to David, who was still manning the barbeque. Frank shook his head in amused disbelief. He made a conscious decision to relax and forget about West Wold and its inhabitants for a while. He collected a plateful of food, talked to his mother, then Nathan, and then had a long conversation with his nephew, Ben, about his imminent trip to Australia.

When the evening turned cooler, the family moved indoors, leaving the youngsters outside. They sat around comfortably on the various sofas and chairs in the large living room.

"How is the West Wold case going, Frank? Terrible thing, a young woman being killed like that," said Joyce.

"They should bring back hanging," said David.

Frank shrugged and said, "There are still relatively few convicted murderers. I don't think that capital punishment is the real issue. It's the five and ten year stretches which worry me. The armed robbers, the GBHs, the fraudsters. The prisons aren't going to cope for much longer."

"I think we should build an enormous prison on a remote Scottish island, and just put them all in there together with a bit of segregation according to the severity of the crime," said David, "Give them dormitories, kitchens, sports facilities, a library, whatever, and let them get on with it. No guards inside, no visitors, no drugs, no contraband. Let them sink or swim. Give them a weekly supply of food etc. Do you think they would organise themselves into some sort of society, or degenerate into anarchy and chaos?"

"It's an interesting question. Interesting idea, too. At least it might be a deterrent," said Frank.

"They could sell it to a television company to screen twenty-four hours a day," said Sophie.

"No, people would commit a crime just to get themselves on the television," said Ali.

"The big muscle-y ones would intimidate the small non-muscle-y ones," said Joyce, "Sound familiar, anyone?"

"Until one of the small non-muscle-y ones had a skill that the others wanted to utilise, and then the negotiations could begin," said Frank, smiling at her.

"Well, the women's version would get themselves organised in no time - into a supportive, communistic society," said Joyce, smiling back at him. She knew she was being provocative. She and Frank spent hours debating modern society, each gently goading the other with outrageous ideas in which they did not necessarily believe.

Joyce had short white hair, the tanned skin which comes from spending a lot of time outdoors, and youthful eyes the colour of bluebells. She was born in York in 1940 but remembered little of the Second World War years except what happened in her own home. Her father worked on the railways, and had gone to fight in France, and mercifully returned intact in 1945. Her parents went on to have four more children and Joyce thrived in a happy family home. She grew up in the safe, if rather stifling, society of the Nineteen-Fifties. As a young teenager she learnt to jive to rock-and-roll music, wore a dirndl skirt and bouffant hair, and fell in love with Elvis Presley. Then The Beatles came along, the world changed and got a lot more exciting. She wore denim jeans and mini skirts, and fell in love with John Lennon. She went to see The Beatles play live at the *Cat's Whiskers* in York, screamed her head off, never heard a note, and went home so happy she could have died right then, and gone to Heaven a satisfied human being. Not long afterwards she forsook John Lennon, and fell in love for real with Jack MacDonald, and never looked at another man. She had just started teaching in a primary school when they met. She was an attractive, outdoors sort of girl with roses in her cheeks. Joyce was as wholesome as Harvest Festival. Jack was ten years older; charismatic and confident. She adored him totally. He was kind and loving and attentive. He had the strength and energy of a stallion combined with the sensitivity and awareness of a cat. They married after a short and joyful courtship. After a year of marriage Joyce gave birth to a son whom they called Paul. He was so small that he fitted into Jack's outspread hand; just a tiny scrap of life. He could not breathe properly. After four days he died in her arms. She never forgot how it felt to hold him; the exact shape and weight of him. In the dark days that followed, Jack and Joyce supported each other and soldiered on. When Alison and then Frank and finally Sophie were born it helped to heal some of the wounds. It was perhaps the loss of their first-born which caused Jack and Joyce to be over-protective and over-indulgent with Alison, to her later detriment. Joyce felt really blessed by the arrival of Frank, her beloved son, and then Sophie, her late baby. She loved her babies. She adored having a newborn to look after. When they were tiny, she felt that her greatest reward was to make them comfortable and happy. If they were hungry, she fed them. If they were tired, she cradled them. If they were dirty, she washed them. If they were cold, she warmed them. If they were hot, she cooled them. If they were fretful, she calmed them. All through the day and night she attended them. When they slept, she slept. When they woke, she rose. If they cried when she slept she could physically feel the sound entering through her ear to wake her, connecting to that place in her head which had not forgotten them, even in sleep. She looked after the layette with infinite care. She washed, she tidied, she folded, she smoothed. Always a step away from where the baby lay, only a heart beat between them. There was a soothing rhythm to their days, and that perfect stillness, which a newborn baby brings, filled the house. She never forgot that she had mothered four children, not just three, nor would she until the day she died. The young children were told about their eldest brother. There was one small, precious photograph in a frame on the mantle-piece. As a family they went regularly to visit his grave, the little ones clutching hand-picked posies. Dedicated to her profession as well as her family, Joyce continued to teach whenever the needs of her growing family allowed her to. She taught in an Infants school and loved her small charges. She got a thrill from watching them learn. Working with the children rewarded her and broke her heart in equal measure. The home lives of some of them was too awful - too chaotic and yet grindingly predictable at the same time - to contemplate for long. She tried, in some small way, to ensure that at least part of their day was spent in a safe, rational and loving environment. It appalled her to think what circumstances some of them returned to when the bell rang at half-past three.

In her late thirties, Joyce read *The Female Eunuch*, *The Women's Room*, and *Fear Of Flying*. These books and others crystallised vague thoughts about the role of women in society which had been running around in her own head. Her own circumstances were favourable; Jack was a kind and egalitarian husband. She could see that other women were far from being so fortunate; that generally girls had their lives circumscribed from the day they were born; that the way that girls were raised was a self-fulfilling prophecy of mediocrity. She did her best to see to it that all of her children were brought up as equals.

In Ali's living room, the family continued with their debate, growing steadily louder and more controversial, until Joyce reluctantly decided it was time that Jack went home to bed, and David took them. Later, Ali cornered Frank in the kitchen, cigarette in hand, and unsteadily poured herself another large glass of wine. Frank loved Ali, but she exasperated him.

"You should go steady, Al," he said.

"That's the trouble with policemen. You always think you're right. I need it believe me, Ben's leaving for a year tomorrow, and I don't know how I'm going to cope." She looked around to make sure they were not being overheard, and whispered, "This whole thing with Robert is putting pressure on me. I'm so fed up."

The latest man invited to break her heart was Robert Jones, a friend of David's. He was faithless and charming in equal measure. Ali had told Frank about her latest infatuation in a series of late-night telephone conversations. She was an insomniac, and, knowing that Frank necessarily kept late hours at times, she often rang him after midnight. Sometimes he let the answering machine do its work, sometimes he lifted the receiver and spoke to her. Frank knew Robert Jones slightly and they had all been at the same party recently. Ali was going to the party alone as David was on a business trip in Japan, and had dragged Sophie with her, as she had known that Harry would be there. She had been thwarted however, as Sophie and Harry, after one hungry stare, had kept determinedly, almost scrupulously, apart. Ali had also asked Frank to go along and he had started to refuse, but then reminded himself that his current monk-like existence was not good for him, nor did it make him good company, so reluctantly he agreed.

At the party, Ali nervously pointed Robert out to Sophie and Frank, and Sophie, who knew his reputation, warned her, "Ali, forget him. If you must be unfaithful to David, at least find someone nice."

"He is nice."

"No, he isn't. He's sexy. He's handsome. He's not nice."

Robert had arrived resplendent in a gold kaftan and black leather trousers. He really was remarkably beautiful. He had perfect skin, dark Byronic hair, blue eyes, a rather large nose and an expressive mouth. He headed straight for Ali, and proceeded to dominate the conversation. She brightened up a lot and started giggling at his *bon mots,* and fiddling with her hair. He was from London, actually Pinner, but he wanted you to believe he had been born within the sound of Bow Bells, or at least of the Stock Exchange trading floor. He was a lecturer in economics at York University, and traded on his winning combination of mock-Cockney charm and intellect to bed every first-year student he could. Second and third years would not touch him with the proverbial barge-pole. But, for all that, Ali liked him. She found that there was something both funny and touching about the way he took himself so seriously, and she liked being in his company. At the party, Frank almost expected him to break into a chorus of *Maybe It's Because I'm A Londoner*, but the cheeky barrow boy was not his style. He was much more the laid-back, urbane Londoner who was the indulgent, if weary, host to some northern simpletons. A bit much really, Frank thought, considering they were standing in the heart of Yorkshire, and it was not even Robert's party.

Frank had allowed himself a couple of glasses of whisky, chatted indifferently to one or two women, got annoyed at the awful dance music that some idiot insisted on playing, and then got bored.

At the end of the party they all spilled out onto the street and everyone started kissing everyone else goodnight. Robert bore down on Ali and she prepared to receive the anticipated 'I-don't-really-want-to-do-this-but-I'm-willing-to-be-polite' peck on the cheek. Instead he kissed her full on the lips. He lingered there for half a second longer than was strictly the form. Half a second when she kissed him back. He looked her straight in the eye for a few seconds, and then turned to link Sophie's arm and walk ahead.

Frank noticed, and pulled Ali to one side. "What the hell are you doing?" he hissed.

"Nothing! It was just a friendly kiss," pouted Ali. She was slightly drunk and pirouetted away from him, giggling, "That kiss was amazing, actually! The whole world suddenly shifted, re-arranged itself and fell back into place, only a slightly different place, like a very small earthquake. I almost looked round to see if anyone else had noticed!" She shook her head in a puzzled way, and walked slowly and quietly by Frank's side for a while. Then she turned to him, suddenly serious, and said, "Look, I don't know where this has come from, and I don't know what I'm going to do with it. I need time to think. Just leave me alone." Frank could see that all her unhappiness and uncertainty about David had suddenly reshaped itself into a huge crush on Robert.

Now, standing in Ali's kitchen, Frank asked her what was going on. Ali wailed, "I haven't heard from him for over a week. I think someone's trying to steal him from me."

"He isn't yours to steal. I thought this was all done with, Ali?"

"So did I but I met him in York Minster, not long after the party," admitted Ali, "He was so funny - he minced around, pontificating and spreading out his arms as though this was his playground and we could play with anything we wanted, you know, the way he does. Then he stopped talking and looked at me really earnestly; he put his face right up to mine. I was trying to suppress my feelings, but my heart just swelled with longing. I wanted him more than anything I'd ever wanted in my life. We sat on some ancient stone seat, side by side. He was dressed in red velvet trousers and a white frilly shirt, would you believe? He turned and gazed at me a little pathetically with big sad eyes, and brushed a curl away from his forehead, in that cute way of his. He said, 'Ali, sweetheart, we need to talk' and I squeaked 'Do we?' I was feeling terrified, for reasons I couldn't quite define. He said 'Something happened the other night - we both know that,' - he was referring to the party - , 'I want to see you - alone. Will you have dinner with me one night,? Just the two of us?' He almost started to pout, but then remembered that he was trying to woo me!" Ali laughed and waved her arms around expressively as she continued, "Frank, I wanted to say no and run out of the building and home to my large red-bricked house in Sheriff Hutton, I really did. I made myself think of David, but he seemed to be a long way off, like looking the wrong way down a telescope. I just stalled and said 'Maybe'. He said 'You're driving me crazy. I think about you all of the time, you never reply to my text messages or calls, and it's affecting my work. When are we going to stop this nonsense and spend some quality time together?' I was appalled that a University lecturer could use an expression like 'quality time' - he may be my putative lover but that was no excuse for bad taste. Anyway, I was paralysed by guilt. I'm a married woman contemplating adultery! I stalled for more time. 'It's difficult with David being away so much - my Mum's around a lot of the time, keeping me company.' 'You could if you wanted to,' he sighed, and touched my knee. That had a very stimulating effect on me, and my resolve weakened. I said, 'OK. Name the day, and I'll meet you.' He smiled and hugged me and kissed my cheek. I looked around to make sure that I was not being noticed by anyone who might recognise me. 'Tuesday then, I'll book a table for eight o'clock.' He tossed those dark curls of his, and beamed. He smacked another kiss on my cheek and off he went. I just sat there with my eyes closed, and wondered what I was doing there. I desperately tried to think of David and the boys and all that I could be giving up if I got permanently caught up with Robert. It was no good - David was hundreds of miles away, physically and emotionally. My boys are growing up, and will leave me soon. Robert mesmerises me. Even his pompousness and silliness are endearing. I know that he wants a lot more from me, and that he probably won't wait too long to get what he wants." Ali had stopped laughing by the end of this speech.

"I thought that you said you weren't going to get involved with him. Al, you're so lazy!" Frank said, angrily. He hated to think of her having affairs instead of tackling the problems in her marriage head on.

"Lazy!" she spluttered.

"Yes. Look at you. Can't be bothered to make anything a success. Can't be bothered to use the brain God gave you to do something worthwhile with your life. Can't be bothered to save your marriage."

"My marriage! What do you mean?" she said, looking uncomfortably as though she knew exactly what he meant.

"Come off it. Everyone can see that you and David are on the skids. Everyone but you, it seems. And you are letting him slip away without a fight or a murmur. And now you're even too lazy to conduct an affair. You can't even be bothered to do that properly," he said.

"How dare you?" she spat back.

"I dare because I'm your brother and I care about you. David's not the greatest husband ever perhaps, but you two were made for each other. You can't even see how unhappy you're going to be when he's gone."

"Gone? Gone where?"

"Can't you see that one of these days he's going to go off to America or Japan or Timbuctoo and just NOT COME BACK! He's probably got a girl in every port already - if he's got any sense."

She sat down on a wooden kitchen chair with a thump as if he had physically hit her. As if it had never occurred to her that David might actually leave her, might actually have alternatives.

Diamonds And Pebbles

"No. No. You're wrong."

"No, Ali. You're wrong. Wrong-headed. Do you think he's going to wait around whilst you come out of whatever muddle-headed fantasy land you've got into. He loved you once and you've thrown it away - through laziness!" Frank said.

"Its not that simple. I'm not happy!"

"Rubbish. Ali, at the end of the day it's up to you what thoughts you allow yourself to think. You can be happy, or you can be sad. It's up to you. I choose to be happy. You've got your head permanently in the sand. Just piss or get off the pot, Ali!"

Mixed metaphors not withstanding, he turned and stalked away, surprised at the anger stinging inside his chest. Then he smiled grimly at the ridiculous picture which he had conjured up, and that made him more angry. He did not understand where the outburst had come from, and promised himself to ring Ali and apologise the next day. It was up to her how she lived her life after all.

Later, Harry dropped Frank off outside his apartment building as the moon rose across the darkened sky, and as they drew up to the pavement Frank, still exasperated by his conversation with Ali, decided to stir things up a little.

"Thanks for the lift, Harry. Look, I've got a favour to ask you. I know it's a bore, but I was wondering whether you'd give Sophie a call, take her out for a drink or a meal or something. She's been a bit down recently, what with Pops being ill and everything. Would you mind?"

Harry looked doubtful, and said, "Are you sure? I mean I'd like to, it's just that I've never thought Sophie really liked me that much. She might be horrified, or worse, say yes when she doesn't really want to."

"Oh, I think she'll be delighted. I really do. I think she likes you. She just doesn't wear her heart on her sleeve, you know."

"Well, if you're sure…"

"Really, I'm sure she'll want to go. Take her somewhere nice. I'd appreciate it. I'd take her myself, but I'm really tied up at the moment with this West Wold case. Let me know how you get on."

Harry agreed to have a try, and, once he had assimilated the idea that Sophie might be in his grasp at long last, a huge grin spread over his face and he cheerily waved goodbye as he drove off.

Frank went wearily inside to have a shower, then settled in his favourite reclining chair to catch up on some football on the television. He did not feel that he had made much progress with the murder case that day, and he still felt unsettled from his argument with Ali. He wondered what the next day would bring.

Diamonds And Pebbles

Monday

Diamonds And Pebbles

Chapter 15

At nine o'clock on the next day, a hot and bright Monday morning, DC Emma Smith walked into Frank MacDonald's office, where he was sitting with Steven Brown.

"We looked at Jane Sinclair's bank statements, sir," she said, "and found regular payments of two thousand pounds per month going out of Jane's bank account into Julia Johnson's account for the last five years."

Frank did the mathematics with amazement. He whistled, and said, "That's a lot of money. It could be something to do with caring for their mother, I suppose. Yesterday, Julia Johnson implied that Jane had not helped her out financially. Unless there's something else, more sinister, going on. Maybe blackmail of some sort, do you think?"

"Maybe," nodded Steven, "I wonder if Roger Sinclair knew about the money?"

"He could be at work now," said Frank, looking up at the clock on his office wall, "let's give him a call." Roger Sinclair had told them that he would still go to work for at least part of the time that week, in spite of Jane's murder;

Diamonds And Pebbles

he felt it was better to keep occupied.

Emma Smith left the room, and Steven rang the phone number and asked to be put through to Roger Sinclair. He put the phone on the speaker setting so that Frank could hear the conversation too.

Roger Sinclair's voice said hello.

"Good morning, Mr Sinclair. DS Brown here, DCI Frank MacDonald is listening too."

"Good morning, Mr Brown, Mr MacDonald. How can I help?"

"We just wanted to check something with you. Were you aware that your wife was paying Julia Johnson two thousand pounds a month, sir?"

"Yes, I was."

"It seems a lot of money, sir. It wasn't blackmail of some sort was it?"

They heard Roger Sinclair laugh, ruefully, "No, nothing so dramatic, I'm afraid. Jane wanted to help her. It was for Julia's children, really. The two eldest have both been through University - it's an expensive business these days. They're both doing really well now, so we felt it was worth it. Jane and I encouraged them. Jane was very fond of them all, and with having no children of her own she always took a real interest and wanted to help. They were about as close as an aunt and nieces and nephew can be. We encouraged them to go to University, but Julia didn't like it. She refused to let them go at first. She wanted them out at work earning money so that they could pay her for bed and board! No-one in her family had ever been to University. We said we would give her a generous allowance to help with the fees if she would agree to let them go. Jason's done well in his "A" levels and he's going to Hull University in September. He's a nice boy underneath all the face-furniture. It will do him good."

And get him away from his mother, thought Frank.

"Thank-you for clearing that up for us, sir. We'll be in touch as soon as we have anything to report."

Steven said goodbye and put the phone down.

"It seems Jane was a very generous aunt."

"Yes - but maybe she'd threatened to stop paying Julia for some reason. Would that have been enough to push Julia into murder, do you think?"

Some time later, Frank was sitting in his office alone. Steven Brown walked quickly back into the office waving a sheaf of paper.

"Just got the forensics and post-mortem report back, sir."

"Anything interesting?"

"Yes, a few things. The pathologist analysed the hairs caught in the inside of Jane's hat and the collar of the coat, and says several of them were not human hair at all, but synthetic, probably from a wig."

The two men looked blankly at each other.

"Why on earth would a woman with long, red hair wear a long, red wig? What else?"

"Apparently, Jane had several fingers broken on the left hand *after* she died. Also, the pathologist confirms that Jane was three months pregnant."

"Curious-er and curious-er."

Steven went to update the team, and Frank leant back and put his feet on his desk; a position he found useful for cogitation. Why would a woman with long red hair wear a long, red wig? The more he thought about it the more he could come to only one conclusion; she would not.

When Steven returned and took the seat opposite him,

Frank put his legs down and sat up straight. "If someone wore a red wig, Jane's Mac, Jane's hat, and took Jane's dog for a walk, who would they look like?" he asked.

"Jane?"

"Exactly!"

Steven saw where he was leading, "So someone deliberately went out dressed as Jane…"

"…to make people think it was Jane…"

"…to make people think that Jane was still alive…"

"…when, in fact, she was dead…"

"…in order to?…"

"…in order to - Oh, I don't know…"

" …in order to?…"

"…Ah, I've got it - in order to obfuscate the real time of the murder and provide themselves with an alibi…"

"…an alibi for the time at which we assumed the murder had taken place…"

"…when in fact it had happened earlier…"

They sat and grinned at each other. This felt like the first real breakthrough.

"It also shows that it was completely pre-meditated," said Frank. "Whoever it was must have planned the whole thing out and taken the wig with them. It shows the killer is pretty cool; it wasn't a spare of the moment thing. Man or woman, do you think?" he asked, "How tall was Jane?"

"About five feet five."

"Not Roger then, too tall. James Powell? He must be about five nine. No, too tall and too ungainly. Even with Jane's voluminous waxed Mac on. Perhaps our BMW driver?"

"No, the high heels rule out its being a man completely, surely?"

Frank thought for a few moments, "Yes, you are right.

Maybe the high heels were deliberately to throw us off course, or maybe the killer had intended to wear Jane's Wellies to complete the outfit, but simply couldn't get them on? Jane had rather small feet if I remember correctly. It's a bit like the Ugly sisters trying to get Cinderella's glass slipper on."

"Glass Wellie, anyway! Yes, that means our killer is probably a woman, then. At the moment, that means Louise, Julia or Stella."

"Well, Julia is certainly as peevish and envious as one of Cinderella's Ugly Sisters. She's a pretty large woman. Could she have disguised her bulk enough to look like Jane - even with the voluminous Mac? So - to recount - one of them, or someone else, a woman at any rate, went to Lilac Cottage, killed Jane at an earlier time than three forty, then dressed up as her, took the dog for a walk and made sure that she was seen. That explains why she had to go, despite the storm, and why the dog was reluctant to go with someone he didn't know. So Jane was already dead by three forty, whereas we've been working on a time of four thirty onwards. That means all of our suspects' alibis are for the wrong time; we'll need to check them again."

"Yes, and it rules out Louise Leighton. She was in the petrol station at three twenty-nine. The timing is still pretty tight though, sir; it was a lot of trouble to go to for not much gain, maybe half an hour, or one hour at the most."

"Yes - so the killer dressed up as Jane, walked the dog, came back and dressed the body in the Mac, and that's why Jane's fingers were broken, because the killer had to quickly get the coat back on to her body to get out of there fast, and establish an alibi. The coat being on was to encourage us to think that she was killed after the walk."

"But, if it hadn't been for the storm, the coat would

have looked completely incongruous in the middle of a heat wave!"

"The storm was widely predicted for Friday afternoon and it did turn cooler just before - perhaps the killer saw her chance. Or maybe 'Plan B' was to wear the wig with big sunglasses and a straw hat!"

"Or maybe Mrs Mountjoy really did see Jane, still alive?"

"Let's just say that we are right. The killer sets up the whole dressing-up charade. Then we come along, and fall for the fact that Jane was still alive at gone quarter past four, when the storm ended. Then she got away down the back garden, and along the path to the side road, and perhaps into a car. Get someone to ask the neighbours again if they saw a car, or anyone walking at the back of the houses."

"Or, if it was Stella, perhaps down the other way towards the stables?" said Steven, looking steadily at his superior.

"Indeed," replied Frank slowly, "What is the time-of-death on the Path report?"

Steven leafed through the pages, "Between two and five," he pulled a face, "that doesn't help much."

"So, if we are right, Jane was murdered some time after two, but before three-thirty, making Stella the last person to see her alive, probably."

"Definitely the last if she's the killer, sir."

Frank frowned; part of him hoped it was not true, but he nodded anyway.

"The whole thing is still a bit elaborate, sir, for not much gain? And nothing that a decent bit of police work couldn't work out."

Frank sat back, pensively. "Yes, but there's something more going on, isn't there? If the motive was envy, not jealousy *about* Jane, but envy *of* her - her looks, her lifestyle, her personality, perhaps even her pregnancy - perhaps, perhaps there was an element of trying on Jane's persona with the coat. It's almost as though the killer couldn't resist the opportunity to *be* Jane, if only for a short while. It certainly fits with what we know about Julia, Louise and Stella and their various relationships with Jane, and with James Powell. The pregnancy is interesting in terms of why the murder happened now. It may have acted as the catalyst. One huge change - the pregnancy, precipitates another - the murder. We will need to find out who else knew that Jane was pregnant."

The door opened and Emma Smith brought in a sheaf of paper for Steven. "Here's the fingerprint report, sir. And the results from the DVLA search for a silver BMW."

Steven took the reports and scanned them quickly, "Ten silver BMWs registered in a twenty mile radius. Someone from the team will be checking them out now." He paused and looked at Frank, seemingly reluctant to continue.

"What is it?"

"The fingerprints on the candlestick, sir. They were Stella Powell's."

They looked at each other in silence for five seconds.

"That puts her at the top of our suspect list then, I suppose," said Frank. "We've got motive, opportunity, and forensic evidence. We'd better go and see her first, when we go to West Wold. We need to find out who knew about Jane's baby. If Stella knew, then maybe that was what pushed her into murder."

He felt a horrible, dead weight in his stomach, and was very weary suddenly. The fingerprints on the candlestick were the only real piece of evidence that he had; and they belonged to Stella. Had he really been blinded by her charm

Diamonds And Pebbles

into believing her to be innocent when she was guilty?

Half-an-hour later Frank MacDonald and Steven Brown were still sitting in Frank's office in York talking, when Emma Smith walked in and said, "We've had a call from Louise Leighton, sir. She says she's had a parcel sent in the post. She wouldn't say what it was, but she sounded upset. Wanted you to go there a soon as possible."

Frank and Steven exchanged a puzzled look.

"Right, lets go and see what the lady got in the post, Steven."

They drove to West Wold separately as they were to split up later, so that Steven could go to question Roger Sinclair in Wetherby. They duly arrived at Louise Leighton's house, and were shown inside by the ever-present Karen Leighton.

"That thing arrived this morning. She's frightened out of her wits. If you were doing your job properly these things wouldn't happen, in my opinion. Still I suppose you've arrested lots of speeding motorists this morning, so that makes it alright," she said sarcastically, leading them through into the kitchen where a white shoe box, surrounded by a square of crumpled brown paper and a quantity of string, sat on the breakfast bar. Louise, looking tense and drawn, walked down the open staircase and joined them.

"It arrived this morning," she said in a quiet voice, "I thought I'd better show you straight away. I simply don't understand what it means, or why anyone would send it to me." She took off the lid of the shoe box and lifted out a long red wig. She splayed it out in front of her like a weird item of underwear.

"It would be better not handle it too much, actually,"

said Frank. Louise replaced it into the box.

"What does it mean, Mr MacDonald? Is it connected to Jane? Is it some kind of threat?" her voice cracked with fear.

"It does fit in with one of our lines of enquiry," said Frank, "how exactly did it arrive?"

"The postman delivered it at about ten o'clock this morning."

Frank carefully put on some thin rubber gloves, and turned over the brown wrapping paper. The address was printed onto a white label, probably using a personal computer. He could not decipher the postmark.

"Not many clues there. We'll have to get forensics to have a look." He dropped the opened parcel into a large plastic bag held out by Steven.

"Did the killer send it to me?" asked Louise. Her voice was apprehensive, but there was little change in her implacable features.

"I really don't know, Miss Leighton. It could just be a practical joke. Not a very tasteful one, of course."

"A bit more than that, in my opinion. You're not safe in your own beds any more, if you ask me. There are so many of them psychopaths running around these days," said Karen Leighton, indignantly.

"Don't worry, Miss Leighton, Mrs Leighton, if there are any forensic clues we'll find them, and hopefully it may lead us to whoever killed Jane. We'll be in touch."

They stayed a while longer to calm Louise down and assure her that she was safe, and to receive a few more insults from Karen Leighton, and then the two men left.

Diamonds And Pebbles

Chapter 16

Steven Brown went to Roger Sinclair's offices in Wetherby to speak to him about Jane's pregnancy, and check the alibis for him and his secretary for the new timings for the murder.

Frank MacDonald stayed in West Wold to find out whether James Powell had known about Jane's pregnancy, and to interrogate Stella Powell about the forensic fingerprint evidence. The gravel crunched as he drove into the semi-circular driveway of Howard House. He walked in the hot sunshine across to the pleasant-looking house. He had abandoned his suit jacket, but still felt overheated and sticky in his long-sleeved shirt and tie. He wondered what Stella's explanation would be for the fingerprints on the silver candlestick. As usual the front door was open and he knocked and shouted hello as he walked in. Stella's voice answered that she was in the kitchen. Bobby, the lurcher, padded towards him as he went into the kitchen. Stella smiled. She was washing her hands at the sink. She was wearing a short-sleeved T-shirt and shorts.

"I'm gardening," she said, "I'm just getting a cold drink. Would you like to come and sit outside?"

"I was looking for Mr Powell, as well."

"Oh, I'm sorry you've just missed him, he's gone to Manchester for a couple of days. Was it urgent?"

"Perhaps."

Stella quickly prepared a tray with some cold drinks, and carried it out into the garden. The lawn was strewn with cuttings from a Pyracanthus hedge which she was pruning. Frank sat down on a wooden bench nearby and Stella put the tray next to him, and picked up her secateurs and began cutting through the prickly branches. The lurcher sat on the lawn nearby and regarded them both placidly. Vito, the Jack Russell terrier, ran happily round the garden chasing imaginary rabbits. The afternoon heat intensified. Bees droned drunkenly from one gorgeous bloom to the next. Frank took off his blue silk tie and placed it over the arm of the bench next to him. He rolled up his shirt sleeves and undid the buttons at the neck.

"I hope you don't mind if I carry on? I'm trying to hack my way through this hedge. It's become much too overgrown and we've had no berries for the last two winters; I think it must be dying."

Frank cleared his throat. "Mrs Powell," he decided to come straight to the point, "can you explain how your fingerprints came to be on the candlestick which killed Jane?"

She stopped what she was doing, and looked at him steadily, "Yes, I can. On Friday when I went to Lilac Cottage she asked me if I wanted to buy them."

"Buy them?"

"Yes. I had admired them in the past. They were beautiful; Georgian silver. I had said, jokingly, that if she ever got fed up of them, or fell on hard times, I would buy them off her. On Friday she asked me if I would like them.

So I picked them up - or one of them, at least - to have another look."

Frank inwardly relaxed, and let out a small sigh of relief, "And you agreed to buy them?"

"Well, we agreed a price - five hundred pounds - and I said I'd think about it."

"Did you apply your 'cave' theory?"

"Did cavemen need Georgian silver candlesticks, you mean?" she laughed. "No, but they might have looked really nice on the cave's mantle-piece!"

"Did she say why she wanted to sell them? Did she give you the impression that she need the money?"

She thought for a moment, "No, not that, I don't think. It was something else; more as if she was clearing out, getting ready to move on." She hesitated as though she was going to say something else, but did not.

Frank asked himself whether she was telling the truth, and decided that he had no choice but to press her. He wondered whether she knew about Jane's baby, but felt that he could not mention it until he had talked to James Powell.

"You say that you knew about the relationship between your husband and Jane, that it had started again, and yet you weren't concerned?"

She stopped pruning the hedge, and regarded him with her large green eyes, "As I've said, James and I are not possessive of each other."

The unanticipated notion that James might have had reason to be jealous of Stella in the past, made Frank the one who had to break eye contact.

"But it's true to say that you and Jane weren't close."

"True." She let the word linger in the air between them, and did not continue with, "But I didn't kill her."

Diamonds And Pebbles

"And what about Louise Leighton? Tell me about your relationship with her."

Stella carried on cutting the hedge. He could not help but admire the rhythmical grace of her movements as she reached and cut off a branch of the shrub, then turned and dropped the cutting onto the lawn behind her. "I wouldn't say that we've got a 'relationship' really. She moved to the village about two years ago. She worked in the pub for a while and got to know the locals including James and me, Jane and Roger, Phil and Samantha Watson, and others. I wouldn't call her a friend, exactly. We go walking together sometimes - we're going to Sutton Bank this Friday, as it happens - it was something Jane and I used to do occasionally, and Louise asked if she could join us. She generally turns up in the pub on Sunday nights as well. I had noticed that she'd taken a shine to James, so I wasn't surprised when he mentioned that he was seeing her," she shrugged, "she's blonde, petite and pretty - it stands to reason, really."

Frank watched her silently for a moment. Looking round at the beautiful, but controlled, wildness of the garden and watching her struggling with the prickly hedge, she reminded him of a princess in an old fairy tale, condemned by an ancient wizard to repeat the same task over and over again. Was she, like a fairy-tale princess, waiting to be rescued?

"It doesn't seem much of a life," he said quietly, "a husband who is not really a husband, and friends who are not really friends."

She flushed, two pink spots of anger appearing on her cheeks, and she said quietly, "I didn't say I don't have any friends. I just said that Jane and Louise weren't particular friends. As a matter of fact, I have some good friends. I love my husband, I love my daughters, and I like my life."

Frank felt wretched at this rebuke. He knew that he should leave, but he so wanted to allow himself to be with Stella for ten minutes on this lovely August day, not as a policeman and a suspect, but as two ordinary people. She interested him. There was a gentle breeze in the garden which dispersed the divine scent of the roses. He breathed in deeply for a few moments.

"Did you know that gardeners are going to save the planet? We're all going to be growing and eating our own potatoes. According to my son, anyway," he said conversationally, by way of an apology.

She stopped what she was doing and gave him a wry look. The colour in her cheeks had faded. She put down the secateurs and came to sit beside him on the bench, seeming to sense that he was temporarily off-duty.

"Really? That doesn't surprise me," she said, picking up a glass of iced water and taking a drink, "What is that saying? 'You're closer to God in a garden than anywhere else on earth'. You should come back at sunset – the scent of the honeysuckles is heavenly at that time of the day. How is your boy? What is his name?"

"Nathan. Nate. He's fine. Just sixteen. He's waiting for his GCSE results. I'm hoping to take him to the Lake District for a few days before school starts."

"A-levels next year?"

"Yes, hopefully. Tell me about your girls."

"They're nineteen and twenty-one, both lovely girls, both at University - one's at Durham and one's in London. I really miss them when they're not here," she said sadly.

Frank allowed himself to admire her raven hair and shining eyes. Surely such an open, honest face could not conceal a murderous heart? Not for the first time, he found himself wondering how James Powell could have affairs when he was married to Stella. Maybe every relationship palls after twenty years? He found himself echoing her own words from an earlier conversation.

"What are your girls called?"

"Ellen is the oldest, and the younger one is called Grace."

"You must be very proud of them."

"Yes. Being a mother is by far the best thing I've ever done," she smiled.

Beside her on the bench was a very old, very battered copy of *Anne of Green Gables* by L. M. Montgomery; its spine was broken and the pages only just still clinging to each other.

Frank nodded at it and asked, "An old favourite?"

"Oh, yes. I re-read books all of the time. Those and *The Secret Garden, What Katy Did, Little Women*. I adored *The Secret Garden* when I was young. I was convinced that there must be a secret garden here. I kept asking my Mum where it was, and kept looking for it, and waiting for a robin to lead me to it. She had to give me a big old-fashioned key to keep in my pocket. Dickon is one of the most lovable boys in literature, I think."

She picked up the book, "It's in a terrible state; I do tend to use books as coasters, door stops, notebooks or whatever. I throw them in the corner as well if they bore me, I'm afraid. There are little book cemeteries all over the house! I even threw *Middlemarch* into the Aegean once, from a Greek pleasure boat on the way to viewing the monasteries of Mount Athos. (From a safe distance of fifty yards of course; no woman has stepped foot on its soil since 1927 - there is separatism for you!)"

Frank smiled and asked, "Which books are in the

cemeteries?"

"Oh, let me think - anything by Gabriel Marcia Marquez, anything by Thomas Hardy (I loathed *The Mayor of Casterbridge* at school, and *Tess of the D'Urbevilles!* - all that business with the letter sliding under the carpet! Enough!), anything with more than six Russian names (except *Anna Karenina*, of course), anything by Graham Greene, anything by Doris Lessing, (I know! I know! I'm lazy and stupid!) anything with a picture of shoes and handbags on the front...I could go on!"

He laughed, "I don't agree with you about Graham Greene, by the way."

She looked down at the book which she was holding, "I suppose this is considered rather sentimental by today's standards, but there is something so real about it; real joy and real sorrow, and Anne is one of the best heroines in fiction," she said tenderly, "and the descriptions of the natural world are superb. I must go to Prince Edward Island one day. It's one of those Things I Must Do Before I Die!"

"Who is the Jilly Cooper fan?" said Frank, remembering the neat row of books in the kitchen.

"Oh, the girls adore her, and I must admit I've spent many a happy hour by a pool with a pina colada in one hand and a Jilly Cooper in the other! - not very challenging, perhaps. To read is the important thing - anything is better than not reading at all. You should come to a session of our book club in the village. Sometimes it's like World War Three. We've just been looking at *Wuthering Heights*. (Don't worry about never having read the Brontes, by the way, and I see from your face that I'm right, I've never met a man who has.) I've read a lot about Emily Bronte, and been to Haworth lots of times. It's an astonishing place. To be able to see the actual settee where she died! I'm writing an article on her, although it's a bit outside of my usual scope. So far at the book club we have galloped our way through *A Hundred Years of Solitude* (torture - thrown into the corner at page 10), *Fingersmith* (courtesy of Julia), *Ulysses* by James Joyce (words failed me - but they obviously did not fail him), *Last of the Mohicans* (Jane's choice, blessed relief). Louise chose *War and Peace* for some reason - I don't think she actually reads much, she just wanted to be there, and she even brought Karen once, who couldn't say anything except how expensive books were these days, and she didn't care for reading herself, in her opinion the telly was better! This month has been my choice again, and I had chosen *Jane Eyre* to much groaning and sighing by my fellow bookworms. Picture the scene - it was at Lilac Cottage, actually - I'd forgotten that - everyone sat there and shuffled self-consciously as they always do at the beginning. Hard to believe that in half-an-hour's time there would be hell-let-loose, as various parties argued about the relative merits of D H Lawrence and Steven King! 'Well,' I said, feeling duty-bound to set the ball rolling, 'To me, *Jane Eyre* is one of the greatest stories ever told. From a purely narrative standpoint not much has surpassed the mad-wife-in-the-attic, the wedding interrupted, the wicked aunt, the progress from lowly governess to gentleman's wife, the horrors at Lowood - '

"'It's hardly relevant for today's woman, is it?' boomed Julia.

"'Sorry?' I said.

"'Well, we don't need a man to validate our position in society, to feed us, clothe us, and patronise us. This is simply Victorian melodrama.'

"'There's no way a man like him would have looked at a woman like her,' said Jane.

"'She was beautiful inside,' I said, 'She was the most challenging woman he had ever met. And what about the sex scenes?' I asked. 'The greatest ever written, surely?'

"'Sex scenes?' they all said.

"I could see Julia and some of the others muttering and riffling through their copies as they seemed to have missed something. You should have seen their faces! It was hilarious, honestly! I was talking about the bit in his bedroom when Jane Eyre rescues Rochester from the fire - the sexual tension is palpable. And that bit near the end where she sits on his knee. Wow! And then there's the jealousy - the whole Blanche Ingram fiasco. Jane's jealousy is enough to start the fire on its own! It's terrific stuff. And the most fascinating thing of all is - how did this torrid love story come to be written by a Victorian spinster, a parson's daughter, living in a remote, storm-tossed part of Yorkshire?"

Stella suddenly remembered something and continued, "I often think I would like to host a radio programme about which eight books would the guest like to take on a desert island? Here are mine;

Number one - *Persuasion*

Number two - *Jane Eyre*

Number three - *Pride & Prejudice*

Number four - *Sense & Sensibility*

Number five - *David Copperfield*

Number six - *Anne of Green Gables*

Number seven - *Peeping Tom (*by Howard Jacobson)

Number eight - possibly *Wuthering Heights* - or I'm considering *Lonesome Dove* by Larry McMurtry - " she counted them off on her fingers as she spoke.

Frank grinned, "You've obviously spent some time thinking about this."

" - you get a lot of thinking time when you're mucking out stables. Call me an old traditionalist, but you can't beat perfection, no matter how old it is. I refuse to be dictated to by the Art élite who think it is so hip and 'cool' to only approve of what is new or cruel or ugly - in Art and Literature. (Also, spare me from so-called gardeners who don't actually like flowers!) On my desert island, Elizabeth and Mr. Darcy would be good company, Jane and Mr. Rochester would be good in a crisis (heaven knows they've been through a few) and David Copperfield, poor motherless David, would provide hours of distraction. I am not sure about included *Wuthering Heights*, although it is undoubtedly in my top eight novels, because I just don't think I could cope with Heathcliff sulking and scowling everywhere, and Cathy would be useless for anything but complaining and reclining. Anne Shirley is so interesting, and Matthew and Marilla so practical and comforting. *Peeping Tom* is there because it's the funniest book I've ever read, and laughter would be important when you're going insane from solitude in the middle of the Pacific. It has to be the Pacific, by the way - I'm not going if it's cold. *Sense & Sensibility* is quietly funny too. When Jane Austen mauls you, you stay mauled. Notice I'm having trouble with number eight. There are so many contenders. Jane Austen has helped me through some testing times. *Pride & Prejudice* is what I read when I'm ill or unhappy. There is something so comforting about knowing that Mr and Mrs Bennett, Mr Bingley and his sisters and all of them will be there, unchanged and unchanging, no matter what the vicissitudes of my life. *Persuasion* is just perfect; the heartache of lost love, a bit darker and less optimistic than some of the other books. Open its pages, and you are there in early Nineteenth century Hampshire. And as for Jane Austen herself, so often portrayed as the frustrated spinster, I do not believe it for a minute. I believe she reached an accommodation, as so many people do, by finding pleasure in small things; her nieces and nephews, her garden, her village society, and sustained above all by her own genius. And it's a good thing for us that she did. Imagine Jane married to a tyrant who would not let her write! And with six feckless children instead of six perfect novels! She may not have enjoyed the pleasures of motherhood, and I do pity her for that, but she knew the ecstasy of creation." Stella paused and sipped some cold water from her glass, "Oh, and in the show I would ask 'what music track would you take apart from Mozart and Beethoven?' Easy. *Twist and Shout* by the Beatles. No contest."

Frank laughed again. "Mine would be *Mannish Boy* by Muddy Waters. You should talk to my mother about The Beatles," he said, and then surprised himself by adding, "I would really like you to meet her."

"I would love to," she said cordially.

To cover his confusion, Frank said quickly, "You don't tackle anything modern at your book club, then?"

"Oh, no. We spit on anything written in the Twenty-first century!"

"Have you read the Pullman trilogy, *His Dark Materials*?" he asked.

"No, but it's on my list," she said.

"Of Novels You Must Read Before You Die?"

"Yes! Would they be in your top eight?" Stella asked.

"Maybe, and the Tolkien trilogy - that's six already. I'll need to think about the other two!"

There was a short silence whilst Frank berated himself for still being there. At least he was doing what Superintendent Drake had asked him to do. Stella suddenly changed the subject, "By the way, when will they be able to have Jane's funeral?" she asked.

"I don't know. We need to be sure that we have all of the forensic evidence first."

"James is terribly upset; it would be better for him to get it over with. He can't grieve properly at the moment. I think he and Jane really loved each other. I don't know if he's told you this - he told me that they were planning to move into his flat in Manchester together." Stella looked upset, suddenly, and said, "It seems as though everything was about to change. I don't suppose that Louise would have been too pleased about that. She strikes me as the jealous type."

"Really?" Frank said, and wondered if she was simply trying to suggest a motive for someone other than herself.

"Oh, yes. I think she fancied herself as mistress of this place," she nodded towards the house.

"With you turfed out onto the street?"

"Something like that. With only my faithful dogs by my side," she smiled and patted Bobby's head as the animal gazed at her adoringly with his strange, orange eyes.

"Seriously, where would it leave you financially, if you and James parted?" It was not a question that he strictly needed to ask, but he went ahead anyway.

"Well, this house is mine as I've said, so I guess he would give me and the girls some money to live on - I don't make much from working at the stables, or the magazine articles - and the rest would be his. I'd have to find a proper job, and stop being a spoilt lady of leisure. I know I'm very fortunate."

Frank nodded. He looked around at the pleasant garden for a few moments, and then shook himself out of his summer's afternoon reverie and decided it was time to get back on duty. "By the way, you haven't seen a silver BMW around the village have you? Someone thought they may have seen Jane getting into one recently."

"No, I haven't," she said doubtfully, "could he be the one? The man who killed Jane?"

"We don't think that it was a man."

She accepted this piece of news with aplomb. If she was the killer she was not letting herself slip.

Reluctantly he decided it was time to leave, said goodbye, and walked around the side of the house leaving Stella to wrestle with the pyracanthus. He felt exhausted by the heat, the lack of progress, and by the struggle to reconcile his inclination and his duty where Stella was concerned. He sighed as he saw Roy Parsons, hanging round outside Stella's gate. The reporter started walking towards him, his flip-flops crunching on the gravel.

"Afternoon, Chief Inspector. Any progress, sir?"

"Another statement will be made shortly - and by the way, you're trespassing."

The man was unrepentant, he said, "We understand that Stella Powell is a suspect, is that true? Are you close to making an arrest yet? Is the trail going cold by now?"

Frank ignored the questions. Don Green, the photographer, took several photographs in a desultory fashion as Frank got into his car as quickly as he could.

"Give me a break," hissed Frank, as he drove off.

Later he remembered that he had left his tie in Stella's garden. Sigmund Freud had a theory that leaving personal articles behind betrays a secret desire to return. Frank held the thought for a moment and chose not to pursue it, but concentrated his mind instead on the hard and cruel facts about Jane Sinclair's murder.

Diamonds And Pebbles

Chapter 17

The journey from York to Manchester via the M62 motorway is a modern nightmare to be avoided at all costs. The journey from York to Manchester across the Pennines, through Skipton, is a joyous experience on a sunny August day, and that is what Frank MacDonald and Steven Brown found themselves doing on the Monday afternoon after Jane Sinclair's death.

James Powell's loft apartment was at the top of a converted warehouse in the centre of Manchester; one of many which had been renovated in the city as it reinvented itself, shaking off the industrial past, and pushing forward to a brighter future. Every square inch of available space in the buildings along the cobble streets and canal-sides had been turned into desirable residences. Frank and Steven found a parking space and walked along narrow dusty streets in the bright sunshine to the address they were looking for. Having gained entry to the building via the intercom, they went up in a luxurious, mirror-lined lift to the fourth floor. They stepped out onto a carpeted landing and rang the bell at a large steel door.

James Powell opened the door and waved them in, padding away in front of them in T-shirt, Bermuda shorts and flip-flops. They followed him through a small vestibule and through frosted glass double doors into a truly impressive room. The apartment occupied the whole top floor of the building and was huge, with floor to ceiling windows around the three exposed-brick walls which faced them. Going round the room clockwise, there was a rectangular pod which Frank assumed housed the bathroom, then an area with king-sized bed and wardrobes, followed by a living area with huge, squashy sofas, gigantic television, and coffee table. This area occupied the corner diagonally to their left, and next to that on the wall facing them, there was a stainless steel kitchen with turquoise American double fridge, and a turquoise, wooden island complete with chrome bar stools. In the corner immediately to their right was another rectangular pod with a door labelled DARK ROOM. The rest of the large space was given over to photography with several large tables covered in photographic and lighting equipment, computers, and photographic prints. There was a rudimentary set with chairs, drapes, lighting gantries, and cameras on tripods.

James Powell led the way over to the living room area, offered them cold drinks, which he duly set down on the coffee table in front of them and then came to sit down.

"Sorry you had to follow me over here," he said, lighting a cigarette. James Powell's features were still flattened and diluted by grief.

"That's alright, sir," said Frank, "we could have spoken

to you on the phone but what we have to say is rather sensitive."

"Sensitive?"

"Yes - we've now had the results of the post-mortem on Jane, and one of the findings was that she was pregnant. About twelve weeks probably." James Powell stared at the floor. "Were you aware of this, Mr Powell?"

James Powell raised his eyes to Frank's. "Yes - I was - actually. Jane told me about a month ago."

"What was your reaction?"

"Well, shocked at first, obviously. We'd only just got back together again. It all happened a bit fast, you know?"

"But you were both pleased?"

"Jane was ecstatic, she never thought she would have a family. So was I, once I'd got my head round it. Jane was going to move in here for a while until we could find something more suitable." Tears glistened in his eyes briefly, as the reality of his situation hit him once again, and he contemplated what might have been.

"And Mrs Powell was aware of the situation?" asked Frank. Steven Brown's interview with Roger Sinclair that morning had established that Roger knew nothing about the pregnancy.

"Yes, I told Stella as soon as Jane and I had decided what we were going to do."

"How did she take it?"

James Powell sighed, and stubbed out his cigarette, "Okay, I suppose. It's tough on her. She doesn't want to break up the family. It's tough on the girls too, you know? She was worried about them."

"Was she jealous?"

"No. I told you. Our marriage isn't like other peoples'."

"But when Stella was actually faced with separation and

divorce - did she react badly? Was she shocked, angry - "

"Look, Mr MacDonald, where are you going with this? Are you trying to say that Stella killed Jane because she was losing me? Because Jane was pregnant? It's nonsense!"

"Why? Sexual jealousy is a very strong motive."

"Yes, in an unstable person, but not Stella…"

"Let's talk about Louise Leighton, then, for a moment, shall we?"

James Powell groaned with exasperation.

"Where does she fit into all of this, Mr Powell? You had a rather complicated love-life, didn't you?"

"I was seeing her for a while, nothing serious, though. Just passing time. When Jane and I got back together I tried to finish it with Louise, but she was persistent, and Jane and I decided it was no bad thing if everyone thought that Louise and I were still an item, you know? Jane didn't want everyone to know about us and the baby until we had actually moved here, to Manchester, and away from the village. Jane didn't want to humiliate Roger. So Louise was a bit of a smokescreen, if you like."

"Very convenient for you, too, being able to see them both with impunity," said Frank.

"It really wasn't like that."

"So Louise knew about you and Jane?"

"Not from me."

"And the baby?"

"Again, not from me. I specifically didn't tell her because she told me once that she couldn't have kids, and I thought it might be touchy subject, you know?"

"Would Jane have told her?"

James Powell shrugged, "Maybe. She was really thrilled about it. Maybe she just wanted to tell someone."

"Rather insensitive, under the circumstances? They

were rivals after all."

"As I said, no, not really, and Louise really liked Jane, sort of looked up to her, you know? She would have liked being Jane's confidante, and she was kidding herself if she thought she was Jane's rival, she knew me and her were finished. She was pretty desperate to be accepted into village life, and Jane helped her, so I guess she just blanked out the other stuff."

"And would you consider her capable of murder? Was she the violent type?"

"You mean, kill Jane out of jealousy over me?"

"And the baby."

"No, this is all crazy. Surely, Jane was killed by some nutcase who was burgling the cottage…"

"Let me put another scenario to you," said Frank, "Were you really so thrilled by the prospect of another child at your age, of leaving your wife and family, of being tied down to a normal lifestyle? Or isn't it nearer the truth to say that it was all Jane's idea? That she was insisting on plans that weren't to your liking, that it was all too much - Jane, Louise, Stella - and that you killed Jane as a way out of a situation which was spinning out of your control…"

Even to Frank's ears it sounded wrong, neither did it fit in with his theory about Jane's killer being a woman, but he was getting increasingly frustrated at having no clear leads.

"No, I've told you. I loved Jane. I wanted the baby. I felt that my life was going somewhere for the first time in years. This is all crazy," James repeated, getting up from his seat, and pacing up and down, "please tell me this isn't what you really think."

Frank relented a little, "Everyone is a suspect at this stage, I'm afraid, until we prove who the killer is."

He felt that he had learned everything he needed for

now, and quickly brought the interview to a close. He was starting to believe that James Powell was innocent, and when they discussed it afterwards on the drive back to York, Steven Brown agreed.

"This seems to let James Powell of the hook, sir," he said, "He has no motive for killing Jane, quite the opposite, in fact."

"Yes, I'm inclined to feel that he's telling us the truth, but he has no alibi whatsoever."

"Nobody does, really. Except Louise Leighton, who was buying petrol and on her way to York."

"Yes, but if it isn't James, isn't Roger, isn't Julia, and isn't Stella," Frank waited for Steven to interject but he merely raised his eyebrows, "then it must be Louise, or the bloody man in the BMW who nobody can find." All of the local owners of BMW cars matching the description which Louise Leighton had given had been ruled out of the investigation by Frank's team. The search area had now been widened.

"Louise Leighton certainly had the motive - if she discovered that Jane was pregnant and about to take James away from her," said Frank.

"Or it could still be Stella..." said Steven levelly, reigning Frank back in.

"Yes," Frank replied quietly. Steven was not stupid. Frank knew that he was aware of Frank's growing regard for Stella.

Tuesday

Diamonds And Pebbles

Chapter 18

On Tuesday morning Frank gave himself a few hours off to stock up on some essential groceries, and go to the bank. Frank's mother, Joyce, came to do some housework every Tuesday. She had her own key and often he did not even see her. He always knew that she had been, however, by the smell of polish as he entered the flat in the evening. She usually left him something tasty to put in the oven. It was as though the fairies had been whilst he was out. At almost seventy years old, Joyce was still hale and hearty, and still helping others, which she had done diligently all of her adult life. She was actively involved with children's charities. The housekeeping arrangement was a source of great amusement to the whole family. Frank's sisters were pretend-horrified and teased him mercilessly. He begged his mother not to come, and said he would pay for a cleaning lady, but she insisted that it was a pleasure. He had too much to do, and she too little, that was her simple rationale. She would not let him pay her either, but he made sure that he seldom arrived on her doorstep without an extravagant bouquet or the promise of tea at Betty's café. In truth, she only did a little light dusting and cleaning, and she loved to be of use to him. Underneath the gentle banter, there was the steady ebb and flow of their mutual love, and of her continuing need to nurture him, which would only cease with her last breath. There was not only his almost subconscious acknowledgement of her needs, but also his own delighted receipt of her ministrations. She had been a wonderful mother to him all of his life. He remembered his childhood in the early 'Seventies as a golden time. The family had regularly gone to Greece on holiday, and Frank remembered long sunny days on golden beaches with his parents and sisters. They had also had regular trips around the beauty spots of Yorkshire - Fountains Abbey, the Dales, Whitby, and Goathland. His father had a fondness for Morris Minor convertibles, and raced jauntily down the country roads. They always took a picnic, spread a blanket on the ground, be it grass or sand, and then the children chased around and played games to their hearts' content. His parents had also taken them to museums and art galleries in London, Hull and York. Every year the MacDonalds made a point of taking the children to the Summer Exhibition at the Royal Academy in Piccadilly.

Frank sat and had a coffee on the balcony overlooking the river and the city with his mother, before setting off. It was a fine, hot, August morning and he dressed casually, left his flat about nine-thirty, and headed across Skeldergate Bridge into York city centre. The River Ouse sparkled in the sunlight as it flowed softly down towards the distant Humber. Already the river was a hub of activity with boats, big and small, preparing for the day ahead, ferrying eager tourists to and fro. The city of York is small, and the centre is closely encompassed by a medieval wall, large parts of which are still intact. The walls are walked with relish by residents, visitors and ghosts alike. Sections of the wall run between Bars, which were the gated entrances to the old walled city, (often decorated in a grisly fashion with the severed heads of traitors) and now allow access to modern traffic; one Bar even has a complete barbican, an ancient form of defence which enabled citizens to trap attackers in a confined space and dispatch them from above with boiling oil. From Bootham Bar, a citizen of York can still legally kill a Scotsman, using a bow and arrow. Confusingly, the streets running from the Bars to the centre, like spokes in a wheel, are called gates, for example Goodramgate, from the Viking word 'gatte', for 'street'. Sitting majestically within the medieval walls is the magnificent York Minster, dominating the skyline for miles around; it is the first sign looked for by York's returning citizens that they are almost home. The oval shape of the medieval city is bisected from north to south by the stately River Ouse, which is traversed by three bridges. The main shopping area lies to the east of the river. Frank's block of apartments was situated on the west bank of the river, close to the most southerly of the three bridges.

York has a long, violent and bloody past. Inhabited by the Romans, then by the Vikings, later besieged by the Royalists and the Scots in the Civil War, it lies a stone's throw from the battles of Fulford, Stamford Bridge and Marston Moor. The citizens of York are used to being at the cutting edge of history. If they have a certain reputation for being correspondingly suspicious of strangers and protective of the contents of their wallets, it is perhaps understandable, if not entirely forgivable. Constrained as it is by its city walls, the centre of York has a cosy and self-satisfied air, like a cat wrapped around itself on a favourite window-ledge. It was mercifully spared the excesses of 'Sixties and 'Seventies rebuilding programmes, and much of its Georgian and Victorian architecture is intact. The tight cluster of medieval streets close to the Minster is still vibrant with commerce. In Victorian times York's prosperity was assured by the coming of the railways and of chocolate. Joseph Rowntree, founder of Rowntree's chocolate factory, was a model employer and benefactor; a true Victorian philanthropist. Modern York is the jewel of the North, set in the glorious North Yorkshire countryside, content to watch the south-east of England choke itself to a standstill, happy to be ignored by southerners who disdain to travel northwards. It has a confidence, bluffness, and self-esteem which is carrying it forward into the Twenty-first century. The railways, even the chocolate-making, may have declined, but the very bricks and mortar of the buildings are steeped in a history which people flock from around the world to breathe in and wonder at. York is full of ghosts, nowhere more so than in its public houses, with several vying to be the oldest and the most haunted. Its warren of small streets and small shops are on a human scale, the antithesis of purpose-built shopping malls situated on inaccessible ring-roads. The narrowest and most famous of all, The Shambles, allowed two people to shake hands across its width, from one Tudor casement window to another. The street's name derives from the unfortunate medieval practice of its many butchers shops throwing their offal into the middle of the street. It is now home to more prosaic tourist shops and tearooms. From the green spaces of the Knavesmire, which is home to the racecourse and where Dick Turpin and countless other felons were hanged, to the towering splendour of the Minster, from the sparkling Ouse to the encircling stone walls, the eye is treated to great beauty at every turn.

Having crossed the nearest bridge, Frank walked towards the main shopping area past the Law Courts and the superb Castle Museum on his right, followed by the quirky Clifford's Tower; an ancient circular structure perched on top of a high grassy mound. The mound is spectacular in springtime when it is encrusted in thousands of daffodils. The tower has a bloody history; in 1190 AD one hundred and fifty Jews were massacred within its walls, rather than renounce their faith. Frank had a great fondness for the Castle Museum, going back to countless visits from his earliest childhood. Built partly in the old debtor's prison, the museum has a series of evocative room-sets from Jacobean, Georgian, and Victorian times, as well as one from the 'Fifties, and a full street set out in Victorian style. It has countless exhibits of household articles, fashions, weaponry, toys, World War Two memorabilia, and the cell where Dick Turpin spent his last night on earth. Frank remembered, as a child, peering in amazement into the rooms depicting bygone eras, and being particularly impressed by the various stuffed dogs placed there for extra authenticity.

He was almost tempted to spend an hour or two in the museum then, but instead carried on along the road and turned right into Coppergate and then onto Parliament Street, a long and wide pedestrianised area which was often home to craft and food markets. Having been to the bank to pay a bill, and a newsagent to buy Nathan a football magazine, he decided to walk through to the cluster of narrow, interconnecting, medieval lanes and alleys close to the Minster. The area was full of bars, restaurants, and small, expensive shops. Down Grape Lane he went to his favourite second-hand record shop. He had come to know the owner of the shop quite well over the years and spent ten minutes chatting to him, before buying an old vinyl album by Robert Johnson which he had been looking for. As he stepped out of the shop into the sunshine, he turned left and was surprised to see the figure of Julia Johnson hurrying out of a narrow alleyway to the right and heading towards Castle Street. She was obviously in a rush, and managing to look both excited and furtive at the same time. She was dressed, as usual, all in black. Frank put on his sunglasses and started to follow her. She walked quickly through the crowds of tourists and shoppers down a couple of narrow streets, and back into the wide open spaces of Parliament Street. He followed as closely as he dared, watching the plum-coloured, spiky hair bobbing through the other pedestrians. Julia crossed over to a building society premises and went inside. Carefully, Frank followed her in, and hid behind a pillar with Nathan's magazine handy for extra cover. Julia had joined a queue of people waiting to see the cashiers who sat behind a glass-screened counter. After several minutes it was her turn to be served and she moved up to the counter. Frank saw her pull a plastic carrier bag out of the large black shoulder bag which she was holding. She opened the carrier bag and produced several bundles of what looked like twenty pound notes. The cashier duly weighed them and recorded the transaction. Frank judged there to be at least six thousand pounds worth of notes in the bundles. He made sure that she did not see him as she turned to leave. He followed her out and watched her go in the direction of Coney Street. He felt there was little point in following her; he was much more interested in where she had been before he saw her, and whom, if anyone, she had been meeting. Was she blackmailing somebody? Had she seen the killer near Lilac

Cottage on Friday afternoon? He considered back-tracking to see if he came across any one he knew from West Wold, but decided it was probably too late; whoever Julia had been meeting would probably be long gone by now.

He decided to go and call in to see his sister Sophie at Smiths café. He made his way back through the little maze of streets which lead from Parliament Street to the Minster. On impulse he entered the quiet shade of the great cathedral. The ranks of wooden chairs which usually filled the knave had been removed and he particularly liked it like this. With the vast expanse of stone floor uncluttered it was so easy to imagine his medieval counterparts strolling on those same flag-stones. It made him feel connected to the past. The staggering height of the ceiling and the richness of the carvings and decorations were enough to stun the tourists into silence. Frank wandered around, head thrown back, gazing at the ceiling. He walked over to the North transept to see his favourite window - the beautiful Five Sisters. Made up of five adjacent lancets or panels each five feet wide, and containing a hundred thousand pieces of glass, it was awe-inspiring. No gaudy mosaic of primary colours this, but the most subtle blend of 'grisaille', or grey and pastel tones, rising up fifty feet above the ground. Frank gazed transfixed at it for a while, before moving and walking around for a few more minutes. It was all superb, and Frank had spent a lot of time there over the years, just sitting and marvelling at what surrounded him.

Presently he left the cathedral. He looked back and paused as always in awe at the foot of the Minster, feeling dwarfed by its magnificent towers, then made his way down High Petergate to Smiths café, and went inside, a large brass bell clanging as he did. Sophie was behind the counter, and one or two customers sat at the tables. To overcome the unchallenging nature of her work Sophie played loud music most of the time, and turned up the volume another couple of notches when things got too boring. It was the music that made Smiths trendy - well at least popular. Whilst most tea-shops had a barely audible Pachelbel tinkling in the background, Sophie's tastes ran more to 'Sixties classics and the odd piece of hard rock, even Nirvana if she wanted to create a particularly down-beat *ambience*. Why a person born in 1979 should have quite such a penchant for the Beatles, Rolling Stones, et al Frank did not know. Played at a decibel level somewhere between loud and deafening, the Beach Boys drew the local fifty-some-things like a magnet. Once in, they settled down with the free periodicals which Sophie so thoughtfully provided, and ordered cappuccinos like there was no tomorrow, which, for some of them, there was not. The men were generally bearded, cordurouyed and indefinably dusty, and the women were similar but usually beardless. The loud music was not a deliberate marketing ploy on Sophie's part, it was simply her way of coping with the extreme tedium of pouring endless cups of café latte to the Bearded Ones. The remainder of her customers were the Japanese and American tourists who, weary from walking the city walls and craning their necks in the Minster, shuffled into Smiths for a rest. The interior of the cafe was stylish with polished wooden floors, chairs and tables, Roman blinds at the ample bay window and a muted shade of yellow on the walls. With the sun streaming in and the smell of fresh coffee in the air, it was a very pleasant place to be. The walls were decorated with small watercolours, painted by Sophie, of stormy seascapes and bleak moors, each with a hopeful price-tag. Cream china, cream linen napkins and silver cutlery completed the rather plush ambience. Sophie was not actually given to inventing marketing ploys because she did not really mind how many customers she had. She wanted to be an artist. She was hopelessly un-materialistic. Hence the self-indulgent opening times at the cafe; some time around nine o'clock until some time around four, and 'Never On A Sunday'. With her working day over, she would go home and paint in the studio she had created in the converted loft at home. One day, she swore, Smiths would be an art gallery selling coffee rather than a café selling art. She left around two o'clock to go home and paint whenever she could, and put Smiths into the tender care of her older sister, Ali. When Ali took over the running of Smiths in the afternoons, she was even less interested in the customers' welfare than Sophie was, and the two hours which she occasionally spent there seemed to tax her considerably. When Ali was in charge the music turned rather maudlin, with Leonard Cohen and Joni Mitchell at their most sombre featuring heavily. Sophie did not ask Ali what she did with the rest of her free time. Looking after Sophie's trendy café in York for a couple of hours a day was the nearest Ali had ever come to working, and she made the most of it by being ever vigilant for unsuitable men to fall in love with (though not amongst the Bearded Ones or the Japanese tourists), and even washing the odd cup.

The café was warm in the August sunshine which filtered through the blinds. A couple of new works by Sophie hung on the walls and Frank paused to admire them; a splashy landscape in dark greens and greys, and an impressionistic view of a crowded beach.

"How goes it, Soph?"

"Okay, sweetie. What are you doing here? I thought you were busy with the West Wold thing?"

"Yes, but I needed a break."

"Did Mum arrive this morning?"

"Yes, I left her there with her duster."

Sophie rolled her eyes, "Honestly! I don't know how you can do it. Letting an old woman skivvy round after you."

"She loves it!" laughed Frank.

Sophie poured him a coffee and they moved over to one of the tables and sat down.

"I have news!" she said excitedly.

"Oh, yes?"

"Harry asked me on a date!"

"No! And there was I thinking you didn't like him. Are you going?"

"Of, course I'm going."

"Well, just be careful. I happen to know he's madly in love with you."

She blushed prettily, "Is he? Is he really?", this seemed to amuse her so much she dissolved in a heap of giggles, "Oh, no. He's much too gorgeous for me, not to mention talented."

"Suit yourself, but I'm telling you, he's smitten. Don't break his heart, because I'm the one who will have to spend months helping him get over it - which will probably involve a lot of heavy drinking."

They chatted for a while, the talk turning serious as they discussed the parlous health of their beloved father, and then Frank left her and set off for home. As he stepped out of the café door into High Petergate, he turned right and strolled towards the Minster, his eyes squinting in the strong sunlight. He stopped in the small paved square in front of the Minster to look at an elaborate pavement painting of Michelangelo's *The Creation of Adam*. As he stood there watching the artist at work with his chalks, he saw a familiar figure leaving the Minster by the West Door. It was Stella Powell. She was dressed in a sundress, flat sandals and sunglasses, her hair tied back and up and exposing the curve of her neck. Frank felt uneasy. Was she the West Wold citizen whom Julia Johnson had been meeting? The one who had perhaps given Julia the thousands of pounds of cash to keep quiet about what Julia had seen on Friday afternoon? Was she the killer whom Julia was blackmailing? She noticed him standing there motionless, and walked over.

"Hello, Mr MacDonald," Stella said affably. If she was shocked to be seen by him in town she did not betray it. "It's wonderfully cool in there," she said indicating the large edifice behind her, "I've just been in to light a candle for Jane - it seems precious little, but I wanted to do something."

"I've just seen Julia Johnson," Frank said, more curtly than he intended, "It must be the day for West Wolders to come to town."

"Oh, really? I could have given her a lift if I'd known," she did not seem disturbed by the reference to her supposed blackmailer. She added, "Actually, I bumped into Louise Leighton earlier, in Stonegate."

He groaned inwardly. Here we go again. The same three women every time, round and round in circles, pointing the finger of suspicion at each other, lying and lying to protect themselves. Or one of them is lying, at least, but which one?

"You haven't seen Julia today, then?"

"No, I went to the bank and then came here to the Minster."

Frank assimilated this piece of information with dismay, and then berated himself for caring so much about her answer. Of the people whom he had suspected of meeting Julia, she was the last one he had wished to see.

"Do you know their mother at all, Julia's and Jane's?" he asked on impulse, wondering whether there was some connection between them all which he had missed.

"Yes, I've seen her often at Lilac Cottage over the years. I hear she's gone downhill a lot recently - totally helpless according to Jane. Such a shame, she was quite a dynamo when she was younger," she replied, "there but for the grace of God, I suppose; we could all end up that way one day."

"Did the two sisters look out for her?" asked Frank, thinking of his own father, and grateful at least that Jack would have the best and most loving care for what little time remained.

"Yes, they spent a lot of time with her until it became impossible for her to live on her own, and they had to put her into a Home. I think Julia felt she always did the lion's share of the work, mind you. It's strange how we change places with our children when we get old and frail, isn't it? They become the carers and we become the weak, defenceless ones."

"If we are lucky enough to live that long."

"Yes - and lucky enough to have children that care about us."

"That's not a matter of luck, surely? I think that we get the children we deserve by the amount of effort we put into bringing them up right," said Frank, thinking guiltily of the years when he neglected Nathan, and hoping he would not be held to account at some unforeseen juncture in the future.

"I agree with you. It's hard work, but it's a privilege also. Personally, I intend to be a very fierce and independent old lady, and not be a burden to my girls, until one day I pass gracefully away during my final reading of *Great Expectations*, with a cup of tea and a chocolate biscuit to hand!"

"A fitting title, perhaps?"

She nodded in agreement, and said, "Or maybe I'll be on horseback; flying over one final fence into oblivion. What about you?"

He considered and said, "Listening to Bob Dylan with a glass of single malt. Or watching a beautiful sunset with my son. Still being our true selves at the end is important; not just some shambling husk of what we used to be. None of us like to think about losing our faculties before we die."

"No, we don't," she said more seriously, "it's the heartbreaking part of being human; we're forced to contemplate, not just our death, but the possible crumbling of our bodies and intellect. Old age makes heroes of us all, I think. Sometimes it feels as though we're all on a crazy fairground ride, hurtling towards our own destruction and helpless to stop it."

"Do you think religion helps?" he asked, indicating the imposing structure of the Minster behind her.

"Faith certainly is a comfort when the going gets tough, and I mean that in the broadest terms, not just Christianity or whatever. I would not call myself religious, but I certainly draw comfort from some higher power, or at least the idea of a higher power. Sometimes when I stand quietly in my garden and just listen, I can almost sense that presence. I lost my parents in a car crash when I was twenty years old. It was indescribable; the pain and drama and sheer chaos that I went through at the time, but it did make me stronger, and it did make me question. But the answer was that I simply could not believe in nothing; however pointless and futile their deaths seemed, to believe in nothing would have made it worse."

"I'm sorry to hear about your parents."

She nodded her head, "Thank-you. It was a long time ago. I love the Minster, don't you?" she said, changing the subject and indicating the magnificent façade behind them, "I haven't seen the Taj Mahal, but until I do I'll believe this is the most beautiful and best building in the world. What do you think?"

Despite himself, he melted under the warmth of her smile, and said, "Like any son of York, I'd have to say you were right."

By silent agreement, they fell into step and began to walk down Petergate towards Colliergate.

She turned to him, and said "Are you alright, Mr MacDonald? You look tired. Is this case more stressful than most? I really don't know how you cope with all the different people that you have to interrogate. I couldn't do what you do."

"Despite your poor opinion of the police?"

She inclined her head to acknowledge his point, "As I told you before, I respect individual policemen very much, but not necessarily the people at the top who have forgotten that the police are there to serve the public, not to oppress them. I hope I haven't offended you. I wouldn't want that," she said, putting a hand on his shoulder.

"No, not at all," he answered, truthfully, feeling the warmth and pressure of her hand through his shirt.

They continued their walk, talking of matters inconsequential, and crossed King's Square into The Shambles, the ancient cobbled street of the butchers. The narrow street was swollen with tourists. Beneath the mullioned windows, Frank and Stella rubbed shoulders with the ghosts of Roman soldiers and Jewish martyrs. Stella usually appeared cool no matter how hot it was, but Frank noticed that even she had some damp tendrils of hair at the base of her neck. The sight of them made him feel an inexplicable tenderness. Lulled by the heat, and strolling side by side through the crowd, Frank found himself wanting to take Stella's hand. This brought him sharply to his senses; he shook his head as if to wake himself from a dream, broke the spell, and politely said goodbye. They went their separate ways. As Frank made his way home he cursed himself for a fool, and considered the pretty little scene he had just been a party to; black memories indeed if Stella turned out to be Jane's murderer.

Diamonds And Pebbles

Chapter 19

"Where on earth did Julia Johnson get that kind of money? And why carry it round in a plastic carrier bag?" Frank asked Steven Brown later when they were in Steven's car on the way to West Wold. Frank watched with satisfaction as they rolled past golden fields. He had reluctantly changed into a shirt and tie and one of his grey suits, when he got back from his walk in York city centre, but already had shed the jacket and rolled up his shirt sleeves. He tugged at his tie and loosened the loop. He really could not remember when he had been so hot and uncomfortable at work.

"Another generous benefactor? Or just more money from Jane?" asked Steven, "or has she started to indulge in a spot of blackmail? Perhaps she knows a lot more than she's letting on?"

"A killer *and* a blackmailer? Very versatile, our Julia," said Frank.

"Maybe she was hanging around on Friday afternoon, and happened to see the perpetrator entering or leaving Lilac Cottage. Perhaps she knows who killed Jane, and has decided to strike quickly whilst she has the chance. Once we've arrested someone she will have lost her chance. She won't be able to blackmail whoever it is when they are in prison."

Frank thought for a few moments, and said, "Or she killed Jane, and then decided to have a quick look round to see whether she could find some cash or valuables whilst she was there?"

"Yes, maybe. Roger Sinclair said that there appeared to be nothing missing, but he did not necessarily know what Jane had in the house. There may have been jewellery in Jane's dressing table drawers."

"Yes - when I saw Julia she may have just been to a jeweller's shop and sold something. But if it is blackmail, and Julia knows who the killer is, she must have been on her way to Lilac Cottage last Friday afternoon, and seen somebody either entering or leaving. She may have even seen the whole dressing up charade. She would have been caught out by the storm, though."

"A bit of a risky business, sir, blackmailing a murderer? It doesn't exactly increase your life expectancy, does it? She needs to be careful, and watch her back, I'd say. On the other hand, maybe she's just a truly upstanding citizen who was transferring her money from one banking establishment to another in order to gain a better rate of interest," Steven grinned.

"In twenty pound notes? Maybe." Frank grinned back, and said, "Still, I'd love to know what she was up to, and I wish I'd caught her red-handed with whoever gave her the money."

"That would be Louise or Stella, if our current theory is correct. If the killer is a woman, if only a woman could get dressed up as Jane and get away with it, then it must be Louise, Stella or Julia. Except that Julia is probably much too large to impersonate Jane. At least they all have a motive for wanting Jane out of the way."

"Agreed, and all three of them were in York this morning. I could just ask Julia straight out where she got the money, and who the killer is, I suppose."

"Yes, and she's bound to tell you because you're such a nice man!"

"Women have been known to fall for my boyish charms you know!" Frank said, and they laughed, and carried on in this vein for the remainder of the journey. They were always careful to be serious and respectful when they were investigating a serious crime whenever other people were around, but when they were alone their natural dry humour came to the fore. They decided to go straight to Julia Johnson's house to ask her about the money that Jane was paying into her account each month, and also her trip to York that morning.

"Mrs Johnson, could you explain why Jane was paying two thousand pounds per month into your bank account?"

The lady was sitting in her usual place in the living room on the sofa, the television remote control in hand, an opened packet of biscuits and an overflowing ashtray next to her. As before, the two detectives had walked straight through the open side door into the kitchen and thence into the living room, where they both sat down without invitation, since the alternative was to continue standing. It was comparatively cool in the shade of the house. Frank looked meaningfully at the blaring television, and Julia reluctantly turned the sound off.

"Yes, I can," she said impassively, "not that it's any of your business. Janey was very well off, (well Roger was), and I wasn't. Our Mum asked Janey to help me out when my husband left me with three kids to feed, and clothe, and look after."

"Your eldest have now left home?" asked Frank.

"The two girls, yes - just got Jason to get off my hands now," she said, clearly relishing the prospect.

"And your sister made the payments willingly? There was no coercion on your part? You weren't blackmailing her?"

"You can't accuse me of that," she spat, looking at him with animation in her normally flaccid features, "I know my rights."

"Two thousand pounds a month is a lot of money. How long has this been going on for?"

"About five years."

"That's a seriously large amount of money. Was Roger aware of this arrangement?" Frank decided to keep his own information to himself.

"I don't know. I didn't care as long as Janey paid me. And it may sound like a lot, but it goes nowhere when you've got all those University fees, and accommodation and goodness-knows-what to fork out for…"

"You would be very angry to lose the money I expect," suggested Frank.

"Well, I will lose it now, won't I, now she's gone and got herself killed," Julia said crossly, and then a more conducive train of thought seemed to cross her mind, "Mind you, Roger was always a bit sweet on me; maybe he will carry on paying me. They were both very keen for Jason to go to University, don't ask me why. Waste of time if you ask me. But if Roger wants him to go, then that will need paying for as far as I'm concerned."

Frank decided to throw something else into the mix, and said, "Perhaps Jane was intending to stop the payments.

She was after all going to start a new life in Manchester with James Powell. I doubt if he would want to fund such an amount each month. Did she tell you?"

Julia looked surprised, or pretended to, and said, "New life? That's the first I've heard of it. That would be typical, leaving me with no money, and Mum to look after on my own. As if everything's not difficult enough to cope with already." Frank speculated that anything that involved getting off the sofa and leaving the house fell into the 'difficult' category as far as Julia was concerned. She continued, "I told her time and time again that no good would come out of getting mixed up with that James Powell."

"What made you say that?"

She looked at him scornfully, and said, "It's obvious, isn't it? He's a playboy. All those models and celebrities he goes round with. Janey was stupid if she thought he was going to change for her. He's made a fool of Stella for years."

"But did she tell you that she might be leaving West Wold to go to live with him - that she would be stopping the payments?"

"No - she didn't say a word," she said glumly, looking crestfallen.

Frank decided to change tack, "By the way, I think I saw you in York this morning. Were you meeting someone?"

Her expression changed again abruptly, her face and neck reddening with anger, and she snapped, "How dare you follow me? Hasn't a private citizen the right to go about their business without police harassment anymore?"

"Hardly harassment - I happened to see you there, that's all. And you are a suspect in a murder case, after all. Did you meet anyone there?"

"No, I did not," she sulked, then recollected, "well, at least, I did see Louise Leighton in Stonegate, all dressed up and nowhere to go, covered in fake tan, trying to look like a model, as usual; and failing, as usual. I didn't meet her on purpose, I can assure you. And since when am I a suspect?"

"Family members are always under suspicion in these cases, and by your own admission you had some serious issues with Jane. You've been jealous of her from the moment she was born. I must ask you, and think very hard before you answer - interfering with the course of justice is a very serious charge - did you in fact go to Lilac Cottage on Friday afternoon? Did you see anything suspicious? Did you see anyone entering or leaving the cottage?"

"I told you before - I was here all afternoon."

"Was Jason here? Can he corroborate your story?"

"No, he was in York, and the bus got caught in the storm on the way back. He was much later than he should have been, getting home."

"Well, I'm giving you a warning, Mrs Johnson; one or two of our lines of enquiry seem to lead directly to you. At some stage soon we all might need to go to the Police Station in York to talk very seriously about all of this. One more thing - what size shoe do you wear?"

Julia was open-mouthed at this, "Size seven, why?"

"Just another line of enquiry."

She laughed sarcastically, "Bloody hell! You are struggling, aren't you?"

Frank decided that he had had enough of Julia's joie-de-vivre and they left shortly afterwards.

As they walked away from the Johnson house, Frank saw Roy Parsons and Don Green waiting across the road. Frank swore under his breath. Roy Parsons swaggered towards Frank.

"Afternoon, sir."

Frank did not even wait for the inevitable question, and said tersely, "There'll be another statement when necessary."

"Is it true that the murderer is a woman? Are you any closer to making an arrest?"

Frank chose to ignore this, as he and Steven got into the car and Steven quickly drove off. As usual Don Green, took several photographs.

"Doesn't he ever have a day off?" grumbled Frank.

Diamonds And Pebbles

Wednesday

Diamonds And Pebbles

Chapter 20

In York, Wednesday dawned hot and humid. After an uncomfortable night, plagued by dreams about the inhabitants of West Wold, Frank was restless and irritable. He and Steven Brown had met in the office at eight o'clock to discuss the case and plan a way forward. Frank, in a sudden revelation, borne more out of middle-aged grumpiness than inspired thinking, had arrived at a simple conclusion; he did not believe that Julia had killed Jane (too greedy, too inert, too just-plain-ordinary), he did not *want* to believe that Stella had killed Jane (too nice, too interesting, too just-plain-*extra*ordinary); therefore it must be Louise Leighton (so needy, so involved, so just-plain-irritating). He was trying, with little success, to convince Steven of this theory.

"Being irritating is hardly grounds for an arrest, sir. Given the new timings, how could Louise have done it? The petrol receipt says fifteen twenty-nine. That means she had to kill Jane, go to the petrol station, go back to Lilac Cottage, dress up as Jane, and get out of the door in time for Mrs Mountjoy to see her at around fifteen forty. How could she have done it?" asked Steven, in a perfectly reasonable way.

They were sitting in Frank's office. It was already stifling hot outside and icily cold in the air-conditioned offices. "Well, there's only one way to find out," Frank picked up the car keys and handed them to Steven, took his jacket off its coat hanger on the back of the door, and opened the door, "let's go."

Arriving in West Wold shortly afterwards, they headed south down the main street and turned left into the short side street before the row of cottages containing Lilac Cottage. They found the path which ran along the back of the cottages, walked along the back of the neighbouring gardens, and stopped at the entrance to Jane's garden, still garlanded with SOC tape.

"So," Frank began, "Louise could have killed Jane sometime before, say, three o'clock, come out of the cottage this way, got into her car which was parked in the side street, and driven to the petrol station, leaving plenty of time in case it was busy, paid for the petrol at three twenty-nine and then got back here as quickly as she could. Right, let's time it ourselves."

They walked back to the car and then back to the side street, drove fairly slowly to the petrol station which was at the north end of the village on the main York road, and timed the journey at six and a half minutes. They drove back as fast as they could within the speed limits, figuring that speeding would have drawn too much attention to Louise's car, parked their car down the side street, and walked quickly down the path to Lilac Cottage and up the garden to the back door. The journey took them four and a half minutes.

"That means that Louise could have been back here by

three thirty-five, quickly got dressed up as Jane, walked up the road with the dog, made sure she was seen, come back here, put the coat onto Jane so that we would think Jane was killed after the walk and not before, broken Jane's fingers in the rush, then back into the car during the storm, and driven to York to keep her appointment at the hairdressers at four fifteen. She always knew that she would be late, but hoped that we wouldn't check what time exactly she had arrived," said Frank.

"She was helped by the storm too, sir - the hairdresser said that everyone was late, or didn't turn up at all that afternoon."

"We need to know exactly what time she did arrive. It would take a good fifty minutes to drive to York and park, even on a good day. She could never have got there quite on time, even if she had driven there straight from the petrol station as she claims to have done. "

"The storm nearly ruined everything, though. If it had hit a few minutes earlier she wouldn't have been able to go out dressed as Jane at all, it would have attracted too much attention, instead of just being a familiar event. And what about the whole shoe thing? Why draw attention to herself by wearing inappropriate footwear?"

"Well, if the killer was Louise, presumably she already had the court shoes on to go into York. Julia or Stella don't normally wear that type of shoe - they would have had to bring the shoes with them and change at the cottage deliberately. In an effort to confuse us? I don't like it; too complicated. I think that Louise had intended to wear Jane's Wellies but her feet were too big so she had to go out in her own shoes, and just hope it didn't look too incongruous. But good old Mrs Mountjoy *did* notice. I'm really starting to think the killer must be Louise. Everything fits. She must have sent the wig to herself to try to throw us off course"

"If it was her, sir, or any of them, it still seems rather elaborate to do all that for an alibi that a little bit of police work could unravel."

"Yes - but maybe she simply didn't think that we would figure out that someone posed as Jane after they had killed her, and thought that we would be too stupid to work it all out. Perhaps part of the point for the killer was to watch us racking our brains and trying to make sense of it all. Maybe she just hoped that we would concentrate our efforts elsewhere. Louise did try to point us towards Stella, James, and the driver of the BMW, who no-one has ever seen but her. She must have made it up to waste our time. I still think that the chance to *be* Jane, even for a few minutes, was just too tempting to give up."

"She took a hell of a risk, though, sir. Someone might have noticed that it wasn't really Jane when she walked the dog. Also, coming back to the cottage after she'd left Jane dead inside. What if Roger had come home early?"

"Well, I guess she would have seen Roger's car, if he had come home, and just backed away quickly. She had already let the dog go by then, presumably, to make sure that she didn't have to go back at all if it looked dangerous, or probably she just couldn't be bothered with it once it had served its purpose."

Steven Brown looked at him seriously and said, "And if all of this was done by Stella, she hasn't even got the petrol receipt alibi. All she's got is that she was hanging round at home during the storm. Seen by no-one, and seeing no-one."

For the first time ever, Frank saw a look of doubt in Steven's eyes that was unmistakable; he clearly believed that Frank was allowing his personal feelings to cloud his judgement. Frank did not like to see that look in his partner's eyes.

"Yes, Steven, I get your point," Frank chided himself again for his inclination to assume that Stella was innocent. "If we dismiss James and Roger, or any man, as being too large to impersonate Jane, we are left with Louise, Julia (also too large?) or Stella, all with a motive, all with no real alibi, and all with opportunity; or else some other woman we haven't yet encountered."

"But not a shred of real evidence except Stella's fingerprints on the murder weapon," said Steven slowly and meaningfully.

Frank knew that sooner or later he would have to tackle the question of Stella's guilt much more meticulously.

"Well," he said, reluctant to let go of his theory for the present, "let's at least look a little more closely into Louse's past. If there's anything at all that sounds odd we'll check it out first, then if that goes nowhere we should get a warrant to search her house, and Julia Johnson's and the Powell's. The killer may just be arrogant enough to have kept something incriminating."

They looked at each other blankly, "We don't have anything else to go on," said Frank, "Let's go and have another chat with Louise Leighton, and then head back to York."

As the two policemen crossed the triangular village green in West Wold, the noon sun beat down on the parched, yellowing grass. They could see a woman walking towards them from the direction of Green Lane. It was Stella Powell. She was dressed in a turquoise silk shift dress and black high-heeled shoes, carrying a fancy, black hat and a small clutch bag. Her dark, wavy hair was worn loose in a way which Frank had not seen before. She walked well in the heels, and Frank found himself watching the sway of her hips. As she reached them she stopped and smiled self-deprecatingly, "Hello, gentlemen."

"Hello, Mrs Powell," Frank did not allow himself to smile back, desperately reminding himself again to be completely professional with her. The black court shoes had not escaped his notice. Was she playing him for a fool? He could not help commenting on her appearance, however. "You're all dressed up, I see. Going somewhere nice?"

"Yes, I'm going to York races. Gambling is another one of my vices, I'm afraid. I don't think you've ever seen me before without mud on my face, have you?" she laughed, clearly exhilarated by the prospect of her outing, "Sorry, I must dash, I'm getting picked up at the pub by some friends."

For a second he held her eyes. He would have forgiven her for some sarcasm at the word 'friends' after one of their previous conversations, but it showed some generosity of spirit that there was none. She turned away and walked towards the public house. Frank stood very still as he watched her walk away from him. He felt a queasy mixture of heat and fear; fear that she could be the killer, and of the catastrophic consequences which would follow if she was. Every unreasoning cell in his body cried that she could not be; every rational cell in his brain confirmed that she could.

Steven Brown looked at him, "Sir, don't you think we should be pressing her more?" he said seriously, "She has a motive, a flimsy alibi, and her fingerprints are on the murder weapon."

"You're probably right, Steven, you're probably right," Frank sighed.

Just as Frank MacDonald was about to knock on Louise Leighton's front door, a shape appeared through the mottled glass, and she opened the door holding a large canvas holdall. She saw him, and jumped back as if startled, "Oh, Mr MacDonald. I wasn't expecting you."

"Taking a trip, Miss Leighton?"

"Oh, no - this is just a duvet for the dry cleaners."

"May we come in?"

"Yes, of course."

She led the way into the kitchen at the rear of the property. Everything was very tidy as before. It was refreshingly cool in the shady cottage. Karen Leighton was sitting at the breakfast bar in the kitchen, drinking coffee, smoking a cigarette and reading a magazine. She was dressed to kill, as usual, in a short black dress and gold sandals. Despite the attempt at glamour, she was as scruffy as a starving hyena.

Frank nodded hello and she nodded back, stubbing out her cigarette. "Good morning, Mr MacDonald. It's too hot isn't it? - much too hot for me. I blame that Global Warming. It's all the Chineses' fault, you know - boiling all that rice. Have you caught poor Jane's killer yet? I've been thinking about that, actually. I thought I'd help you out. Three brains on the case must be better than two. You need look no further than that Stella Powell, in my opinion. Louise has been telling me what a jealous bitch she is. Louise and James make a lovely couple, I think, especially with him having all that money and jet-setting lifestyle and all. Stella just can't stand the fact that James is in love with my Louise, so I reckon it was her that done for Jane; she was jealous of Jane too. Brian Sykes agrees with me. Mind you Jane got no better than she deserved by the sound of it; she was a trollop by all accounts. James wasn't her first affair by a long chalk. She was always carrying on behind Roger's back. And he's such a lovely man as well."

During this speech, Frank and Steven exchanged a complicated look which began as shared amusement, and faded into something which acknowledged their growing difference of opinion over Stella.

Louise, who had stood silently by whilst Karen delivered her diatribe, offered them a cold drink and they accepted. Steven Brown sat on one of the bar stools at the breakfast bar.

Frank wanted to take a look upstairs if he could; he wanted to see if the upstairs of the house revealed anything more about its inhabitant, but also now whether Louise was, in fact, planning a trip away from West Wold. Was she, for instance, going to join James Powell? That would imply that he had been lying to them. Frank asked for the bathroom, and Louise directed him upstairs. He climbed the open-tread steel staircase, turned to the left and had a quick look into the back bedroom. It was small and sparsely furnished, with a single bed. There were signs of the occupancy of Karen Leighton; clothes draped over a chair, a towel dropped carelessly onto the floor, and a jumble of cosmetics on the small bedside table. Frank was surprised to see a rather prim-looking, long-sleeved nightdress laid out on the bed. He quickly entered the bathroom, also at the back of the building; nothing out of the ordinary there. He flushed the toilet noisily, turned on a tap and left it running, then stepped quietly across the landing and looked into the larger bedroom at the front of the house. There was a double bed, wardrobe and chest of drawers. On a small desk there sat a neat row of Geography text books, and some piles of exercise books. Stacks of clothes and toiletries were on the double bed, and on the floor there was a large suitcase with its lid open, currently empty. He quickly went back to the bathroom to turn off the tap, and then turned to leave the bathroom again. As he walked out of the door back onto the small landing, he almost jumped out of his skin when he found Karen Leighton standing there.

"Ok, Mr MacDonald? Can I help you with anything?"

How on earth had she crept up the stairs in those shoes without him hearing her? "No thank-you, Mrs Leighton, I'm fine," he said, crossly. He was in no mood for being startled. He made his way downstairs, followed by Karen Leighton, and joined Steven Brown at the breakfast bar.

Louise sat with them on one of the high stools. "By the way, you've reminded me," she said," I *might* be going away for a few days, soon. I'd like to get away before school starts again. This business with Jane has been so upsetting - I keep bursting into tears whenever I think about it. I need to clear my head. There won't be a problem will there?"

"I'd rather you stayed here, at least until after the weekend, Miss Leighton," said Frank evenly, having regained his composure, "but of course we can't detain you. I'd appreciate it if you would leave and address and phone number with one of my constables if you do decide to go somewhere. We feel we are close to making an arrest." If only, he thought. This piece of information seemed to cause no disturbance to her placid features.

"That's okay," she said, "Of course I'll let you know."

Steven Brown had taken out his note book and placed it on the breakfast bar, and Frank nodded at him to start taking notes.

Frank decided to catch her off-guard, "Were you in

York city centre on Tuesday morning by any chance?"

She paused, "Well - yes I was actually. Why?"

"Oh, I was there myself and I thought I saw you." (Can't always be truthful, he thought.)

"Oh, I didn't see you," she said doubtfully. "Pity, we could have had a coffee together." She tried to narrow her eyes into an approximation of a provocative stare.

"That would be quite irregular behaviour between a policemen and a suspect," he said coldly, trying not to think about the illicit hour he had spent with Stella in her garden, and his stroll through York with her. "I also saw Julia Johnson - you two didn't happen to meet up I suppose?"

She left a silence; she probably dare not risk denying it, in case he had seen them together.

"I did bump into her briefly, yes. Only to say hello, and how sorry I was about Jane. My life just won't be the same now, I know, and I thought she must be feeling the same."

"How well do you know Julia?"

"Not well at all, really."

Clearly, despite Louise's desire to be fully integrated into village life in West Wold, she drew the line at Julia Johnson.

"I need to ask you again about the relationships between you and James and Jane," Frank began, "You say that you had only a suspicion about the fact that they might be seeing each other again?"

"That's right."

"She hadn't confided in you?"

"No."

Is she telling the truth? Or did Jane tell her, and unwittingly bring about her own demise? he thought.

"How did you feel when James admitted it to you? When was it that he told you, by the way?"

"On Sunday at the cricket match. He was so upset about Jane, too upset almost, that I was suspicious. I was angry of course, and embarrassed, to think that other people knew about him and Jane, and I didn't."

Frank remembered the fraught conversation he had seen in the cricket pavilion.

"But he also told me he had been trying to get out of it. Jane was being desperately clingy, she wanted him to divorce Stella and live with her. It was all too much for him."

"That contradicts his own statement. Also, he seems genuinely upset about Jane. Perhaps the truth is that he really loved Jane, and was going to make a new life with her?"

"You'll have to ask him, Mr MacDonald."

"But I have, Miss Leighton. That is my problem. I can only conclude that one of you is not telling me the truth."

Her expression did not change. She said, "Well, our relationship is over now. I won't let him make a fool of me twice."

"If what you say is true, and Jane was becoming too demanding, do you really think he was capable of killing her?"

She tilted her head to one side and considered, "Oh, yes, I should think so. He loved his globe-trotting lifestyle, he wasn't going to give that up easily," she said, "There's a side to James that you haven't seen."

"You think he's capable of violence?"

"Look, I really don't want to get James into trouble. I've said too much."

"It's much more than just 'trouble', though, isn't it? This is a murder enquiry."

If she was the killer, she was trying to be clever;

pointing the finger elsewhere, and feigning reluctance at the same time. If they were right that the murderer was a woman, then clearly James Powell was innocent and Louise was lying. But was she lying because she was the killer, or out of spite because James was no longer interested in her? Frank did not know.

He decided to play along, "Well, Miss Leighton, if you have suspicions it is your duty to tell us about them. You must overcome your scruples, if necessary."

She nodded, "Yes, I will."

He changed the subject, "I believe one of my constables came to tell you that we now believe that the murder may have taken place a little earlier than we first thought. I'd like to go over the timings with you again. Where were you between two o'clock and four o'clock last Friday afternoon?"

"I was here alone up until about three fifteen, then I went to get petrol and headed into York about three-thirty. I was due at the hairdressers at four fifteen, but I was delayed by the storm; it was more like four forty, I think."

"In fact, the hairdresser said it was more like five o'clock."

She held his gaze steadily, "Oh, I'm sorry, I hadn't realised it was as late as that."

"So no-one saw you between those times?"

"No, I'm afraid not."

Frank sighed inwardly; the initial impression of coolness in the kitchen had evaporated, and it suddenly felt suffocating with the four of them sitting around the small breakfast bar on silly stools. It really was too hot for all this, especially for talking to the likes of Louise Leighton, who had the charisma of a blancmange, despite a certain superficial attractiveness. "Okay, that's all for now. One last thing - what size feet do you have?"

"Size six, why?"

"Just a line of enquiry. Thank-you, for your help, Miss Leighton."

They left soon afterwards, and as they were walking away from the cottage across The Green, they heard a voice calling behind them. It was Karen Leighton. She had come out of the house and was wiggling after them, dragging intently on a cigarette at the same time. They stopped and turned back towards her.

"Mr MacDonald, I needed to speak to you alone," she said, glancing back nervously towards the house, "It's Louise. She's behaving very oddly. I'm beginning to think that she could have been Jane's killer, after all. She's got a very jealous nature you know, and a violent temper. She's attacked me in the past. I've had to defend myself. I've seen her fighting with her friends too, in the past. Proper cat-fights with hair-pulling and scratching and everything. That James Powell has got her into a right state. I wouldn't put anything past her. She'd probably go for me if she knew I was saying this, but finding the murderer is more important than thinking about your own safety, isn't it? I thought it was my duty to tell you. I put my civic responsibilities before being a mother, you know. Of course, if she has to go to prison, I'd just have to look after everything here for her."

"Thank-you, Mrs Leighton, we'll bear what you have said in mind. We are pursuing several lines of enquiry." Frank remembered what Louise had said about Karen's being a liar. Karen Leighton gave them a conspiratorial wink and wobbled back into the house.

Walking across The Green, Frank and Steven saw Julia Johnson walking down the main street in the direction of her house. When she saw them she changed course and headed across the road towards them. She stopped to speak.

"I'm just popping in to see Roger at his mother's house. He appreciates a bit of company. His mother can be hard work. He's so cut up about Janey; he's taking the whole thing very hard. Her being pregnant has knocked him for six, I can tell you. I think James Powell had better stay out of his way or I wouldn't like to think what might happen," she said, with relish, "As soon as we can get into Lilac Cottage I'm going to help Roger sort some of Janey's things out. Shame she wasn't my size really, I could have had her clothes. Mind you she's got some lovely jewellery, and that fits anyone doesn't it?"

"Indeed," was all that Frank could manage to say.

"Roger and I make a good team, actually. It's like old times, me and him spending time together. At least he won't be lonely with me around to help him, and keep him company and all that," she said. *(Helping him spend his money too, no doubt, thought Frank.)*

Julia paused, and her jaunty mood seemed to pass, "I'm going to see Mum later. I haven't managed to tell her about Janey yet, and I don't know how I'm going to tell her, I really don't. She was asking after Janey the other day. I tried to tell her, and I couldn't. I think it might kill her. I don't like to think of her being upset. She always treated us equal, after all, when I think about it," she said. Julia actually had tears in her eyes, the first real emotion which Frank had seen her display, and he realised that, despite outward appearances, she was capable of loving her mother deeply and sincerely.

Then, as they walked along, Frank saw his old adversary walking towards him across the street and frowned as Roy Parsons ambled across the road.

"Afternoon, Chief. Got a statement, sir?"

"No, Mr Parsons."

"We understand the victim was hit over the head with the silverware, is that true? Going to arrest anybody, are you?"

Frank turned away as he and Steven got into the car, and Steven quickly drove off. Again the tall man called Don Green took photographs.

"Oh, marvellous," Frank exploded, as they drove off, "I'm sick of having my photograph taken by that man."

They went back to York and started re-reading statements, and looking again at all of the other data, to see if there was some important fact which had been overlooked. Whilst they were there, Frank received a phone call from his mother to say that his father had been taken ill again, and asked him go to the house in Sheriff Hutton that evening, if only for a short while. At about seven o'clock he set off from York city centre.

As Frank drove he thought about his father and his recent decline in health. Jack MacDonald had been a teacher, a respected man in his small community, and a patient and loving father. Frank particularly remembered family holidays in Robin Hood's Bay and the Dales, where his father organised energetic and argumentative games of rounders and cricket with them all, or taught them the names (English and Latin) of the flora and fauna that they encountered. The family had spent countless hours wandering around art galleries and museums, with his father on hand to discuss the masterpieces they encountered. The previous summer, aware that his father had started to become less hale, and that their opportunities to travel together were coming to an end, Frank suggested to Jack that they go on a trip to Paris together; something they had long talked about and planned. It was Jack who had given Frank his love of fine art, and the trip was intended to give them a chance to tour the Louvre and Musée d'Orsay together. Jack particularly wanted to go on the train via the Channel Tunnel, which neither had done before, and they had made their way by train from York to Kings Cross station, and thence made the short walk across the road to St Pancras International station. They stood for a few moments outside of St Pancras to admire its imposing Victorian architecture, and then made their way to the train. In the station there was that atmosphere of nervous excitement connected with foreign travel. Safely ensconced on the train, they chatted excitedly about the forthcoming trip, and exactly what the itinerary in Paris should be, as the Kent countryside sped past. Frank worried that his father would get too tired, but Jack seemed fine, enjoying the change of surroundings. He had had some long spells confined to home, unable to do much more than sit in a chair or have a short tour around the garden, but he was going through a better patch. Frank knew that the good patches would get shorter as the bad ones got longer, which was why he had decided to arrange the trip sooner rather than later. It was a benign May day, with similar weather forecasted, perfect for sightseeing.

They slipped into the darkness of the tunnel for some twenty minutes, trying not to think too much about the tons of earth and cold Channel water above them, and duly passed through Lille and arrived in Paris at the Gare Du

Nord. They made their way by taxi to the hotel which Frank had chosen close to the Louvre. It was a large, old-fashioned, and luxurious place which had cost Frank the proverbial fortune but he thought *what-the-hell* to the expense. They had a twin room with long, heavily-swathed windows overlooking the street, and an en-suite bathroom, all solidly and handsomely furnished. Jack was delighted with the room, particularly a comfortable armchair placed close to one of the windows where he could look down on the busy Parisian street below. Frank suggested that they go and relax with some refreshments, and they went down to sit in a sumptuous lounge with brass chandeliers, gilt mirrors, glass lamps, and a selection of large, comfortable sofas, chairs and tables arranged in cosy clusters. They ordered coffee and cakes, and this was duly brought to them by a smartly-dressed and imperious waiter. They both enjoyed trying out their schoolboy French, but this was largely useless in Paris, where the Parisians famously disdained the English and their attempts to converse, professing an inability to comprehend unless the words were spoken in perfect, idiomatic French.

Their first museum trip was not to be until the next day, so they went for a short walk as far as the Seine, and then went back to the hotel to relax until it was time to have dinner in the elegant dining room.

The next day was fine and mild, and after a breakfast of coffee and croissants, they took the short walk to the Louvre. It was a massive and impressive building, with its magnificently domed roofline ranged around three sides of a huge courtyard. In the centre of this was Ieoh Ming Pei's inspired and controversial glass pyramid, built in 1989 to provide a modern and spacious entrance to the museum. They had both seen it before separately, and reaffirmed

Diamonds And Pebbles

their unqualified approval. Father and son had a liking for the statue of Venus De Milo, so they decided to go there first whilst Jack was still fresh from a good night's sleep, and they made their way down stairs to the gallery where she was situated. It was still quite early, so there were only one or two other visitors, and they managed to get very close. Larger than expected and exquisitely sculpted, she was fabulous to behold. What particularly thrilled Frank was the sheer age of the statue, some two thousand years old, and the series of fortunate events which must have conspired to preserve it for all those years, albeit in a damaged form. He imagined the joy of those archaeologists who had discovered her in Greece in 1820. He would have loved to touch her. Frank and Jack walked around her and stood in awe for a long time. Next, they decided to go to the main galleries, which housed the paintings, including the Mona Lisa, Leonardo Da Vinci's famous portrait of the unknown smiling woman. It was protected behind plate glass and surrounded by tourists, and since neither Frank nor his father cared for it particularly, they quickly moved on. They wandered enthralled along the long, high-ceilinged salons whose walls were covered in masterpieces. Frank kept an eye on his father and made sure that they had plenty of rest breaks. After a long morning spent in glorious self-indulgence they made their way back to the hotel, where they had lunch, and Jack slept for a couple of hours. Frank had been to Paris many times before (generally, he admitted to himself ruefully, to impress a romantic conquest), and did not feel the need for breakneck sightseeing at every opportunity. Therefore, he settled down on his bed, and made the most of a rare opportunity to read a novel. He had been persuaded by his sisters to read the Philip Pullman trilogy *His Dark Materials* and, having started *Northern Lights*, he blessed them for their insistence.

When Jack awoke they pressed on with the next part of their plan; to fulfil Jack's lifelong ambition to go to the top of the Eiffel Tower. They took a taxi to the Champ de Mars and joined a sizeable queue to buy tickets and get the lift to the first stage, then the second stage, and finally into the lift to the top, some one thousand feet above ground. As they stepped out onto the metal walkway which encased the structure they felt a cold, sharp wind. There were far fewer tourists at this level than at the lower ones. They looked down at the ground from a dizzying height, and saw the white buildings of Paris and the winding River Seine spread below them. A group of teenagers were making paper aeroplanes and launching them into the air. Frank and Jack stood for several minutes watching the frail structures swoop and bank on their way to the ground far below. Jack reminisced about the trip to the top of the Empire State building which he and Frank's mother, Joyce, had made on their honeymoon, and how this visit made a pair. Jack did not say it, but Frank knew that he was thinking that the two trips linked the start and end of a marriage and a relationship which would soon be severed by death. Frank turned away from his father for a few moments to hide the unshed tears which burned his eyes. At that moment, Frank felt a sorrow as deep as a grave. He and his father stayed for a while longer, walking around all four sides of the structure and marvelling at the city spread out before them.

The next day was to be their last full day, and was to be devoted to the Musée d'Orsay which housed the works of the Impressionist painters. After another breakfast of coffee and croissants, they set off again by taxi. Frank was relieved by the shortness of the queue, and they soon entered the magnificent ground floor of the former railway station. Frank marvelled, as always, at the ability and ingenuity of the French when designing their public buildings and spaces. The main ground floor gallery was dominated by the high, curved roof of the former railway station and a magnificent clock, and separated into smaller galleries by low dividing walls which leave the towering walls of the original structure in full view. They wandered around contentedly for an hour, Frank particularly admiring Monet's winter landscape *The Magpie*. He found Jack resting on a bench and then they made their way up to the upper galleries with their overwhelming riches of Renoirs, Degas', Pissarros, Gauguins, Monets, and Manets. Frank particularly admired Alfred Sisley's *The Snow at Louveciennes,* Camille Pissarro's *Red Roofs,* Gustave Moreau's *Galatea,* Claude Monet's *Hotel des Roches Noires, Trouville,* Edgar Degas' *The Ballet Class,* and *Ballet Rehearsal,* Gustave Caillebotte's *Toits Sous la Neige.* (Perhaps it was having Northern blood in his veins that attracted him to pictures of snow? he wondered.) He liked Alexandre Cabanel's *Birth of Venus,* preferring its soft and idealised nude to Edouard Manet's *Olympia* with the cold, modernistic handling which was considered so scandalous in its day. (He did not need to ask himself why he was attracted to pictures of naked women.) Frank stood and admired, and marvelled, and delighted, and respected, and thrilled, and smiled, and wondered, and criticised to, literally, his heart's content. Occasionally, he and Jack would arrive in front of the same painting at the same time, and have a brief discussion of its merits, but mainly he liked to wander round alone in an almost trancelike haze of happiness and amazement. Though he knew he might forget most of the individual detail of the paintings which he had seen, he knew he would never forget the feeling of joy they gave him, a feeling made all the more life-affirming by the presence of his father. Frank knew that this would be their last such trip together, and it heightened the experience almost unbearably.

They stopped for a sumptuous lunch in the gallery's restaurant overlooking the Seine. Frank was pleased that Jack was in high spirits, analysing and commenting on what they had seen. After lunch, they continued their cultural wanderings amongst the best of mankind's endeavours, until Jack was exhausted and they went back to the hotel. He laid on his bed and slept again. Frank made sure that his father was warm by pulling a blanket over him, and then stretched out on his own bed to read his book; Lyra Silvertongue and Iorek Byrnison were already becoming lifelong friends whose company he would return to again and again.

The next day they made their way back to the Gare Du Nord, and started the long and tiring journey back to York. They were mainly companionably silent this time, with Frank reading his book, and Jack alternately sleeping and reading a copy of the Guardian which he had managed to purchase at the Parisian station. When they arrived at the house in Sheriff Hutton, to the anxious enquiries of Frank's mother as to whether they were exhausted, Jack thanked his son profusely for his generosity and company. Frank shook his father's hand and hugged him, and kissed his mother goodbye as he left.

Frank's reverie ended as he shortly arrived at his old home. Joyce and Jack lived in a substantial Nineteen-Thirties bungalow, on a good-sized plot which they bought as newly-weds. They were both prolific and creative gardeners, and the garden was skilfully tended, with lawns, shrubs, pergolas trailing with roses and clematis', a greenhouse, and a vegetable plot. The bungalow was surrounded by riotous pots of nasturtiums, Busy Lizzies, and petunias, which also lined the various paths and patios. After a brief consultation with Joyce, Frank entered the bedroom which his father now used so that he could have a double bed to himself in comfort. It used to be Frank's own bedroom, but the trappings of his youth had largely disappeared. He noticed that a football trophy he had won as a boy had been placed on the bedside table alongside bottles of medicine and a glass of water. The lamp which also stood there had not yet been switched on, and the daylight was fading slowly into long shadows. A breeze which blew through the open window fanned the net curtains into the room. In the bed, his father cut a heartbreakingly small figure under the bedclothes. The dapper and elegant man of Frank's childhood, who had had a penchant for fancy bow-ties and waistcoats, had gone.

"Hello, Pops, I hear you've been in the wars again," he said gently. It was his father's own phrase, used in his boyhood to describe accidents and the like.

"Now then, Frank. Good to see you, son," Jack MacDonald smiled with an effort and patted the bedclothes to indicate where he wanted Frank to sit. His breathing was slow and laboured. Jack had become more ill recently. Frank and his family watched his deterioration with foreboding; the unspoken knowledge that he was heading towards death leaving them feeling helpless and already bereft. Doctors had left them in no doubt that medical intervention was not only pointless but needlessly painful. It had been tacitly decided amongst them that Jack would end his days here in familiar surroundings, as comfortable as modern medicine, kind nursing and loving solicitousness could make him. On good days he could still sit in the sitting room with them, on less good days he lay in his room and listened to the radio. Long gone were the high days when he pottered round the garden, or polished his beloved cars.

"How are you feeling?" asked Frank.

"I've felt better, I must say. You must be really busy. How is it going - the killing over at West Wold?"

"Early days yet," Frank said, his thoughts immediately turning to one particular inhabitant of West Wold. He would have loved to tell his father about Stella Powell and her wondrous eyes. Perhaps next time. They chatted for a while about cricket, and the storm, and the state of the nation. Frank could see his father's energy ebbing away, and wondered if he should go.

"You look exhausted, Pops, shall I leave you to sleep?"

"Not just yet, son. The sight of you makes me feel better. You and those crazy sisters of yours," he laughed and coughed, and coughed and wheezed, and wheezed and sighed. "I am really tired, Frank. I don't think I've much fight left."

Frank took his father's hand, "One day at a time, Pops. One breath at a time."

A comfortable silence fell, and they both watched as a rosy twilight filled the room. Frank remembered lying awake in this room as a boy on summer nights, when it was still too light to go to sleep. He had felt safe, listening to the sounds of family life still going on in the rest of the bungalow. His father's breathing deepened and Frank was about to tiptoe out of the room, when his father's voice, much stronger and clearer than of late, suddenly broke the silence.

"Frank, promise me that you'll look after your Mum when I've gone."

"Don't talk like that, Pops."

"No, son, it won't do. I know that I'm dying. I can feel it in here," Jack patted his chest with his hand, "it doesn't feel right. I can feel my heart fading away. It's alright. You don't have to pretend."

Frank squeezed his father's roughened hand.

"I've had a good life," Jack continued, "Better than most. Your Mum has made me a happy man. You and your sisters have made me so proud. All I want now is to die at home in your Mum's arms - and yours, Frank. When the time comes, tell your Mum not to worry about me - I'll be looking after baby Paul for her until she arrives."

"We'll be there, Pops, I promise, but don't go yet, not yet." Frank promised himself that nothing would prevent him from being at his father's side when death came. He thought of the contrast between the death that his father had just envisaged and Jane Sinclair's death; hers was lonely and frightening and violent, at the hands of someone she had trusted, maybe even loved.

Jack fell asleep then, as though satisfied that he had said his piece. Frank made sure that his father was warm and comfortable, then left him and went to talk to Joyce in the kitchen. If Frank's whole body shook and his knees felt unaccountably weak as he walked away from his father's bedside, he could not bear to ask himself why.

Chapter 21

When he finally arrived home on Wednesday evening, Frank had a message on his telephone answering machine from Ali. He felt too tired and too hot to engage in the sort of long, meandering conversation favoured by his neurotic sister, but felt it was his duty to call her back. She was sensitive, and highly-strung, but she was his sister. He poured a tumbler of single malt whisky. He had not eaten since lunchtime, but he preferred to get the phone call out of the way before he looked into his almost empty fridge. He took off his shoes and jacket, leant back in one of his reclining chairs, and dialled her phone number.

"Thanks for calling me back, sweetie," said Ali when she heard his voice, "I was hoping you would get time to call." They exchanged enquiries about the family and Ali's son, who was now on his way to Australia, then she continued, "Frank, I'm sorry I snapped at you on Sunday. Listen to what's happened to me since. I met Robert in a restaurant in town last night…"

Ali described to Frank how nervous she had been as she

got dressed, and once or twice almost changed her mind about going. What does a wife wear when she is going to meet her maybe-lover? The usual nothing-to-wear problem is multiplied by a hundred. She did not even know what she was trying to say. Nothing too revealing (in both senses), nothing too off-putting. Yes-I-will, No-I-won't. She decided on a black sleeveless top, a smart pair of beige trousers and flat black shoes. No clues there, she thought. She was always fairly liberal with cosmetics, so a lick of bright pink lipstick to finish was not out-of-the-ordinary. When she arrived at the door of the restaurant, Robert was already sitting at their table with a bottle of red wine and two glasses, his full and hers empty. She took a breath, and plunged in still not knowing what her decision was going to be.

Ali turned Robert down. He was not happy.

After lots of small talk, Robert had suddenly launched in with "Ali, this is driving me mad. I must see you again soon."

"I really don't know, Robert."

"You can't deny how I feel about you - you know because you feel it too."

"I'm a married woman."

"Does David really care about you the way I do? Face it, Ali, you've been married too long; it's just become a habit."

Ali considered this for a moment, and said "*If* I loved you, and *if* I no longer loved David, it's still not that simple - what about my boys. Nothing on earth would separate me from them."

"OK. I've never been interested in fatherhood in the past, but this is different. This is you."

"I can't. Don't ask me why, I just can't."

"You married women are all the same," he spat. "Scared of living, scared of rocking the boat, scared you'll discover you've missed something all these years, scared you'll find out you're stuck with second best," he sneered.

"No. You're wrong. My life's fine. David is my life, my rock, as it happens. He has his faults, but he *is* right for me. He always has been. Always will be." As she said the words, she realised that for her, at that moment, they were true; David was exactly what she needed, or at least he provided her with exactly what she needed, and she wondered how she could have behaved so badly. How could she have let it come to this? She suddenly became aware that there was a deathly hush in the restaurant. She had become so carried away by her little speech that she had been speaking more loudly than she had realised, and the fact that she had stood up and was pointing her knife at Robert had somewhat added to the thrust of her argument. A faint ripple of applause began next to the sweet trolley and spread around the tables, and before long everyone in the restaurant was clapping...

On the phone with Frank, Ali paused. After a few moments she said, "So, I did the right thing after all, didn't I, brother?"

"Good for you, Ali," said Frank, chuckling as he imagined the scene. He actually had his doubts that this would be the end of the affair. He had seen Ali nurse her obsessions before, and she did not give anything up easily.

"Sorry, I've got to go now, love. I'm sleepy and hungry. Speak to you soon." He put the phone down, drained his whisky and went to look for some food.

Diamonds And Pebbles

Thursday

Diamonds And Pebbles

Chapter 22

Early on Thursday morning, there began another parched and scorching day in North Yorkshire. Frank got up at six o'clock, too hot and fidgety to stay in bed, and made his way to his office on foot, turning his face to the sun and soaking up the sunshine as he walked along. When Frank got to work he found DC Emma Smith already there, working in the incident room alone. She made them both a coffee and they sat down together. The earliness of the hour and the unusual silence in the office seemed to create a strange intimacy. Emma sat opposite him flicking her shiny blonde hair, and smiling a smile which showed a mouth full of perfect teeth like little white grave-stones. She was an enigma to him. She was ferociously intelligent, and relentless in her quest for perfection. These qualities made her a magnificent organiser. She was also tall and leggy and had a copy of Vogue sticking out of the top of her Dolce & Gabbana tote-bag. She had always made it plain that she was interested in him and once, during the previous winter, she had asked him to go for a drink with her as they were leaving work one cold, miserable evening. Frank was tired, fed up and lonely, and thought *what-the-*

hell and accepted. He made sure that it had gone no further, however. She was a valuable member of his team, and he only found her attractive at the most clinical level. He was not going to do anything stupid. Particularly as he was convinced that she was going to be his boss one day. Emma already dressed as though she was the Chief Constable, in expensive and sharply-tailored black suits, or, as a concession to warmer weather, expensive and sharply-tailored navy suits. She was now staring into his eyes, which felt a little like being probed by an alien and having the contents of his mind sucked out against his will.

"How are you, sir?"

He shrugged, "Mustn't grumble."

Emma, who was a Londoner, said, "I just love you Yorkshire men - you're all so -"

"Handsome?"

"Yes, that's just what I mean - so cool. You hide behind humour so that nobody really gets to know you."

Frank said nothing.

Emma licked her already glossy lips.

"So where do you see yourself in five year's time?" she asked, out of the blue.

"Um. Pretty much the same I suppose."

"Oh, you must have a plan. You'll never get anywhere if you don't have a plan."

Frank considered this for a moment.

"So what is your plan?" he asked.

"Oh, I aim to make it to at least DS by the time I'm thirty and DCI level by forty."

"What about marriage and children?"

"I'm not going to get married until I'm about thirty-five - any earlier would be a distraction. I'm pretty ambivalent about children at the moment. I'm going to review it when

I'm forty."

"How old are you now?"

"Twenty-five."

Frank finished his coffee, and asked, "What if you fall in love?"

"What do you mean?"

"What if you fall in love before you are thirty-five?"

"Oh, I don't really see love as a necessary ingredient in marriage. It's more about shared aims and mutual benefit, surely?"

"Okay, what if you meet someone with shared aims before then?"

"I'm just going to just keep dating until then. It's really just a matter of self-control. I'm very careful about contraception, so sex isn't a risk and I can pursue it from a recreational point of view," - she paused, and saw her chance - "if you know what I mean," she said, with a pout and another toss of her shiny hair. Frank quickly withdrew to the safety and comfort of his office. He thought she was making fun of him, but he was not prepared to stay around long enough to find out definitely, one way or the other.

"It will just be a small gathering, you understand," Roger Sinclair's voice on the phone had sounded friendly, "Mother and I are both upset that we can't give Jane a funeral at the moment, so we thought that this would be better than nothing. Father Wrigglesworth, our local vicar, has kindly agreed to say a few words. It will be held at Lilac Cottage, as it is no longer off-limits. We thought it would give people an opportunity to pay their respects and also have a chat. People are upset, and obviously a bit frightened, until someone is arrested. I've invited everyone I know from the village. I thought it might be useful for you to be there."

Frank MacDonald was sitting at his desk in York, "Yes, Mr Sinclair, I'll be glad to come. I'm very sorry about the funeral but it really can't be helped at the moment. Unfortunately, Steven Brown has gone home for today - his baby isn't well and his wife was a bit concerned, but I'll be there."

"Thank-you, Mr MacDonald. It will start at seven o'clock tonight. There'll be some refreshments afterwards," Roger said goodbye, and rang off. Frank reflected that it would be a good opportunity to mingle with the good people of West Wold, and hopefully some of his suspects too. Just before he was preparing to leave York to go to West Wold, DC Emma Smith opened his office door, then walked in and handed him several pieces of paper.

"Just got this sir. It's the forensic report on the wig and the parcel that was sent to Louise Leighton."

He scanned the report. The only human DNA deposits had belonged to Louise Leighton, whom they knew already to have touched both the parcel and the contents. He continued to scan the text until his eyes were riveted to a sentence which read; 'The string (which was used to tie the parcel); particles analysed contained traces of a linseed-type oil normally associated with the grooming of horses, tack and other stable paraphernalia'.

He leant back and put his feet on the desk. Running his hands through his hair, he groaned. This was another piece of forensic evidence pointing directly at Stella Powell.

Shortly afterwards Frank drove to West Wold, parked near The Green, and as he walked along the road to the Sinclair's house he saw the familiar figure of Roy Parsons, still hanging around in his quest for a scoop. He wandered over, full of self-importance as usual.

"Evening, Mr MacDonald. Got a statement, sir?"

"Chief Inspector MacDonald, Mr Parsons. I have no intentions of making a statement."

"We've learnt that the victim was impersonated after she was dead, is that true? Have you got any idea who did it?"

Frank kept his head down. Don Green took photographs.

"How I detest that man," seethed Frank, to himself.

At Lilac Cottage, he walked up the short path past the lilac trees and into the hall, through the open front door. The sitting room to his right was full of people, mostly standing, and Frank could get no further than the doorway leading off the hall. Some of the gathering were dressed respectfully in black, some had been mindful of the heat and were more casually attired. It had been another very hot and humid day, and was still warm, although the evening sky had turned dull. There was a tense atmosphere with not much conversation, and what there was in hushed tones.

The mantle-piece had been cleared and a wreath of cream roses had been placed there next to a small, framed photograph of Jane. Someone had tactfully moved a rug to hide the blood stain on the floor. Roger Sinclair went to stand beside the mantle-piece, and almost immediately the room fell silent.

"Thank-you all so much for coming here this evening," he said in a quiet voice, "I don't need to tell you how upset I am about this terrible business. There will be a proper funeral for Jane in due course, but we thought this might help people to express their grief and bewilderment in some small way. Father Wrigglesworth will say a few words and lead a prayer. Then please join Mother and me for a drink and something to eat in the garden. Father?"

The vicar, dressed in clerical black and a dog-collar, stood next to Roger. He was an older man of about sixty, with untidy grey hair and a kindly face.

"Good evening, everyone," he said, in a surprisingly deep, baritone voice, "Let us spend a few moments together to remember our sister Jane. She was a hard-working member of this community as you all know, a loving wife to Roger, a beloved daughter, a dear sister to Julia, and a dear aunt to Julia's children. She will be sadly missed by all those who live in West Wold, and by her many friends elsewhere. We have all been affected by this dreadful crime, and let us hope that the police will soon apprehend the perpetrator, with God's help. Let us pray that Jane's soul is at rest, as her body cannot yet be. Let us pray that the violence done in this room can be dispelled, and that God's peace may take its place. Let us pray that this village, where such evil was committed, can be restored to the goodness of God's love. I will give you a few minutes silence for you to remember Jane, grieve for her, and pray for her. Then I will lead you in the Lord's Prayer."

A heavy and sombre silence filled the room. Frank scanned the faces of the people he knew. Roger had his eyes shut and was clearly moved. Roger's mother, Daphne, was grim-faced; death was a familiar fact at her time of life. Julia Johnson, her black clothes suitable to the occasion for once, stood impassively with her eyes open. Her son, Jason, looked uncomfortable. Jane's neighbour, Sadie Mountjoy, looked sad and tearful, and prayed earnestly. Brian Sykes was there, no doubt gathering gossip for his bar-flies. Stella Powell was unusually pale with downcast eyes. James Powell was absent, perhaps in deference to Roger's feelings. Louise Leighton had her back half-turned to him and Frank could not see her expression, but he could see her dabbing a tissue at her eyes. (Crocodile tears? he wondered.) Karen Leighton, looking scruffy and scrawny as always, seemed totally indifferent to the proceedings. Phil Watson looked serious. Samantha Watson was fighting back tears.

After a few minutes, the deep baritone voice of the vicar resumed with '*Our Father, Which Art in Heaven*', and those present joined in and mumbled their way through *The Lord's Prayer* in that peculiarly inept, English way. Then, in silence, Roger ushered the vicar and his mother out of the living room, through the kitchen and out into the garden. Everyone else slowly followed them out, and Frank made his way after them.

A teenaged girl in black blouse and skirt was handing out glasses of sherry from a tray to everyone as they stepped out of the porch onto the large patio. On the large octagonal wooden garden table there was a small buffet of food, and bottles of wine and spirits, and rows of glasses. As the guests collected a glass of sherry they broke into small groups and began to talk, quietly at first, but after a few minutes the mood lightened and people started to enjoy the food, drink, and livelier conversation.

Roger Sinclair escorted his mother to one of the chairs near the table. A pleasant-looking woman in her early forties was officiating over the food and drink, and chatting to Roger, and Frank assumed that it was Sarah Smith, Roger's secretary. Julia Johnson was standing as close to the food and to Roger as she could without actually pushing Sarah out of the way. Roger, as always, was as chivalrous as a Knight of the Round Table.

Frank accepted his glass of sherry and went and stood on the edge of the patio. He looked around. Stella Powell was standing near to the table. She was wearing a black shift dress and black sandals. She caught his eye, nodded, and gave him her ready smile. Frank allowed himself the brief luxury of remarking to himself what a lovely face she had. He smiled back, and then turned his attention elsewhere. Roger noticed him and came over, "Thank-you for coming, Mr MacDonald. Was it alright, do you think?"

"Perfectly alright, Mr Sinclair. I really am very sorry for your loss. We are still doing everything we can to find Jane's killer, and we won't stop our efforts until we do. DS Brown sends his apologies."

"Thank-you," Roger said, and paused, "What do you think happens to us when we die, Mr MacDonald? Is there an after-life, do you think? Jane was so lively, it's hard to think of all that energy just dissipating, as it were."

Frank reflected, and said, "I think you must believe in something or it would be hard to keep going. There must be an incentive to behave as well as you can, otherwise life would just be anarchy and chaos; every man for himself."

"You don't think that mankind has a basic instinct to look out for his fellow man?"

"Perhaps," Frank conceded, "even if purely from an evolutionary standpoint - what's good for one man is good for everyone, in terms of survival of the species. The Church certainly used the promise of Heaven as an incentive for hundreds of years, and as an instrument of oppression; 'the opium of the people' as Marx said. Unfortunately, it seems that basic altruistic instinct is being subverted into apathy and disrespect at the moment, in Western society at any rate."

"I wonder why?"

"I can only think it's the old rats-in-a-laboratory syndrome - too much overcrowding makes people turn on each other. Our cities are becoming intolerable."

"Yes," agreed Roger, "We are very lucky to live

somewhere like West Wold. Anyway, please stay as long as you like and help yourself to refreshments." He moved away, and went to speak to the Watsons.

Frank resumed his surveillance. By the table, Julia and Jason were tucking into their food with gusto. If Julia is the killer it certainly hasn't affected her appetite, he thought to himself.

Just then, Louise Leighton threaded her way through the various groups towards him, a glass of wine in her hand.

"Hello, Mr MacDonald. A good idea this, don't you think? It gives everyone a chance to pay their respects," she said. She seemed to have recovered from her upset in the sitting room, and her eyes were not at all red. She was, as always, immaculately made-up and her hair was shiny and well-cared for. She was wearing a beige trouser suit, and high-heeled, beige, strappy sandals.

"Are you any nearer to catching poor Jane's killer?" she said, trying to look very serious, "I'm very upset by all of this. Have you found out who sent me that vile parcel? Was it the killer? It makes me feel so vulnerable. You don't know who is hanging around, do you?"

"We are happy with our progress, in general," said Frank, blankly - if only that was true, he thought, "but, no, we don't know yet who sent you the parcel."

"I'm sorry to say this, Mr MacDonald, but maybe my mother is right, and you really don't know what you are doing?"

She was a little too smug for his liking, and he decided to get a little tougher. "Actually, I needed to speak to you. Would you mind walking down the garden with me so that we can talk privately?"

"Of course," she nodded.

They made their way down the long garden. He paused

about half way down, when they were well out of earshot of the people on the patio. Brian Sykes was watching them and so was Julia Johnson.

"Miss Leighton, we've reason to believe that you misled us in your original statement. Isn't it true that you were actually fully aware of the renewed relationship between Jane and James Powell, and furthermore that you knew about Jane's pregnancy - because she had told you herself?" It was sheer conjecture, but he tried it anyway.

For the first time since he had known her, she lost her composure and stammered, "P-pregnancy? Wh-what pregnancy? No-one told me! No-one!"

"And isn't it also true that you yourself cannot have children?"

"Who told you that? Oh, that bitch Stella, no doubt," she snorted.

"It seems that Jane had everything you wanted - and couldn't get, doesn't it?"

"Rubbish! I have a wonderful and rewarding career, not something that Jane could have said! Why should envy her?" Even in a state of heightened emotion there was little change in her expression. She breathed hard for a few moments, and got herself under control. She forced a thin smile, "Sorry, Mr MacDonald, it's just a shock that's all. I swear I didn't know about Jane's baby. Do you seriously think that I killed Jane out of jealousy? She was my best friend."

He ignored the question, "I feel I should tell you that we shall be looking into your past very conscientiously."

"That's fine by me," the mask was fully back in place now, "is that all?"

He nodded, and she turned and made her way back up the path towards the others. No sooner had Louise left him than Karen Leighton waved at him from the patio and teetered down the path towards him, glass of wine and cigarette in hand. She was dressed dramatically in black trousers and jacket, with the same gold high-heeled sandals as before. The black outfit made her look even smaller and skinnier than usual, and had the effect of making her look like a demented scare-crow.

"I take it you're having no success catching Jane's killer," she began, "it seems obvious to me, but there you are. Stella Powell must have done it. Stands to reason. She was furious about Jane taking James away and killed her. It's lovely here, isn't it?" she indicated the cottage, and the patio full of people, "Roger Sinclair is such a gentleman. I like a tall man. So handsome. Shame about Jane being murdered. Bet he got a nice life insurance pay-out though. Quite a catch now, being single and loaded as well. I'd love to live in West Wold. Who knows what might happen? That Brian Sykes is a gentleman as well. I quite fancy myself as a pub landlady," she laughed, "Louise should have got herself a man by now. Too skinny that's half the problem. Men like something to get hold of." (A case of pot and kettle, surely? thought Frank.) "She's wasting her time with that James Powell, in my opinion. Stella will never let go. All that money he's got! Louise always looks in the wrong places. She's too selfish to look after a man properly, anyway. Too busy doing her hair and make-up. Always trying to draw attention to herself. Well, I'll just go and get another drink," she shuffled away, as always, before he could reply.

The sky had turned pigeon grey by now, and people were beginning to go indoors as the first rain drops started. He followed Karen back up the garden at a distance. He could not see Stella anywhere, and presumed that she must have gone. As he crossed the patio he said a brief goodbye to Roger Sinclair, ignored everyone else, stepped through the porch into the kitchen and made his way through the cottage to the front door.

Chapter 23

As Frank walked back up the dusty high street towards The Green under a low sky, it began to rain violently with large, heavy raindrops the size of ten pence pieces. Ahead of him he could see Stella running for shelter. She dipped under the pitched roof of the wooden lych-gate at the entrance to the churchyard on the corner of Green Lane. She saw him and waved.

"Come and join me," she laughed, pushing back her dampened hair.

He joined her under the shelter, and they stood facing each other whilst the rain bounced off the roof and the pavements. A small silence ensued which neither of them seemed to know how to fill. What Frank did know was that he should not be talking to her alone again, but he did not feel like playing the policeman. It had already been a long day. He noticed her shiver; her dress was thin and her arms and legs were bare.

"Here," he said, "have my jacket." She protested, but he took his suit jacket off and placed it around her shoulders. They both leant back against the wooden structure, facing each other.

"Thank-you. I think that went pretty well, didn't you, Jane's little service?"

Frank nodded, "Yes, nicely done. I like Roger Sinclair. He seems like a real gentleman."

"Yes, poor Roger, what he must be going through. This week has seemed extremely unreal," Stella said. "To have a murder committed in this village is strange enough, but to have known the victim really well, and for the whole thing to be intertwined with your own life, feels very odd indeed. It's brought a lot of things out into the open between James and me. It seems that *our* lives will never be the same either. We've asked both of the girls to come home this week-end, so that we can talk to them. They are old enough to be told what's been happening to James, so that they can understand his grief. He needs their support at the moment."

There was another small silence. The male in him could not help but relish the sight of her wrapped in his jacket, her face wet and her heart-melting eyes shining.

She put a hand up to stroke the worn old oak of the lych-gate, and said, "They built these to shelter the bodies at funerals, you know. There were no coffins in medieval times; bodies were just wrapped in a shroud. So they used these to shelter the bodies and the mourners whilst they waited for the priest to come out of the church and start the funeral service. This is a very fine one - quite ornate."

Frank nodded, and said, "I didn't know that."

Another silence ensued. The rain continued its staccato beat on the roof and the pavement.

"What shall we talk about to pass the time?" Stella asked, with a wry smile.

"Tell me about your childhood," Frank said, more seriously.

She considered for a moment, and then nodded, "Okay. Well, I had a good childhood on the whole, I suppose. Growing up in a small village, ponies, good school - all that; a privileged life, I know. I've almost always lived in the same house; it's been in our family for generations. My parents were reasonably well off; my father was an accountant. My Mum was lovely, but my father drank," Frank was flattered that she was not merely passing the time with small-talk, "I remember him being out of the house a lot, and then as soon as he came home the atmosphere changed. It didn't affect me much directly; I didn't understand, but I sensed how much he hurt my Mum. It made me distrustful, I think - " she paused, " - I think I always knew that James would not commit himself fully to a marriage, and that's why I chose him; because it meant I didn't have to either. I kept a big part of myself back. I was scared. I know that I hide behind my marriage so that I don't have to put myself at risk. It's strange really; I can jump a five foot fence on the back of a horse, but I've been too scared to let myself fall in love. I'm the loser. And so is he - never committing to anything. Dreading losing his precious freedom. Freedom to do what? Save the world? Do something good for mankind? No - just look for the next conquest."

"It seems he might have finally decided to settle down with Jane?"

"Yes," she conceded, doubtfully, "Yes, it does."

"There do seem to be a lot of unhappily married people," he said, thinking particularly of his sister Ali.

"Yes there are. And do you know why? It's because they marry the wrong person in the first place, and for all the wrong reasons. They hate living at home, or they want to marry money, or they can't bear being alone. But that's no good. It has to be for the right reasons or it's bound to fail. People don't achieve married happiness because they're too scared to even try it, too scared to dip a toe in the water. And I include myself in that category, I'm afraid. Because it takes hard work and risk, yes, even tedium at times, but without the hard work you don't get the rewards. You don't get the bliss."

"Bliss?"

"Yes. Bliss. When you love someone and they love you. When you look after someone, and they look after you. When you respect someone, and they respect you. When you've made love to someone for the thousandth time. Total contentment. Total bliss. I can describe it, but I've never achieved it. Except the kind you get from being a mother. That is total love, total commitment."

"But the bliss, the married bliss, doesn't last surely?"

"No, you're right, but maybe remembering the bliss is what gets you through the bad times when they come."

"And the bad times always come?"

"Probably."

She left a long pause, and then gestured towards the small graveyard surrounding the church, "They're both in here, my parents. It sounds mad, but I often come over here and have a chat to my Mum. I bring her the roses from her garden."

"Do you believe that she can hear you?"

"That she's in Heaven, you mean? Yes, I can believe in a sort of Heaven, but I can't believe in Hell. How many people are really that wicked that they deserve eternal damnation? A few hundred in the whole of history, probably. Isn't eternal oblivion enough of a punishment? Perhaps we are already in Heaven but we just don't know it, and that's why the dead seem so close. Perhaps this is

Heaven on Earth," she said, indicating the pretty village, and the green and golden and purple hills beyond. "Sometimes when I'm in my garden, particularly early in the morning, it feels like a kind of Heaven. I'm at my happiest there. There's always something new to discover; some gorgeous flower opens up overnight, or something you thought was dead puts out shoots. It's a good place to think, as well; there's something very soothing about digging and weeding!"

"Tell me about you and James. How did you meet?"

"I met him at a party in Manchester. I went to live and work there for a while with some girl friends. He was just breaking into the big-time with his photography. I was eighteen. He wanted to take my photograph (that old corny line!); I went to his studio the next day, and pretty much never left! We had a wild time for a while - it was the late 'Eighties and everyone was on the up, or so it seemed. We bounced around the world for a while - travelling light, and looking for the next party. Then my parents were killed, and I got pregnant at more or less the same time. I was totally shattered. We decided to move back here just before Ellen was born. James brought me here and just cared for me and the baby, for a long while. Like Dorothy in *The Wizard of Oz*, I discovered that there's no place like home. James was very good to me then. He's not a bad person, despite what you might think," she stopped speaking, and stared at the ground, "How about you?" she said, lifting her head and changing the subject, "Did you have a happy childhood?"

"Very, I think. Very happy, and very ordinary. I have an older sister and a younger, and they always kept me on my toes! Stopped me from becoming too full of myself, which boys are inclined to do, I think. They were very good at squashing me; sometimes literally!"

"I always wanted a sister," she said.

"I have two - take one of them, please!"

She smiled, "What about your parents? Do you get on?"

"My parents are still together and still happy. They live for their children and grandchildren. They're getting on in years though; my father is very frail, and we can't help but worry about them."

"What about Nathan's mother? How did you meet?"

He told her the history of his marriage, trying to match her own candour, and concluded with, "I wonder now whether I ever gave her a real chance; I was so taken up with my career. I was constantly torn in two."

"I can see that it must be difficult; always putting your public duty before your private inclinations," she said sympathetically. "I was never ambitious. I was clever at school, but I had no direction. I went to work full-time at the stables and I loved it; being near horses is as natural as breathing to me. I was just marking time until I met James. Being a mother was all I ever wanted to do, really. I know that women are expected to want to do more these days and I applaud those that do, but what could be more important than raising the next generation? Especially when so many people seem to do it so badly at the moment; they don't care about their children, they neglect them, they care so much more about themselves. To me, parenting means putting your children's needs above your own *all of the time*. I don't mean a return to the bad old days, when women were tied to the home and given no voice, no equality. There has to be a better way; one where women are valued in all of their roles. I adored my babies, even being pregnant! But being a parent is sad too. I had two babies, two toddlers, two schoolchildren; where are they now? I miss my babies, so much. Parenting is a continual process of bereavement, nobody ever mentions that. That was the best time of my life, when the children were young. I suppose it's that feeling of being needed, of knowing that you are the centre of someone's world..." She held a hand out beyond the shelter, "Oh, look, the rain's stopped! I'd better go," she said reluctantly, looking into his eyes. The shower had left a clear sky, like a silver dome, now washed pink and orange by the twilight.

Stella took off Frank's jacket and pushed it into his hands. For a moment, he thought she was going to kiss him. For a moment he almost responded; he did not care if she had killed a thousand Jane Sinclairs. She did not kiss him. Instead she smiled, and said goodbye, and he watched her walk around the corner into Green Lane.

Frank felt a kind of despair then; she had completely unravelled him. He walked across the road to collect his car, then he saw *The Prancing Pony* public house, and suddenly longed to sit somewhere quiet with a whisky in his hand. He went inside. There were only a few diners in the bar, waiting to go into the restaurant for their meals. He ordered the drink and took it to the darkest, coolest part of the room. Luckily, Brian Sykes had still not returned from Lilac Cottage. Frank groaned inwardly at the thought that he and Stella might have been seen during their tête-à-tête by Brian Sykes, or worse, one of the newspaper reporters who were still hanging around in the village, especially Roy Parsons. He sat at a round, brass-topped table, facing the room, and gratefully removed his tie, laid it and his wet jacket on the seat next to him, and opened up the neck of his shirt a couple of buttons. He sighed and tried to turn his mind back to the case; he felt on safer ground there. He chided himself that he was getting nowhere; getting nowhere, and being led, literally in one case, down the garden path by a handful of women. He could not find a way through the lies, conjecture, rumours, half-truths, and basic lack of concrete evidence in which he felt mired. He ran his hands through his hair in frustration. Julia Johnson seemed innocuous on the surface, but there had been a primeval struggle going on between her and Jane throughout their lives. There was no doubt that family rivalry could lead to desperate acts, on occasion. Julia had no personal attributes to make her attractive to an impartial mind, but that did not make her a murderer, and he had not a shred of evidence against her. There was also something about Louise Leighton that he did not like. On the one hand, she was friendly and anxious to please, but there was also something guarded and watchful. Some eyes invite you in, some have depths you could drown in, but hers were like steel shutters; designed to keep you out. Frank knew better than to follow his instincts completely. Just because he did not like Julia or Louise did not make either of them a killer, nor did Stella's charm absolve her automatically of guilt. He was too experienced to fall into that trap. He had been beguiled before by people with attractive personalities which had hidden implacably dangerous minds.

Frank sipped his drink, and made himself switch off from the case for a few minutes. By the time he was half way down the glass he felt calmer; no doubt they would get a breakthrough soon. He stared at nothing for a while and allowed his thoughts to drift where they would. This was a mistake as his thoughts, when left to themselves, could only reveal what he was so desperately trying to hide from himself. He suddenly made an astounding discovery; that he was in love with Stella Powell. In fact, he probably had been from the moment that she had bowled out of her front door and almost knocked him over. He realised that ever since Saturday, somewhere in the depth of his hidden heart, he had spent every moment waiting for the next sight of her. He thought about sitting in the sunshine in her garden, watching her, the rhythm of her movements as she cut down the branches of the hedge, and again just now sheltering from the rain with her. He had rarely felt so happy. He smiled to himself ruefully. Stella; she had overwhelmed him so completely in so short a time. She had bewitched him somehow. She had pierced the armour which he had so carefully constructed, both professional and personal, and wounded him, flesh and bone. With that realisation came the prospect, as dreary as November, that she would never be free, could never be tempted to leave the safety and comfort of her marriage, never leave the husband whom she called her best friend, never trust Frank enough to give herself unreservedly. But far, far worse than this was the irrefutable truth that Stella could still be the person who had killed Jane Sinclair. He found it almost inconceivable that someone who appeared as open, warm and loving as Stella could be a killer. If she was Jane's murderer, then either she was the most consummate actress and cold-hearted villain that he had ever met, or she had the kind of terrifying multiple personality which could simply compartmentalise itself, and carry on with daily life whilst one of the personalities nursed a dreadful secret. Either way, this thought appalled him, and robbed him of the little calmness that he had achieved whilst sitting there.

He drained his glass and left the public house; a different man to the one who had entered it.

Diamonds And Pebbles

Chapter 24

Extract from a diary;

IT WON'T BE LONG NOW. SHE'LL GET WHAT SHE DESERVES. SHE THINKS SHE'S SAFE BUT SHE ISN'T. SHE CAN'T HAVE JAMES. HE'S MINE. I CAN'T WAIT. JUST ME AND HIM, ALL OVER THE WORLD. IT'LL BE WICKED. SHE'S GOING TO BE SORRY. I'M GOING TO GET HER. JUST LIKE THE OTHER ONE. REALLY SOON. I'LL BE CAREFUL, THOUGH. IT WILL LOOK LIKE AN ACCIDENT. I'LL STAND ON THE EDGE WITH HER AND PUSH HER. THEN I CAN KEEP HIM. SHE WON'T STOP ME. SHE'S NOTHING. LESS THAN NOTHING. THAT POLICEMAN WON'T CATCH ME EITHER. HE'S USELESS. I CAN'T WAIT. AT SUTTON BANK TOMORROW SHE'LL GET WHAT'S COMING.

Diamonds And Pebbles

Friday Again

Diamonds And Pebbles

Chapter 25

It was nine o'clock on Friday morning, a week after Jane Sinclair's death. Frank MacDonald and Steven Brown were in Frank's office in York Police Station. Frank was unsure how to move forward. If he was honest with himself, the forensic evidence, the circumstantial evidence, and public opinion were pointing him towards Stella, but his instincts, his inclination, and (heaven help him) his emotions were fighting against this. For something to do which was not associated with going to arrest Stella (which was what he ought to have been doing), he had decided to look more closely into Louise Leighton's former employment history. Frank was sitting with his feet on the desk, whilst Steven Brown sat across from him using the telephone.

"Yes, that's fine. We'll be there in about half an hour," Steven said, putting the phone down after four or five calls. "It seems that Louise Leighton was on a six-month contract in the last nannying job she did before she started her teacher training degree, but they let her go after three months. They are called the Allinsons. She's a doctor, he works in computers. The wife didn't want to talk on the phone - she said it was complicated. They live in Harrogate. They're about to fly off on holiday to Madeira for a fortnight, so I said we'd go there straight away."

Frank felt a thin trickle of excitement in his chest. Was this finally a breakthrough? Did Louise Leighton have a dark secret in her past which would indicate a personality capable of murder? He could not wait to get to Harrogate.

"Good work, Steven. Let's go."

As the two policemen made their way to Steven's car, Roy Parsons and Don Green were waiting outside of the police station, having got bored with waiting for something else to happen in West Wold. The rest of the media had long departed, preferring to find out what was happening in North Yorkshire by phone, from the comfort of their London offices. Frank rolled his eyes. He really wished something interesting would happen in London. The man made his way slowly over to where they stood.

"Morning. Any statement today, sir?"

"As always, if and when necessary."

"We understand the victim was pregnant, is that true? Are you any closer to making an arrest? Isn't it true to say that you have no idea who killed Jane Sinclair? Are your superiors planning to take you off the case?"

Frank said nothing, as he and Steven got into the car and Steven quickly drove off. Don Green snapped a couple of photographs, just for old times' sake.

"A mine of information, as usual," said Frank, as they drove off. "He'll keep dogging our footsteps until we find this killer, or I retire, whichever is the sooner."

Stephanie Allinson showed the two detectives into a sunny living room. The weather had become unbearably hot again, and the room was uncomfortably warm. The house, with at least five bedrooms Frank guessed, was large and imposing. It stood on its own plot on the outskirts of Harrogate.

"Thank-you for making the time to see us. I know you are going away." He could see the holiday paraphernalia collected on the dining table through an archway into the adjacent dining room; camera, passports, sun-tan lotion, and beach towels.

"Not at all, Mr MacDonald, your sergeant said it was very important. How can we help? Shall I get my husband?" In her early forties, she was a plump, no-nonsense type, rather matronly, with short greying hair and glasses which she pushed up her nose from time to time.

"Please do."

She went into the hall and called softly, "Martin, they're here."

They heard footsteps on the stairs and a tall, handsome man, prematurely-grey, also in his early forties, walked diffidently into the room. He shook hands courteously with them and they all sat down; the Allinsons side-by-side on the sofa, and Frank and Steven on an armchair either side.

"What exactly is this about, Mr MacDonald?" asked Martin Allinson, nervously. He seemed reserved and cautious.

"We are investigating the death of a woman in the village of West Wold - you may have seen the newspapers. We are following several lines of enquiry and this is one of them." Frank decided not to startle them too much; they both seemed rather ill-at-ease. "Louise Leighton lives in the village, and was known to the victim. We understand that Miss Leighton is a former employee of yours. According to her statement, she worked here as a nanny for three months in the summer of 2001. Is that correct? What was she like?"

Mrs Allinson sat up in her seat slightly in preparation for answering, "She was a very good nanny - pleasant, efficient, hard-working; the children liked her - we have three - and she seemed to care about them."

"But you let her go after three months instead of finishing the six month contract?"

"Yes, she - how can I put it - things became a little intense, and we decided that it couldn't go on."

"In connection with the children?"

"No," she took a deep breath and plunged on, "I'm afraid she developed a crush on my husband."

Martin Allinson blushed slightly, and wriggled uncomfortably in his seat. "She was fine at first," he said, swallowing hard, "but then she got more and more friendly. She took every opportunity to be alone with me, sometimes quite inappropriately, for instance she would follow me into the bathroom. She eventually told me that she loved me."

Stephanie Allinson sat composedly throughout her husband's admissions. She had obviously heard everything before. Martin Allinson looked at her frequently as he spoke, as if for reassurance that it was alright to continue. "I was flattered at first, I'll admit. She was an attractive girl," (He searched his wife's face; she nodded encouragement), "I didn't touch her. Well, just a kiss and a cuddle a couple of times. I'm ashamed of myself, of course. But then she started saying weird things."

"Such as?"

"Louise wanted me to divorce Steph, get custody of the children, and live with her - in this house, preferably - " (Echoes of what Stella said in her garden, thought Frank) " - and she even started talking about 'getting rid' of Steph, about her meeting with a nasty accident, that sort of thing, sorry darling," (with a look at his wife), "it was always semi-joking, semi-serious, you know? A few times she said that she would make a good mum to the children. She told me that she couldn't have children of her own because of some incident in her teens. I came to realise that it wasn't actually me, or sex, that she was interested in. It was more that she wanted to take Steph's place. To *be* Steph, almost," (Frank again felt a fluttering of excitement in his chest; this, surely, proved that Louise Leighton was the killer?), "Luckily, I decided to tell Steph what was happening; we are always honest and open with each other; we have a solid marriage," (he took his wife's hand in his) "and we decided to sack her there and then. We had to give her three month's pay to get rid of her but it was worth it. Steph virtually packed her case, and escorted her off the premises; and she went."

"And that was the end of it?"

"We got a lot of phone calls in the middle of the night where the other end went dead when we picked it up, and we were plagued by junk mail for a while, but then it all went quiet. She left us in the June and we assumed that she started University in the September; that's when the nuisance stuff stopped."

"You didn't think to let the police know?"

"What could I say? What had she really done? It was mostly innuendo. I was ashamed, and it was her word against mine."

Frank looked enquiringly at Steven Brown, who raised his eyebrows and nodded. "Thank-you for being so open with us. I know it can't have been easy, raking up the past. I'll have to ask you to make a formal statement."

"That's alright, Mr MacDonald." Martin Allinson relaxed and smiled, relieved to have made his confession.

As they left the Allinson's house, Frank and Steven discussed the implications of what they had heard. Steven said, "Louise certainly had the motive - if she discovered that Jane was taking James away from her, as she saw it, and expecting his baby."

"Yes - poor Jane - she may have signed her own death warrant if she made the mistake of confiding in Louise."

"What about the parcel with the wig in, sir?"

"She must have sent it to herself to try to throw us off the scent, and laced the string with linseed oil to throw suspicion onto Stella. Right, let's find Louise Leighton as quickly as possible, get her taken into the station, and lean on her to see if we can get her to confess. Let's also get a search warrant for the house. She may have been stupid enough to keep something that will incriminate her. I'm just afraid that everything we have on her is too circumstantial to stick."

"We could try getting Julia Johnson to come clean about what, if anything, she saw that day - she could be an eye witness; we may have to go easy on any blackmail charges. I'll get somebody to pick her up too," said Steven.

He picked up his mobile phone and rang Emma Smith to explain what he wanted. Several minutes later she rang back. He listened and nodded for a few moments, then looked at Frank in alarm.

"They've located Louise Leighton, sir. James Powell said she and Stella have gone walking on Sutton Bank. They left West Wold over an hour ago. They planned to get to Kilburn for lunch."

Frank suddenly found it hard to breath. "Yes, I remember Stella telling me that they were going walking today, even though Louise doesn't seem to actually like her very much." He ran his fingers through his hair distractedly. "If Louise is the killer, Stella could be in danger. Louise has got just as much reason to want Stella dead as she had for Jane, and she must suspect that we're onto her after my conversation with her last night. I hope I haven't pushed her into doing something rash." A feeling of absolute dread engulfed him. He leant against the car for support.

"And if we're wrong and Stella is the killer, then Louise could be in danger," Steven said quietly, looking at his watch, "We can get to Sutton Bank in thirty minutes from here."

"Right, let's go. Get somebody over there quickly, and an ambulance just in case."

Diamonds And Pebbles

Chapter 26

Sutton Bank forms part of the southernmost promontory of the Yorkshire Moors which stretch from Darlington to Thirsk. Its sheer face rises perpendicularly from the valley below some three hundred feet and is clearly visible for miles around. It provides incomparable views westwards towards the Vale of York and the Yorkshire Dales and Thirsk. Approached from the west, a windy road twists its way up the steep climb. From the east, the road comes on the flat from Helmsley, and passes close to the exquisite Rievaulx Abbey, before arriving at the edge of the dramatic drop. On the gentler descent of the southernmost face of the outcrop, in 1857, a local schoolteacher, John Hodgson, decide to create a White Horse in chalk with the help of his pupils and other local people. The White Horse is three hundred and twenty feet long by two hundred and twenty feet high, and is said to be the largest and most northerly in England. Sutton Bank is formed of limestone, and the horse was created by removing the topsoil and exposing the underlying rock. Six tons of lime were used to whiten the exposed rock, and the White Horse is now formed of off-white limestone chips. During World War Two it was covered over to prevent it from becoming a conspicuous navigation landmark for the enemy's bombers. This White Horse can be seen from over forty five miles away. At its base lies the village of Kilburn. Visitors to Sutton Bank can leave their cars close to the edge, in a car park next to the Helmsley road, and walk along the top to the north, or to the south. The southerly path leads past an airfield which is used to launch gliders, and eventually leads to the top of the White Horse as the land starts to dip towards Kilburn.

Frank MacDonald and Steven Brown raced towards Sutton Bank with Steven driving as fast as safety would allow. The flick of a switch turned their innocuous-looking grey Volvo saloon into a police car, bristling with lights and technology. As the minutes ticked away, Frank's heart was thumping in his chest. He was in agony at the thought of what they might find. He shifted distractedly in his seat, and cursed the harvest tractors which slowed them down on the country roads. As he and Steven approached from the west via Thirsk, some of his team were also on their way from York via the Helmsley road. The weather was gradually deteriorating; clouds of gunmetal grey were beginning to block out the sunshine, and a blustery wind agitated the trees.

"How about going straight to Kilburn, sir, and walking up the hill to meet them? They can't be far away from the White Horse now. The local officers and our lads will follow them from the Helmsley road, and we should all meet in the middle somewhere."

"Good idea, Steven."

They duly arrived in Kilburn, and hurriedly left the car parked at the side of the lane which led to the open, green grass of the hillside. They quickly found the mud path which led towards the White Horse, and began the steep walk across the vast, white shape. It was unrecognisable as anything at all at this proximity; they were merely surrounded by a huge expanse of white chalk edged with grass. Layers of thick cloud gathered and merged overhead, and the rain started to drizzle as they walked. The wind buffeted the rain into their faces as they struggled up the hill. In the distance they could hear ominous cracks of thunder. They ran uphill as quickly as they could with Steven slightly ahead, his long seven-league legs propelling him quickly up the steep slope. Frank kept scanning the horizon at the top of the hill, hoping to see Stella and Louise walking towards them. Frank's heart began to pound with the effort of climbing and the fear that they were too late.

As he jogged up the hill, his mind automatically started to piece together the facts of the case into a coherent whole. If Louise was the murderer, then she had deliberately pointed the finger of suspicion at James, whilst feigning reluctance, made up the man in the BMW to waste police time, sent the red wig to herself and laced the parcel with linseed oil to throw suspicion on Stella, and set up the whole charade of dressing up as Jane in order to fudge the time of the murder and give herself the plausible alibi of being at the hairdressers. There was also, he knew, a more pathetic reason for dressing up as Jane; a deep-seated feeling of inadequacy which had driven Louise to hate Jane, to kill her for being the woman that she, Louise, could never be.

Scrambling up the chalky hillside, Frank also realised that if Louise was the killer, then at last he knew that Stella, finally and categorically, could not be. Yet Steven Brown had voiced that last little nagging doubt that, in fact, the truth was the other way round; that Stella was the killer.

Diamonds And Pebbles

That it was Louise who was in danger on the cliff-top, not Stella. Frank urged himself to keep running upwards, even though the pain in his chest was burning into his heart.

Suddenly, they saw two female figures heading towards them along the ridge beyond the top edge of the White Horse. Louise Leighton was dragging Stella along by the arm and heading straight for the sheer drop at the edge of the promontory. Stella was staggering and holding her head with her free hand. Frank could see blood on Stella's hands and down the front of her shirt. He shouted at Louise to stop, but the wind snatched his words away. Louise must have heard him, however. She stopped and turned; as she did so, Stella seemed to gather her wits and managed to break free with one tremendous push. She started to stumble awkwardly towards Frank. Louise stood frozen for a moment, then turned and ran in the other direction, back the way they had come towards the edge of the airfield. Steven Brown bounded after her whilst Frank ran towards Stella, catching her as she finally fell to the ground.

"Are you alright, sweetheart?" he supported her in his arms.

She looked at him with fear in her eyes, gripping his arms as he held her. She closed her eyes, and started to lose consciousness. Frank could hear the whine of a siren in the distance along the road into Kilburn at the bottom of the hill. A fine mist was forming in the valley below him as the rain continued. He knew he had to leave Stella to go after Steven and Louise.

"Stella! Stella, look at me! I've got to go. Stay still. You must try to stay awake. The paramedics should be here soon," he gently disentangled himself, and lowered her onto the white stones as softly as he could, leaving her lying there, holding her head with both hands and moaning. Her hair was matted with blood, and soon the blood ran in red rivulets in the rainwater and soaked into the white chalk which surrounded her.

Frank chased off in the same direction as Steven Brown, up the steep incline that brought him to the brow of the hill. He ran onto a path through a swathe of low trees which grew over the edge and down the west face of the high outcrop. As Frank approached, Steven Brown had stopped. As Frank caught up with him he could see Louise standing twenty feet off to the left of the path on the very edge of the perpendicular drop. Steven was standing still and talking quietly to Louise, trying to persuade her to move towards him. Frank walked very slowly and carefully to where Steven stood, so as not to startle Louise. She stood, not moving, half turned away from the two men.

"Louise," said Frank, gently, "Come away from the edge. We can talk. We can help you."

She turned her head, and looked at him with no expression in her blank eyes. She looked unusually dishevelled; her hair for once untidy and flattened by the rain, and her make-up smudged. She cut a forlorn figure standing there alone in the pouring rain. She did nothing for several seconds, then turned away from them, and as she did so she seemed to lose her footing and plunged out of sight. They raced forward, but when they got to the edge they saw her crumpled body sprawled fifty feet below on a rocky ridge.

As he looked down, Frank felt sick at the sight of her small, almost childlike body, lying curled up on the ground below, looking more asleep than dead. He breathed hard to try to slow down his heart rate. He sat down on the wet, grassy bank, too shocked to move. Steven Brown joined him. Frank looked at Steven, and shook his head in disbelief and dismay. He had found the killer at last, but he could take no pleasure in it, nor even, yet, a sense of the satisfaction of a job well done. He wanted to go back to Stella, but did not trust his knees to keep him upright. The two men sat silently side by side on the grass, high up on top of the rocky outcrop of Sutton Bank, and stared out across the Yorkshire landscape, seeing nothing. After several minutes Frank said to Steven, "Better get someone to get Louise's body sorted out. I'll go back and make sure they've found Stella." Steven nodded, and started to make arrangements with the team on his mobile phone. Frank slowly got up, and made his way back along the wooded path to the top of the White Horse and started to walk down, oblivious to the magnificent view before him. Below, down the steep slope, he could see one of his team and a couple of paramedics looking after Stella. They were lifting her gently onto a stretcher and covering her with a blanket in preparation for carrying her down to the waiting ambulance. There was no movement or sign of life from Stella. He could see the lights of the ambulance flashing below in the gloom, lighting up the valley intermittently with garish blue. The rain was lashing down now, still whipped up by the blustery wind which blew it into Frank's face. He sat down on the white chalk and put his head in his hands, heedless of the rain. He cried with relief that he finally knew for certain that Stella was not the killer, and also, in no small measure, with pity for Louise Leighton, lying doll-like on the rocks, like a toy left out in the rain. He felt regret for her life cut short; regret for the bitter edifice of hate, built from the particular circumstances and events of that difficult life, which led to the killing Jane Sinclair. Mixed in with relief and sorrow, there was also a growing anxiety about Stella's survival, and the pain of knowing that, if she lived, he had no rightful place in her life. He remembered how it felt to cradle Stella in his arms; something he had wanted to do so much. He could never have envisaged the terrible circumstances in which it would happen. Once the tears came, the agony he was also feeling about losing his beloved father welled up from the dark place where he kept it hidden. Sitting there alone in the cold rain, surrounded by the expanse of chalk of the White Horse, Frank had never felt so miserable in his life.

Diamonds And Pebbles

September

Diamonds And Pebbles

Chapter 27

It was eight o'clock at night as Frank MacDonald walked across the hospital car park and shivered in a chill wind. August was rolling into September, and already it felt as though that astounding summer was over. It was three days since the incident at Sutton Bank. He wanted to see Stella, indeed it was his professional duty to do so, but he had stayed away; he did not know what to do with the feelings which she stirred up in him. As soon as he had heard that Stella was alright, Frank sent DC Emma Smith to take a formal statement from her. Finally, he relented and allowed himself to see her for what would inevitably be the last time. Normally cheerfully optimistic about the future, on the rare occasions when he thought about it at all, at that moment he felt as though there was only a lonely, mournful autumn to look forward to, and a silent winter to follow. He entered the building and followed the signs to the ward he wanted. He checked at the nurse's station to find out which side-ward Stella was in, and walked along the darkened corridor until he found the correct door. He knocked and entered.

Stella was lying in one of four beds in the room; only one of the other beds was occupied. She lay in a pool of soft light in the dimly lit room. Stella was awake and smiled when she saw him. James Powell sat on a plastic chair to Stella's right, one foot casually resting on the opposite thigh, trying to relax by reading a car magazine. He looked even more tired and bewildered than he had before Stella's injury. It was the first time that Frank had seen him since the day of Louise's death.

James Powell jumped up and came to shake Frank's hand enthusiastically, "Hi, Mr MacDonald, good of you to come. I can't thank you enough for what you did for Stella. She might have been killed but for you."

"I'm just glad we got there in time, Mr Powell."

"Look - do you mind if I just go and stretch my legs for five minutes whilst you keep Stella company?" They both turned to look at Stella, and she nodded approval.

James Powell left the room, and Frank took the chair to Stella's left, pulled it up close to the bed, and sat down.

Stella looked pale, and the bandage around her head made her eyes look enormous. She looked at him with gratitude in her eyes, "Thank-you so much, Mr MacDonald. You saved my life, I'm sure."

"Please," he said gently, "call me Frank. I think we can be a little less formal, now, don't you?" He smiled, and handed her a package which he had been carrying. She opened it with enthusiasm, and was delighted to find the Pullman trilogy.

"For your convalescence," said Frank.

"Thank-you so much," she said, and paused, "so the

killer was Louise all along? I can't believe it."

"Yes, I think we got to you just in time," said Frank, "You shook Louise off yourself in the end though. What exactly happened?"

She frowned with concentration, "Everything seemed normal to start with. She offered to drive, and we parked at the car park just off the main road. We walked along the path past the airfield towards the White Horse. We were going to go to Kilburn for lunch and then walk back."

"Was Louise acting normally?"

"She was a bit tense and quiet in hindsight, but we were chatting a little. I wasn't alarmed or anything. Then the path narrowed and we had to walk in single file for a while. I went in front. Then suddenly I felt an enormous blow from behind and my knees buckled. I couldn't think what had happened. In my confusion I thought I'd been kicked by a horse! There are bridle paths all round that area. It was the only explanation that I could think of. I put my hand to the back of my head and felt blood. I presume it was actually a rock that she used. She grabbed me by the arm and started dragging me along. I couldn't understand why she wasn't helping me - I was still upright - just - and stumbling along - I think I almost lost consciousness a few times - and then I could see she was dragging me towards the edge - I panicked - I felt terribly sick and woozy - that's when I saw you - and suddenly a small voice inside my head said 'Fight! You're stronger than her! Fight her!' - she was only a little thing really - so I just gathered all my strength and twisted away and pushed at the same time. I managed to get away and - well - you know the rest…"

They were both quiet for a moment as they thought about Louise's fate.

"I keep replaying it in my mind," said Frank, quietly, "I

still can't decide whether she fell or she jumped. She turned to face me for a few seconds, and then she was gone." He remembered the small, twisted body lying on the rocks below him in the rain.

"And it was definitely Louise who killed Jane?"

"Yes. She played us along for a while; feigning grief, concern, ignorance, surprise, or whatever was needed to appear innocent. She kept trying to point us at you, or James, or anybody except herself. We were convinced it was her by Friday morning, and we were looking for her to take in for questioning. Then James said that she was with you on Sutton Bank. I was really worried about you then. We got there as quickly as we could. We've since found a vitriolic diary in her car which prove it beyond doubt. At first, she obviously thought we were never going to catch her. She may have been right, we had precious little to go on; just conjecture, really. But the boot of her car had suitcases in it; she was obviously planning to get away after she killed you. She must have known that simply telling us that you'd fallen over the edge wasn't going to work, or she just wasn't thinking straight by that time. Poor Louise, Jane was her nemesis. She was so desperate to make a new life for herself in West Wold, and she might have too, if she hadn't met Jane. Jane was everything Louise aspired to; exotic looks, a kind husband, money, a role in a community, then an affair with James Powell the handsome playboy - sorry! I know he's your husband, but it is the truth - and finally, a baby. It was too much for Louise to bear and that, combined with her own particular psychological make-up, which we can only guess at, sent her over the edge - in both ways. She was a cold-hearted killer at the end of the day. Nothing more, nothing less. Apparently, she was medically unable to have children of her own. At the age of sixteen she contracted an infection from a boyfriend which left her infertile. She also seems to have had psychological problems from a young age. Her mother is hardly the nurturing type."

Stella nodded, "James told me that Karen Leighton is living in Louise's house permanently now. Louise is still in the mortuary, and she has already moved in."

"That doesn't surprise me. From what Louise told me, Karen certainly never had Louise's interests at heart. Anyway, Louise found out that James and Jane had got back together again – " he paused and looked at Stella, " - I hope this isn't too upsetting for you?"

She shook her head and asked him to go on.

" - that stoked up the jealousy even more, but what really seems to have made her murderous was when she found out that Jane was having James's baby - poor Jane - the one person she should not have told. Louise pretended to us from the start that she didn't know, but she obviously did."

"I keep thinking about Jane," said Stella. "I don't think I was right when I said that she wasn't a friend. We've known each other most of our adult lives, and she could be irritating, but I know she would have helped me if I'd ever needed her to. I dismissed her as a friend because she wasn't a soul mate, but that's not right. I'm afraid that I may have taken her for granted. One of my best friend lives in Scotland and I rarely see her, but we are still very close. I've realised that friendships come in all shades; just like marriages."

Frank wondered briefly whether he would be satisfied to have Stella as a dear friend and nothing more, but dismissed the notion; he knew it was not possible.

"Yes, I know what you mean. Steven Brown is actually

one of my best friends, but we hardly ever see each other out of work hours, and I have a friend in America whom I haven't seen for years, but I know that he would get on the first plane if I needed him."

Stella looked very tired suddenly and changed the subject, "James has been devastated by all of this. He feels responsible somehow."

"Where does this leave you and James?" Frank desperately wanted to know.

"When I get out of here, and things settle down, we are going to talk. It's too soon now. Everything is topsy-turvy. I must think about my girls, as well," she looked at him steadily, her eyes full of meaning, perhaps even love, as if she understood and acknowledged what was behind his question.

Frank knew that if Stella was free he wanted to try to get to know her better, but that he would not attempt it whilst she was still married to, and living with, James Powell, no matter how unconventional her marriage. He could not share her. The thought made his heart squeeze with jealousy; he knew a little of the torment that Louise Leighton had suffered in her obsession. He also remembered Stella's own admission that she was too frightened of love to risk her happiness in pursuit of it.

"Will you make a full recovery?" he asked.

"The doctor thinks so, but he's pretty much banned me from ever riding again. Even a slight riding accident could be fatal, it seems. My poor skull will always be a bit tender," she felt the top of her head gently, and smiled, "so it looks as though I'll be taking up knitting."

"I need a scarf for the winter," he smiled back.

"You obviously haven't seen my knitting!"

She laughed, but the effort had hurt her. She turned

serious, suddenly, "The thing about almost losing your life is that it makes you stop and think; think really hard about what you want to do with the rest of the life that you nearly didn't have. My girls have been here all day - you just missed them. I so want you to meet them. I'm so grateful that I will have lots more time with them than I might have had, if you hadn't arrived at the White Horse when you did. James is very upset at the moment - we need each other. But things are going to change, I'm sure," she said, and again she looked at him with something close to love in her eyes.

"You'll be booking that trip to Prince Edward Island soon then?"

"The minute I can drag myself out of this bed and get to the airport!"

There was a silence then which seemed to go on just a little too long.

"Stella – " he began.

At that moment James Powell returned with a cup of coffee in his hand and walked over to the chair which he had vacated earlier.

"I should go," said Frank.

His right hand was on the bedspread palm down, and Stella reached over with an effort and squeezed his hand with hers. He turned his hand over to hold hers tightly. The shock of touching her flooded him with delight and despair in equal measure. Stella looked into his eyes, "Thank-you again, Frank. I owe you so much. Please keep in touch with me."

He noticed that she said 'me' and not the more conventional 'us', which gave him a little relief and hope. He released his grip and stood up, nodded at James, said goodbye to them both and left. He felt that he would never see Stella again.

Chapter 28

The summer held one more golden day. The following weekend the weather was good enough for the MacDonald family to go for a day out at the coast. The day of the picnic was fine and sunny, and they all met on the cliff top at Cayton Bay at the appointed time. Cayton Bay lies on the glorious East Coast of Yorkshire, some three miles south of Scarborough, and is an unspoilt bay of smooth sands and towering cliffs. Frank, nursing his anguish over Stella, had almost refused to go, but Ali, on the telephone, had persuaded him by reminding him that Nathan would come too. Ali and Sophie led the way down the steep mud steps to a long sweep of sandy beach. Nathan led Joyce by the hand, and Ali's younger son, Daniel, helped Steven Brown and his wife carry their daughter, Daisy, and the new baby. Behind them, Frank helped the elderly couple who were the MacDonalds' oldest friends, with their son Harry. David, Ali's husband, and his friend Robert Jones brought up the rear. David muttered dark forebodings about the weather (going to rain), the sand (gets everywhere), the midges (spread diseases), the sea (polluted) and the sun (causes cancer). They were all carrying bags, wind breaks, rugs, deckchairs, buckets and spades, cricket bats and balls, and the other paraphernalia essential to having a good time on the beach. Frank had been dismayed to see Robert Jones. He suspected that Ali was still interested in Robert, and had probably had a hand in securing the invitation. Frank's father, Jack, was too poorly to go with them all, and was being looked after by a trusted neighbour, who had promised to play cards with him.

Everyone arrived safely on the beach, and they set off towards the sea's edge. To the right, the cliffs swept round high and majestic towards a headland several hundred yards away. To the left the bay stretched for half a mile or so, backed by lower cliffs towards another headland, and, several bays to the north, Scarborough was visible. The whole bay was empty of buildings except for, to their left, one lone house, a temporary toilet block, and a kiosk made of white wood which sold teas and snacks during the summer. There were a few other families on the beach, mainly further up and closer to the amenities. Rock pools would be revealed later as the tide receded. Children of all ages loved to search amongst the seaweed and crevices for crabs and starfish, ankle-deep in sun-warmed water. They set up camp on an empty and inviting stretch of sand, and rugs and windbreaks were arranged with due regard for the prevailing wind. They settled Joyce, Steven Brown's wife and new baby, and Harry's parents into deckchairs. Joyce asked if she could hold the baby, and chatted easily to Steven's wife as she cradled the child in her arms. Sophie and Ali sat down companionably on the rugs, and then David started a game of beach cricket with Nathan and Daniel. Daisy played nearby with her bucket and spade.

Harry and Steven went off for a brisk walk up the beach towards the northern headland. Robert Jones was just making himself comfortable near to Ali on the rugs when Frank grabbed her by the arm, and hauled her off for a walk in the opposite direction to the others, towards the sheer cliffs which formed the southern headland.

"What's he doing here, Ali?" Frank hissed, "You're making a fool out of David, bringing him along."

She shrugged, and said nothing.

"Promise me you won't tell anyone if I tell you a secret?" she asked him presently, as they scuffed along the waters edge.

"Of course, what is it?" he said, knowing what she was going to say.

"Last week Robert asked me to leave David and live with him...Robert still wants to be with me."

"Ali, you should be careful. What if David finds out?"

"It doesn't matter if David does find out."

"What?"

"Robert wants to live with me, so then everyone will know everything anyway."

"Oh Ali, you're not serious - that womanising, philandering, egotistical....I thought it was all over between you."

"It was...but I still want to."

"I thought you had made a decision."

"I had, but now I don't know, again. I just want to." The breeze caught Ali's long hair, and she brushed it away from her face.

"What about David?"

"David...everything's gone," she said, lamely.

"Oh Ali, please don't. You're risking everything for - for

him."

"I just want to feel something - anything. I just want to feel different."

"Ali, you could lose David; everything. Don't, just bloody don't."

"You know Mum's saying. 'Better a flawed diamond than a perfect pebble'. I just want to find out if Robert is a diamond or a pebble."

"But David *is* a diamond, however rough. You already know *that*."

"Seeing Robert is the only pleasure I have in life."

"That's nonsense, it's all in your head. Even if it were true, it's still your choice. You're so lucky - you have time and you have money. You should be having the time of your life - instead of doing everything by halves."

"I'm too depressed."

"That's up to you."

"That's easy for you to say. With your perfect life."

"No, Ali, it's far from perfect." His throat tightened, but he told himself it was just the salt air. A fresh breeze blew his shirt as they walked, and he could feel the sun on his back. "Look Ali, I don't want to talk about this now, let's just enjoy the day. It's too nice to spoil. Please?"

Ali took his hand briefly and gave it a squeeze. They continued strolling down the beach for a few minutes, then they turned and walked back in silence for a while, until Frank put a hand on her shoulder.

"Look, just make sure you know what you're doing, okay?" he said, gently. Ali nodded, and patted his back. They walked companionably back to join the others.

When all of the walkers had returned to the 'camp', David organised another lively game of beach cricket, leaving Joyce and her friends to snooze in their deckchairs.

They tossed Daisy high from a blanket for fifteen minutes, an adult holding each of the four corners, until even she could take no more, and had giggled and squealed herself to a halt. Then everyone settled down in a circle on the rugs and deckchairs, and started opening bags and containers, and pooling sandwiches and salads and bread and dips and fruit and cakes on a table cloth spread in the centre. Food and cutlery and drinks and napkins were handed back and forth until everyone had a plateful to start, and they all tucked in hungrily. After lunch, people settled down to nap or read. Sophie and Harry simultaneously pulled copies of *Captain Correli's Mandolin* from their bags and enjoyed a lengthy chat about Kefalonia, Pelagia and her ill-fated lover, and whether Nicholas Cage was brilliant or awful in the film adaptation. Robert looked at Ali meaningfully, and said in a loud, casual voice, "Coming for a walk, Ali?"

She looked around to see what David was doing, but he was busy building a sandcastle with Daisy so she agreed. Frank watched them go with irritation. During the afternoon various alliances formed and went their separate ways. Joyce and Nathan took Daisy for a paddle, and to look for crabs in the rock pools with her fishing net. Sophie and Harry went for a walk, shyly holding hands. Harry had plucked up the courage to ask her out for dinner the previous week, and they had surprised themselves by finding lots to talk about. Steven Brown and his wife relaxed with the baby. Later, Frank and Daniel volunteered to go to the kiosk for teas, coffees and ice-creams. The others lay and sat on the rugs and talked, or snoozed. They grouped and re-grouped as the afternoon grew older, and hotter, and more mellow. Ali and Robert returned from their walk, and then sat separately. He watched Ali constantly, but seemed resigned to having to share her company for the rest of the day. David seemed oblivious to the relationship between Ali and Robert. Frank watched his mother closely for any sign that she was tiring, but she seemed very happy. She was enjoying spending time with Harry's parents and Steven's children.

Frank beckoned to Nathan to join him for a stroll, and they set off along the water's edge in bare feet, with their jeans rolled up to keep them dry. Nathan was as tall as Frank but slimmer, and he had brown eyes and a shock of long, brown hair. In the first burgeoning of manhood, Nathan was as beautiful as a medieval knight in a Pre-Raphaelite painting.

"What's new, Nate?"

"Oh, this and that," said Nathan with a grin. He liked to tease Frank with a pretence of secrecy and guardedness, when in reality he had every intention of telling Frank everything. He had finished school for the year, felt that he done well in his GCSE exams, and was enjoying a long break without responsibilities or pressure. He was a boy with passion and sensitivity in his nature, but also enough humour and confidence to make him a popular friend with both sexes at school. Having found a subject which interested him, the natural world, he had lost no time in exploring it, and had had many conversations with Frank about it. He liked to tell Frank of his recent discoveries.

"Permaculture is the new thing. It's going to save the planet, the human race, everything," said Nathan, as they stood ankle-deep in the lapping waves.

"What is it?" asked Frank.

"It's a kinda new idea that's actually been around for awhile. It's short for Permanent Agriculture. It's about a system of food production for human beings that is sustainable, that supports human life without impacting in a bad way on the Earth and other species. Basically, when the oil and other fossil-fuels run out, we are going to have to completely change our ideas about how we farm and produce food. There won't be any farms as we know them now. We will have to produce our food locally, because there won't be any way of transporting it long distances. The idea of bringing food in by plane from around the world will be seen as just stupid. In a hundred years time they will look back at what we've done and just be baffled. Huge fields with one crop and no hedgerows will be gone. In fact, it's the hedgerows which will be producing the food, not the fields! We've got to go back to as much bio-diversity as possible, or else we'll all starve!"

"Do you think it's possible - to keep humanity going like that?"

Nathan screwed up his eyes, and pondered with the seriousness of youth, "It should be, if everybody buys into it. The really exciting thing is the permaculture idea - basically you grow everything you need in a wooded area, and the wood looks after itself as part of its natural cycle - you know - the leaves drop and the nutrition goes into the ground, where the fungi and the worms convert it to liquid nutrients and the tree roots take it up, and the whole cycle starts again. It's a natural thing. It looks after itself, so there's no intensive labour for the humans. We'll just make sure that the things we want grow there. Everything edible can be grown in small amounts, vegetables, fruit from the trees, salad ingredients, small areas of grazing for the animals. It's an extreme extension of the allotment idea. We'll be gardening and not farming. We'll all be smallholders; keeping chickens, ducks, pigs. Everyone will eat local produce - meat and vegetable. Did you know that animals can winter outside if you grow the right combination of grasses? So then you don't need to use petrol for a tractor just to make hay – ", his eyes shone as he explained the theories to Frank, " - it all fits together. The idea is to use small parcels of land for people and their animals, and return the rest of the land to wilderness, which is what it started out as, and what it naturally returns to, if we let it. They way we grow crops like wheat on the same soil year after year means we have stripped all of the nutrients out of the soil. Nothing useful would grow there, unless we fertilised it each year before we sow the seeds. One of the most interesting areas will be how we help the wilderness to re-grow by making sure that diversity is introduced."

"So England will revert back to The Greenwood?"

"Yes, exactly."

"Wonderful. You should talk to Joyce about it," said Frank. "She remembers her mother growing most of their food during the Second World War, and afterwards."

"I'm hoping there is a University that will let me specialise in it."

"So you're going to be an Eco-warrior, then?"

"Oh, yes. Hope so. I'll be fighting to save the planet while you're fighting the criminals. How about you, old man? How is fighting crime going?" asked Nathan, slapping Frank on the back.

"I'm fine, and less of the 'old', thank-you."

Frank felt anything but fine, but did not want to spoil the day, or make Nathan anxious. They stayed and looked out to sea for a while, chatting and exchanging their latest news, and then headed back to the others.

At about four o'clock another game of beach cricket was suggested, and the more energetic joined in. Frank particularly enjoyed playing sports with Nathan, and liked to see him with his cousins. Nathan was excellent with the bat, and enjoyed spraying shots far and wide for Frank and the others to run after. There was something relaxing about the repeated rhythm of the game; the throw, the strike, the fielding of the ball, the protestations of the batsman when caught 'out'. They all had an easy relationship, borne out of many such gatherings and outings, and they gently ribbed each other at every opportunity. Even David's attempts to instruct them in the finer arts of cricket did not spoil the camaraderie. At about five o'clock, the breeze turned cooler and sharper, and by common consent they began to pack up their belongings, climb back up the steep steps to the top of the cliff, get into the various cars, and start the hour's drive home.

Everyone agreed it had been the perfect day.

Diamonds And Pebbles

December

Diamonds And Pebbles

Chapter 29

The public house was crowded as Frank walked in. Cold and grey outside, there was a warm and welcoming atmosphere inside. It was *The Prancing Pony* in West Wold, and many months had passed since Frank had been there; since he sat alone in the cooling shadows of an August evening, and realised that he was in love with Stella Powell. It was the Sunday before Christmas, and there were festive lights and tinsel decorating the room, as well as Christmas cards dotted at random on the wooden panelling. The dark walls and dimmed lights gave a cosiness to the room. Most of the customers were singing Christmas Carols from song sheets; a lusty chorus of *Deck The Halls* was in progress. Frank made his way to the bar, scanning the room for a familiar face, but saw no-one he knew. Standing behind the bar, Brian Sykes said hello with an inquisitive look, and Frank ordered a pint of best bitter. Frank stood next to the bar, holding his drink, and waited; he hardly dared to turn around and look again. He was expecting to see Stella, and he did not know what he would do if she was not there. He had not seen her since the evening in the hospital in early September.

Frank had grieved for Stella through an autumn of bonfires and decay. During the long, grey days he had kept himself busy. He had had a very long and complex fraud trial to take to court, and he had immersed himself in it. Luckily, this had left his weekends free to be with Nathan and, with the onset of colder weather, they had abandoned the camping trips in favour of watching football on the television in Frank's flat, and ordering take-away pizzas, whenever Nathan was not busy with his friends. Nathan split his week between his parents now, and came and went between the two. Frank was very happy with this arrangement, and it gave him great pleasure to go home, open his front door, and find Nathan waiting for him.

For all this, Frank could not ignore the restlessness of his heart in the quiet hours of the night. In the end, it was to his beloved mother, Joyce, that Frank had unburdened himself about Stella. It was a relief just to tell someone about the loss he was suffering. Joyce stroked his hand, and told him that everything would work out for the best.

One sombre November day, Sophie, Harry and Frank set off for a long walk in the country lanes around Sheriff Hutton. Sophie was very happy now that she and Harry were together. Once Harry had cut his way through the forest of their mutual shyness and diffidence, he did not hesitate to kiss his Sleeping Beauty.

"I'm going to have to go back - I'm tired," she said. They had barely walked five hundred yards. Frank looked at her closely.

"Sophie, you're putting on weight!"

"I know!" she said, pulling a face, and glancing back towards Harry. "Too many cosy nights in! And too many bloody cocktails, darling!"

Sophie and Harry got married in early December, as

soon as it became apparent that Sophie's supposed surfeit of cocktails was actually a baby. Harry proposed immediately, and they quickly arranged a simple wedding; quickly so that Jack MacDonald, whose health was failing fast, could give his radiant daughter away, albeit sitting in a wheelchair. Afterwards, at a small but raucous reception, Sophie danced and swirled in long, unfamiliar skirts until her lungs ached. Harry threw back his head and laughed more than was usual, and tossed small, giggling bridesmaids into the air, luckily being surrounded by people who remembered to catch them. Like all weddings, it was a happy day of meetings and greetings, private thoughts, public speeches, confetti, jokes, unexpected drunks and appalling fashions. A wedding is a strange occasion, where the acting out of ancient rites and rituals calls up un-named and unknown forces, and unleashes them on those assembled to witness the union. Weddings release unbridled emotions; the accidental overlooking of a cousin from the guest list can cause a family rift so deep that the ensuing generations are forever strangers to one another. Even supposing that the marital couple can organise the ceremony to celebrate their love for each other without offending a solitary member of either family, the reception furnishes endless opportunities for long-buried grievances to be re-aired; for wine-mellowed reminiscences to turn to drunken accusation; for long-held grudges to boil over into gnashing, no-holds-barred exchanges; for a wife's gentle forbearance to be catapulted into shrieking desperation; for a husband's secret guilt to be prodded into confession. It was a poignant and tear-filled day for Sophie and her family, and one that Frank would long remember, not least because it made him ache for Stella.

Ali was still prevaricating between her husband and her

lover; never quite making up her mind, and all the while falling deeper into unhappiness. She had those riches that most of mankind aspires to, but does not have - companionship and affluence and good health - but she did not know how to count these blessings.

Jack had rallied again, of late; the joy of seeing Sophie happily married and expecting a child seemed to invigorate him a little. The family were allowing themselves to look forward to a Christmas with him at the centre of the celebrations.

During those autumn months, Frank had spent a lot of time at his parents' house, spending as much time as he could with his ailing father, and his anxious mother, to give them his help where he could, as well as for the comfort it gave him to be there. Frank had found himself unaccountably drawn to his mother's pile of recent Yorkshire magazines, and had come across a gardening article by Stella, obviously written earlier in the year;

Garden Diary

It is the first week of March and the first daffodils are finally out. It has been a cold February – we had ten inches of snow covering the garden for over a week. This seems to have made the daffodils really late. Now my borders are suddenly full of green shoots for crocuses, grape hyacinth, chionodoxa, scilla as well as my favourites - the daffodils. They seem to grow inches every day. I walked right down to the far wall yesterday, past the small kitchen garden that I created a few years ago (the vegetable beds look so sad at this time of year - only a few winter onions left now); by the wall there is a particularly sheltered and sunny spot as the ground falls away south-facing, and as I turned the corner there they were – several groups of February Gold *lifting up their heads to the watery sunshine. Of all the varieties, I particularly like the small* Tête-à-tête *, and also*

Professor Einstein, *and the late-flowering* Old Pheasant's Eye *which I would call a true narcissus; round white petals with a flat orange trumpet. Daffodils are always so cheery of course but particularly so this year; a sign of sunnier days after a long, hard winter. In April it will be time for my annual pilgrimage to Farndale; a bracing walk amongst thousands of yellow flowers following the twist and turns of the river, with a country pub at the end of it. What more could you want? The valley is quite cold and shaded there, so the majority of the bulbs flower comparatively late. If you like walking amongst antiquities, then go to York and see the wonderful daffodil display at Clifford's Tower and around the city walls. I feel as though I have really hibernated this winter – Persephone cannot have longed more for Spring to arrive. I cannot wait to get out into the garden and start the year's work. Spring cannot be long now; those few clumps of daffodils in my garden lifted my heart as much as Wordsworth's host.*

On one seemingly endless Sunday, Frank found another article by Stella in the Observer;

The End of Democracy

We have a Government which seems hell-bent on dismantling our democracy, and our way of life. We are on the edge of an abyss of parental neglect, yobbism, laziness, sponging, disrespect, racism, drug-addiction, intolerance, child sexualisation, apathy, selfishness, surveillance, petty interference by officialdom, serious encroachment of fundamental civil liberties, and basic lack of freedom of speech. The behaviours which make the moral majority feel so beleaguered are actively encouraged by the Government. They want you to feel afraid. They want us to fear our neighbours. They want everyone, not just women, to be so terrified of stepping out of their own front doors that they just stay at home and don't cause any trouble. Above all, don't ask any questions. Don't vote, don't canvas, don't voice an opinion, don't heckle, don't march, don't riot, don't demonstrate against unnecessary wars, don't go putting rubbish in your rubbish bin.

Stay at home, get the beer out, and watch the television, is the Government's message. And if you do happen to defy us by stepping outside, we've got you on a CCTV camera. It could be Orwell's 1984. They want us to be the most surveilled society in the world, not because anyone is going to bother looking at the films, but because they want us to think that if we need all those cameras it must be dangerous out there, mustn't it? Make no mistake, they want us to be frightened. The Government uses the threat of terrorism to bring in measures which oppress us all. Anyone who spent time in London during the IRA attacks of the 'Eighties and 'Nineties knows what it is like to live under the shadow of a terrorist attack. We all politely agreed to have our handbags searched as we entered public buildings and that was that. The current Government did not stop to ask us whether we were prepared to accept the numerically small risk of terrorist attacks in order to preserve our freedoms. If they had bothered to ask us, we would have said yes. I ask you, is the nation which took on the Nazis to protect Poland really that risk-averse? I don't think so.

As for the terrorists themselves, I say, if you genuinely believe that your way of life is the right one, then fight through the ballot box. Let the people of this country decide for themselves whether they agree with your beliefs...

On another occasion, Frank found an article by Stella on the Brontes;

One of the problems with Emily is that there are so few known facts about her that biographers over the years have been desperate to flesh out the little we do know with wild theories and assertions. But it is obvious if you think about it. She lost her mother at the age of three, but let us assume that the quality of mothering up to that point had been 'good enough'. This would have ensured that the adult Emily would be free from psychosis and major neurosis, or perhaps the loss of her mother at this rather important stage did leave her with some neurosis that later manifested itself in her rather reclusive habits. From the point of her mother's death, Emily was looked after by a relatively indulgent father and an aunt, who if not loving, was certainly diligent in feeding, clothing and generally looking after the comfort of the young Brontes. Also, she had the company and love of three like-minded siblings. So there is not much there to suggest major neurosis. The main thing to remember is that Emily had an exceptional intelligence, which, though restricted by the social mores of Victorian society in regard to women, had certainly an outlet and opportunity for stimulus through contact with her immediate family and through her reading and writing. Other than the bare facts we simply do not know how she passed her minutes, hours or days. Let us not besmirch her with idle conjecture, I say. Her early twenties were perhaps her worst years; the unremitting toil and lack of freedom as a governess must have taken their toll on her spirits. She is portrayed as a frustrated spinster, but she may at least have experienced unrequited love of the sort that blighted Charlotte, and she possibly believed that, at twenty-nine years old, there was still the chance of meeting a suitable match. Or she may have simply accepted that there was little chance of meeting a man whose intelligence, wisdom and nature would have made her happy. She was even portrayed by Victorian critics as 'masculine' and there have been suggestions that she was a lesbian. This is, of course, nonsense. The Victorians hypocrites could simply not stomach the possibility that a normal woman could have written Wuthering Heights; *it challenged their status quo too much for comfort. The novel is the product of a free spirit, a towering intellect and a literary genius which just happen to belong to a woman. She would not have been so reviled in the late Twentieth century. Another comfort which she had was, of course, Nature. She loved her moor-land home for its wildness, its beauty and its confirmation of God's bounty. Just as her heroine Cathy said 'I am Heathcliff!', so Emily could have said 'I am the moors!'. I believe that both her solitary and companionable walks alike gave her a great and abiding pleasure and satisfaction; her wild, free soul was filled to its depths by the landscape. How she must have loved to hear the wind roaring off the moors at night, and rattling the windows. Emily does not need justification or pigeon-holing or pity. She bequeathed to us one perfect novel and some beautiful poetry and the rest is silence; let us not wish for more. Let us leave her undisturbed on her beloved moor-land with her sisters, for that is surely where she is.*

And Charlotte? Well, although the image of a gloomy existence in a cold, dour parsonage prevails, this is far from the whole truth. Yes, Charlotte suffered terribly during that awful year when she lost her three surviving siblings. She had lost her mother at the age of five, and formed an unwise and heartbreaking attachment to Monsieur Heger in her twenties, but when Emily, Anne and Branwell were alive she lived a happy and fulfilled life writing, collaborating and discussing Literature and Art, and later was happily married for a short while. Also the portrayal of Charlotte as a quiet, shy parson's daughter is false; she was Jane Eyre to all intents and purposes, with her feistiness, self-belief, determination and intelligence. It was Mrs Gaskell who first created these falsehoods about the Brontes in order to try to lessen the distaste which Victorian readers had for what they saw as the 'courseness' of the Bronte fiction. The subject matter and portrayal of womanhood in Jane Eyre was far too racy for Victorian upper class society to handle. Mrs Gaskell tried to deflect this by presenting the Brontes themselves as beyond reproach; shy, demure, parson's daughters. As for Jane Eyre, there are those critics who suggest that Rochester actually intended to marry Blanche, and that Jane was merely second choice. This is obviously nonsense. From the time of her rescuing him when the fire starts in his bedroom, he is clearly in love with Jane. The Blanche episode is merely the following through of a social process (which he had begun but now regretted) to a polite conclusion, and, given that he cannot immediately get out of the obligation, he sees it as an opportunity to test Jane's feelings and reactions...

Then Frank came across a short review which Stella had written in the Yorkshire Post;

...Why is Persuasion *the best and most serious of Jane Austen's books? Anne Elliot is the most tortured of Austen's heroines. She suffers a traumatic break-up of her relationship with Captain Wentworth, made all the worse by its being her choice, albeit unwilling. She then endures eight years of regret and solitude, bearing the loss of her looks and vitality, neglected by the very family whose will she bowed to in ending her engagement to a man of whom they did not approve. Eight years later, she is thrust unwillingly into the company of the man she has thus hurt, and has to tolerate his seeming indifference, at best, and contempt, at worst. Finally, and almost most cruelly, her heart is broken again as she is forced to stand by and watch as he falls in love with another woman. So many coals heaped upon her undeserving head! The vicissitudes of Emma Woodhouse's life seem trivial in comparison, except perhaps for the nightmarish spectre of having to live the rest of her life as a spinster with her feeble-minded father. There is a horrible parallel with Miss Bates here; she is already living Emma's nightmare. Perhaps that is why Emma boils over into nastiness at Box Hill, when confronted once too often with her own possible fate. No other heroine is forced to suffer as much as Anne Elliot, save perhaps for Marianne Dashwood, whose agony is acute but of a much shorter duration. Anne's family circumstances are similarly amongst the worst an Austen character has to endure. She has lost*

her beloved mother to an early death. Her father and oldest sister are vain, ridiculous figures incapable of warmth or concern for others. Her other sister is an envious, neurotic creature, too selfish even to put her children's needs before her own. The Dashwoods' loving mother and even the neglectful Mr Bennett are model family members in comparison. In her friendships, Anne fares no better. The dubious Lady Russell is one of the people who made Anne doubt her own judgement in her engagement, and coerced her into abandoning it, through reasons of snobbery. There is darkness too in Louisa Musgrove's accident on the Cob at Lyme Regis. She is in real danger of imminent death. Those witnessing the affair are deeply shocked and affected. Frederick Wentworth's life is almost ruined by it; his guilt almost precipitates him into an unfortunate marriage. Just as Anne's suffering is the greatest, so perhaps her ultimate joy is the most heartfelt, her ability to feel the deepest, her future happiness the most assured. This was Austen's last novel, written as she slid towards ill-health and death, and bears the fruits of the author's maturity and experience. So, it is the most serious novel certainly, but why the best? The reader is invited to share Anne's heartache and triumph. Although we rejoice when Elizabeth Bennett gains the felicity of marriage to Darcy, we have not suffered too greatly with her beforehand. Her angst after her first refusal of him is short-lived and easily overcome. In comparison, Anne's sufferings are deep indeed…

During the long winter nights, Frank had listened to a lot of Robert Johnson's blues music, and even found the time to read Jane Eyre for the first time.

Standing at the bar on that Sunday evening in December, Frank felt a touch on his arm and turned to see Stella there, grinning widely. She was dressed in a thick blue sweater and blue jeans. Frank grinned back, enormously glad to see her again. He was there because a few days before he had received a parcel at the police station. Steven Brown had brought it into Frank's office with a curious look, "Something for you, sir. Sorry, it's been opened. The desk sergeant thought it might be a bomb!" Steven placed it on Frank's desk, then turned and left the room. The squashy, brown paper parcel was addressed to Frank in a flourishing hand, and had been slit open at the end. Frank lifted up the parcel curiously and extracted the contents. These were a knitted scarf, ridiculously multi-coloured and haphazardly constructed, and a Christmas card with a robin on the front. The message inside the card read;

Thought you might like this.
Seems a fair exchange for saving my life!
With Love and Thanks, Stella.
PS. There will be Christmas Carols in The Prancing Pony *on Sunday night.*
PPS. James is now living permanently in Manchester.

Frank had tried not to read too much into the message, but it was impossible to quell the impetus which it had given to his hopes. He had found the few days since he got the message very difficult. He was in a state of torment; both looking forward to, and dreading, Sunday. Here he was at last, looking at Stella's lovely, beaming face - and wearing her gift.

"Nice scarf!" she said, mischievously.
"Somebody I know knitted it."
"Very badly!" she smiled.
He laughed, with real joy. It was such a relief to be

finally here with her, without suspicion, without constraint, without fear. But he still did not know how she felt about him. He needed words.

"Thank-you for getting in touch with me, Stella. I've thought about you a lot since September."

"I just thought you might like to know about me and James. Was I right?"

"Yes, you were," he smiled. He lifted up one end of the scarf and examined it, "and now that you have finished your masterpiece, what's next?"

"I have a new project in mind."

"Oh, yes?"

"There's a certain man I know with soulful, brown eyes; he looks like he might be worth spending some time with."

Thinking how lovely this would be made his heart swell, but he said, "And perhaps you could fashion a matching pair of mittens, as well?"

Stella giggled, and it was the best sound that he had heard for a long time. Then she hesitated and fished something out of her jeans pocket. It was the blue silk tie which Frank had left in her garden on that hot sunny afternoon in August.

"I've been looking after it for you," she said, looking earnestly into his eyes. "I kept it under my pillow, I hope you don't mind."

Brian Sykes was hovering close by, looking at them nosily, and suddenly Frank longed to be alone with Stella. He put down his drink, grabbed her hand, and led her outside into the porch around the front door of the public house. It was bitterly cold, and the skies were heavy and low with grey snow clouds. They stood facing each other, almost touching, their breath visible in the cold night air. Stella put her head back, and he could see the whiteness of her throat in the dark. She looked at him with a kind of desperation, "If you don't kiss me right now, I'll die," she said.

Frank gently kissed her forehead. "No, don't do that," he said, in a low voice, "we've had enough of that."

He pulled her close, and kissed her, and they whispered words that he would remember for the rest of his life.

Frank pulled away slightly, and looked into her eyes, "Stella, are you still married?"

"Yes, but not for much longer. Why?"

He felt his throat tighten. "I was wondering if you'd like to marry me."

Stella said gently, "We'll see."

Frank held her close again. He sensed that her hesitancy contained a warning; they really knew each other so little. But he had no doubts. He was happy. After all of the false starts, the mistakes, and the wrong-headedness of the past, all he wanted now, all he earnestly desired to be, was a husband, a father, a son, a brother, a friend.

After a while, Frank turned away from Stella, and looked up, and saw that the snow had started falling. Already it was blanketing the village landscape with white.

"Look, Stella! It's snowing. You know, I have a feeling that it's going to be a wonderful Christmas!"

THE END

Coming soon

The Power Of Love

**By
P. B. Slater**

The second Frank MacDonald novel